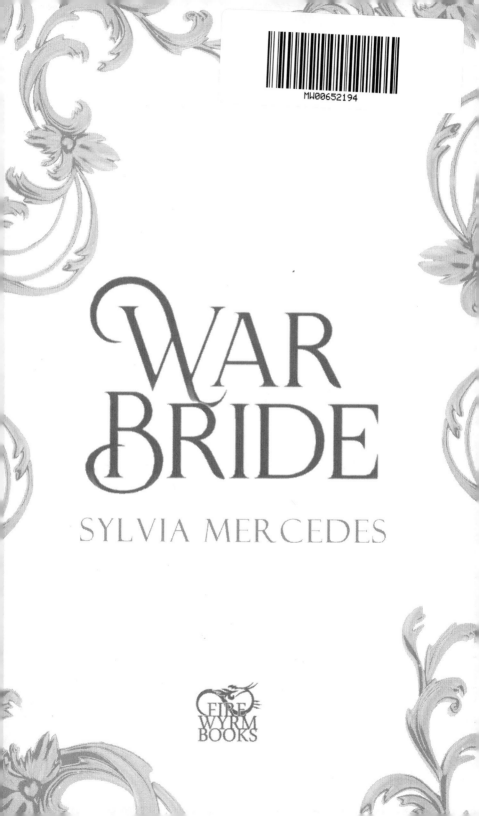

WAR BRIDE

SYLVIA MERCEDES

FIRE WYRM BOOKS

PRAISE FOR BRIDE OF THE SHADOW KING

"Sylvia Mercedes hits every note romantasy
readers want in a novel."

DANIELLE L. JENSEN
Bestselling Author of
The Bridge Kingdom

"Utterly swoon-worthy!"

ELISE KOVA
Bestselling Author of
A Deal wtih the Elf King

© 2024 by Sylvia Mercedes

Published by FireWyrm Books

www.SylviaMercedesBooks.com

Cover design by Fay Lane

Interior Art by TrifBook Design, Panna Mara, and Skadior Art

*This one is for those of you
who are looking for escape.*

ALSO BY SYLVIA MERCEDES

BRIDE OF THE SHADOW KING

Bride of the Shadow King

Vow of the Shadow King

Heart of the Shadow King

WARBRIDE

WarBride

(more to come)

OF CANDLELIGHT AND SHADOWS

The Moonfire Bride

The Sunfire King

Of Wolves and Wardens

PRINCE OF THE DOOMED CITY

Entranced

Entangled

Ensorcelled

Enslaved

Enthralled

WAR
BRIDE

PROLOGUE

T HE BARRED DOOR BURSTS OPEN, SCREECHING IN
protest like a soul ripped from a corpse. It hits the side
of the cage with a bang which reverberates through every
bone in my body. I cannot help the scream that escapes my throat
as I throw my arms up over my head.

Hands reach inside: large, pale-skinned, and tipped with black
talons. Grasping, eager, greedy hands. The last time they reached
through that opening, they grabbed a young priest and dragged
him forth, struggling and blaspheming like a heathen. None of
us tried to stop them, none of us tried to help. We're beyond such
pathetic resistance.

So when those hands latch down hard on my shoulder and the
front of my bodice, when those talons dig through the rough fabric

of my cloak and into my flesh, I'm not surprised when no one moves to defend me. I don't bother with either begging or pleading, nor do I cast my fellow prisoners a final, desperate glance. They cannot help me. No one can. Not anymore.

I hold my tongue, my last scream still choked in my throat. My only hope now is that whatever my captors intend for me will be done quickly. I've heard tales of the fae and their prisoners, stories of torments and tortures lasting for days on end. Crucifixions and bloodlettings, great burning pyres surrounded by wild figures singing in hideous harmony with the screams of the dying. I used to listen to such stories in my father's hall, relishing the horror and the gore, hanging on each word from the minstrel's mouth. Waiting for the moment when the hero arrived on his white horse to topple the pyres, to vanquish the foes, to make right all that was evil.

There are no such heroes left in this world. I learned that bitter truth the hard way. No champion riding in on a white horse to save me. If I cannot save myself, no one will.

But I could not save Aurae. They took her. My sister. They took her, and I could do nothing but listen until her screams were drowned out in savage roars.

Now it's my turn.

Though I'm determined to face my end with courage, my body rebels. My knees give way as I'm hauled from the cage, and I collapse in a trembling heap. Raucous voices growl in a language

I do not know, and the grip on my shoulder releases momentarily, only for those long fingers to snarl in the hair atop my head. A painful wrench, and I'm back on my feet.

"March!" snarls a voice close to my ear. Forced into motion, I stagger through the churning crowd. Strange faces close in around me. Some are hideous, like monsters born of nightmares, all greenish mottled skin, seeping warts, and gnashing teeth. Others are beautiful—pristine masks sculpted to perfection, radiating glamours that dazzle the eye and intoxicate the senses. These beings are more terrifying by far. They speak to each other, monsters and men alike, motioning at me, pointing out my various attributes, while their eyes travel up and down my figure in lewd appraisal.

It's all too much. Too many voices in my ears, too many faces swimming before my eyes, the stench of blood in my nostrils, and bitter terror coating my tongue. We reach the foot of eight crooked steps leading up to a scaffold. They seem so big, so insurmountable. I stop, unable to make my feet obey.

It doesn't matter. The hand on my head shifts to the back of my cloak and gown, propelling me onward and upward to the top of the scaffold, where I'm tossed roughly forward. The clasp of my cloak rips open, and I fall to my knees. Barks of laughter erupt from the crowd. Clenching my jaw, I push upright and swipe wild strands of hair out of my face as I look around. I'm alone up here—no brutalized corpses of my fellow captives for company. No sign of Aurae.

"On your feet," the taloned creature growls. He stands at the top of the stairs, my cloak still in his grasp. When he takes an aggressive step forward, I hasten to get my feet under me, to stand tall. If this is to be my end, I won't snivel and shrink from it. I am a daughter of warriors and kings. I will face death with dignity.

So I brace myself before that vicious throng, painfully aware of every rip in my gown, every bruise purpling my body, and the dried blood matting my hair. I draw my shoulders back and lift my chin as though even now I wear a queenly diadem and robes of royal silk. Turning slowly, I survey all those leering faces surrounding the scaffold. They look ready to rend me apart and lap up my blood. I hate them. I hate them for making me so afraid I'm ready to piss myself. I hate them for taking my sister before me. I hate them with all the force and fury I can summon. Hatred is my only remaining shield.

"Here, brothers!" the creature behind me, the one holding my cloak in his awful hands, roars, his voice rising above the din of growls and snarls. "Here is a fine specimen of human womanhood!" He speaks in a strange tongue which I do not know, but which transforms as it strikes my ear into words I can understand. "A tasty warbride for the man lucky enough to win her. What'll you give for her, my savages?"

"Five silver heds!" a voice bellows back immediately from the front of the scaffold.

"Ten!" another snarls from the right.

Another voice and another, one after the other, and the bidding has gone up to twenty silver before my dulled brain finally comprehends what is happening. Oh gods. I'm not to be killed. I'm to be sold.

As a bride.

1

ILSEVEL

A TRICKLE OF GOAT BLOOD RUNS ACROSS THE AGE-cracked sacrificial stone. I watch its slow progress, oddly fascinated. It oozes to the edge of the slab, seems to pause for a moment, before spilling over in a gory streak to finally pool in the gutter cut around the altar's base. A stink of copper mingles with the sting of incense in my nostrils. My lip curls faintly, hidden behind my demure prayer veil.

Then I draw a deep breath, close my eyes, and brace for what I know must come next.

It hits like a blow—a whole chorus of holy prayersong erupting all around me, flooding my senses. Wincing, I bow my head. I can only hope I look solemn and reverent rather than nauseated. Of course, in that assembly of two dozen devout voices, there's one that is just *slightly* off-key. That's the one I hear, singled out from all others. He might as well be singing a personal solo just for my benefit. It's impossible to concentrate on anything else.

Not for the first time, I bite back curses aimed at the very gods who blessed me with the gift of song on the day of my christening. I'm pretty sure they were having a laugh when they did it, amused at the prospect of how often my ears would be offended by less than perfect pitch. It's a useless gift as far as I'm concerned. Sure, people like to hear me sing. Sure, I can play any instrument I put my hand to. So what? Anyone could learn to do the same with a little bit of effort. I don't see why the gods felt the need to get involved . . . unless it was to spite my father.

They tell me that King Larongar went on a quest when he was young—back when he was just a prince, and a younger son at that, not the sovereign he is today. Supposedly he climbed to the summit of Mount Helesatra, defeated the dragon which sleeps there, and claimed the right of gods-gifts for his future offspring. No doubt he hoped the gods would dole out useful sorts of gifts which he could use according to his ambitions. A war gift, especially. A gift for strategy would have been acceptable as well. Even an affinity for spellcraft would do. Something exciting. Something worthy of divine bequeathal.

Instead he got the lot of us: my older brother, Theodre, who is beautiful as the day; my older sister, Faraine, who gets headaches from other people's emotions; and my younger sister, Aurae, who dances like a dream.

Then there's me. When I sing or play an instrument, people see pretty pictures in their heads. Worth a little mountain-climbing and dragon-slaying? Perhaps not.

To say my father was disappointed as each new gift manifested, doesn't come close to communicating the level of disgust we inspired in his heart. At least my gift he's always found a bit more to his liking; he can trot me out to perform for courtly visitors on command.

In the end, however, I could only serve one ultimate purpose in his eye: a bride. A commodity to be bought and sold, a choice fruit with which to tempt other kings into alliance.

Which is exactly what happened. Which is exactly why I find myself in my present position, kneeling before this altar, watching the remains of a slaughtered goat burn on a blood-stained altar stone. Completing the rites of my Maiden's Journey before my new husband comes to claim me and carry me off to his kingdom.

I'm supposed to be singing along with the priests. This service is for me, after all, a sacred and significant moment. But I won't sing. I'll do no more than mouth the words. Peering out from the gauzy folds of my prayer veil, I study the statue of the god I am here to petition. Lamruil's visage, carved in a block of black marble, is all hard edges and severity, his unsettlingly long teeth bared in a grimace. The God of Darkness—the first of the seven gods to whom I must make sacrifices in preparation for my wedding. His is not the most cheerful shrine to visit while on pilgrimage, but it's an important one. Certain things are about to happen between me and my intended bridegroom in the darkness of my bridal chamber . . .

Hastily I drop my gaze from the god's stoney stare and squeeze my eyes shut. But that's no use; my future husband looms large in my mind. Massive, rock-skinned. A veritable mountain of a man. Not human; that would be unpleasant enough.

No, the husband my father picked for me is a *troll*.

"The high priest knows you're not singing."

Startled, I turn to my sister, who kneels beside me at the altar rail. Aurae's face, what I can see of it behind the filmy fabric of her veil, is the picture of piety. But her eyes flash, catching me in a quick, sidelong glance before shifting to the high priest. He stands on the far side of the altar, his arms, stained with sacrificial blood, upstretched over his head in a great V. His hard gaze is fastened on me, however. Disapproval scores every wrinkle of his ancient brow. Though he continues leading his brothers in prayersong, there's nothing worshipful about that expression.

"He can't see me through my veil," I whisper back a little uncertainly.

"I don't think it matters." Aurae leans closer so that she can speak into my ear. "Please, Ilsevel, try to sing. You look as though you're preparing for your funeral rather than your wedding."

"Maybe I am. For all we know, trolls devour their brides on their wedding nights."

Aurae dips her chin to hide a smile, though I'm not entirely joking. "The Shadow King seemed courteous enough," she persists. "Faraine, at least, believes he will make a good husband."

"Let Faraine marry him then," I mutter. There'd been a brief point in my hurried courtship when I had hoped my terrifying suitor would choose my elder sister instead of me. I'd seen the two of them dance together on the first night after his arrival. He had seemed unusually taken with quiet, serious Faraine.

Ultimately, however, he knew he would be better off allying himself with me: Larongar Cyhorn's favorite daughter. The apple of the king's eye.

I squeeze my prayer-clasped hands tightly, my knuckles standing out white. It doesn't pay to be the favorite of a tyrant. Not in the long run. I've known all along my fate would be something like this. It's simply the way of it for a woman like me, a king's daughter. *Princess* . . . Gods, how I hate that title! A princess is not a person, not an individual. She is a representation. Of power, of loyalty. Of entire nations when need requires. She is an instrument to be used at the discretion of mighty men. Men like my father. Men like the Shadow King.

"Why are you grimacing like that?" Brow puckered, Aurae pushes her prayer veil back to study me more closely.

"I'm not grimacing." I firm my lips and jut my chin at the priest. "We're praying here, remember?"

"Ilsie . . ." she begins in a warning tone, but I don't hear whatever she's about to say, for a plucking at my sleeve steals my attention. I turn from her to the round-cheeked face of a young novitiate, who has just appeared at my other shoulder. He holds out a slip of paper. Frowning, I accept it, turn it over in my fingers. Who would send me a message in the middle of this sacred ceremony? Certainly not Wulfram, captain of my armed escort. He is far too devout to risk the high priest's wrath.

Aware of the priest's gimlet eyes fixed upon me, I drop the note behind the altar rail, flick it open, and hastily scan the contents by the dancing light of the sacrificial blaze:

Ilsevel, I have come for you. Leave the chapel at once and meet me in the temple courtyard.

Artoris

My heart skips a beat. Artoris! Here, at Ashryn Shrine? Folding the note, I press it against my breast, unable to think, even to breathe. For weeks now I've teetered between hope and fear, wondering whether the message I sent would ever reach him. But he's here. Artoris is here, all the way from Evisar Citadel. My prayers—my true prayers, not the ones I pretended to sing before this bloody altar, but those I whispered into my pillow each night—are answered.

I might just get out of this betrothal in one piece after all.

Aurae, no longer trying to pay attention to the service, pushes back her prayer veil to stare at me frankly from her wide doe-eyes. "Ilsie, what is it?"

I shake my head, pressing my lips together. Now is not the time for explanations. Half-afraid the high priest will call down the power of his dark god to smite me on the spot, I rise, make a hasty holy sign with one hand, and back down the long chapel nave, head bent, hands folded. No one moves to interfere with me. The priests go on singing, and Aurae remains kneeling at the altar rail, watching me go. I reach the shrinehouse door unhindered.

Then I turn and race out into the glare of sunset. I lift my hand, shading my dazzled eyes. How many hours have I knelt in that dark chapel? The whole day seems to have passed. But it doesn't matter. None of it matters, for that red sun now sets on my last day of captivity. Artoris is here. I will be free—free of my father, free of the Shadow King. Free of marriages and alliances and being treated like a valuable broodmare. I will flee this place and never return.

A smile breaks across my face. Though I want to spread my arms like wings and simply fly from the hilltop, I force my gaze down to the temple complex, built on the lower slopes of the shrine hill. A series of peak-roofed dwellings stand in a semi-circle around a central well. A dozen or so horses, all tacked to ride, fill the yard, but my eye goes immediately to a powerful white stallion which paces back and forth, hooves ringing against the paving stones. This fine beast is mounted by a broad-shouldered figure in black mage's robes. Though his hood is thrown back to reveal his face, I'm too far away to discern features. But I recognize him: Artoris Kelfaren. The man I've held in my heart these last seven years, in defiance of all my father's wishes.

The next moment I'm racing down the narrow stairs leading from the gloomy chapel of Lamruil. It's like I'm escaping darkness itself and my grim, terrible future as the Shadow King's bride. Hope surges in my veins, and I run and run, heedless of any danger. A new, unknown future awaits, and I'm ready to meet it with open arms.

I'm panting so hard by the time I near the bottom steps, I can't even shout his name. Artoris does not see me. He has his back to me, his attention fixed on the door of the guest house where I and my entourage have been housed during our stay at the temple. Just as I reach the base of the stairs, the door opens, and ten solemn figures emerge. Not priests—no, these figures are not clad in priestly cassocks but in bloodred cloaks, long and sweeping, their faces hidden by deep hoods.

My pace slows to a stop. Why did Artoris bring so many men? In the weeks since I sent my desperate letter, when I dared to envision his arrival, I always saw us making a covert escape. Just the two of us, racing off into the sunset. The daydream certainly didn't include a full company of crimson-cloaked mages in tow.

"Is it done?" Artoris demands. His voice is a cold bark.

The foremost of the hooded figures bows its head, wordless.

"Excellent. Now we must find the princess, and—" He breaks off when the crimson cloak raises a gauntleted hand and points. Directly at me.

Artoris turns in his saddle, eyes flashing.

For a moment the air goes still. It's as though the whole world has inhaled sharply. I'm caught in his stare, in that space of existence between us which seems to stretch across the long, lonely years. Years during which I've had nothing to hold on to but a few secret letters and my own determination to thwart my father's control. Years in which this man before me has been little more than an idea in my mind, not a living, breathing person.

He's aged since last I saw him. His face, still square and handsome, has acquired a new sternness that doesn't fit on the remembered face of the young man I knew. Seven years makes a difference. I suppose it has in both of us.

"The beard is new."

The words are out, hanging in the air between us, before I can think better of them. My voice seems much too loud, echoing against the solemn stone buildings. Gods, was that really the best I could come up with? The first words spoken to the man I've cherished in my most forbidden dreams these seven long years? Too late to take them back now.

I motion to my own face, tracing a line around my mouth and chin. "You look very . . . mage-like."

Artoris blinks. His stallion paces uneasily beneath him.

"It's not bad," I hasten to add. "I've never been kissed by a man with a beard." I smile and tilt my head a little to one side. "I might let you give it a try."

His lips part. No sound emerges, just a little stream of cold air. Then suddenly he dismounts in a whirl of heavy mage's robes and strides across the courtyard. He seems much bigger, much older, and I take an uncertain step back. Before I can take another, his arms are around me, crushing me to him. "Ilsevel!" his voice is rough, speaking into my hair as his hand presses my head against his chest. "At last!"

The relief in his voice is enough to make my own stiffened limbs relax a little. I wrap my arms around his neck and breathe him in. I used to love the smell of him, that combination of balsam and cinnamon. After he was sent in disgrace from my father's house, I found an old handkerchief of his and kept it under my pillow for years, pulling it out every now and then to catch trace remnants of his scent.

A different aroma fills my nostrils now: something cold and a little bit sulfurous. Almost . . . rotten. It's unpleasant enough to make me want to jerk back. But I don't. I used to feel safe in his arms, protected. I lean in now, eager to reclaim that feeling, and refuse to acknowledge the way his grip feels more like a cage.

Finally he pushes me from him just enough to look down into my face. Close up, with the last of the sunset glow bathing his features, I can see something of the young man I once knew.

His deep-set eyes are the same mix of brown and green, framed in dark lashes. His features are even, his jaw square and strong, emphasized now by the addition of that beard. He's built like a warrior, though he spends his days bowed over great tomes of magic, studying the secret lore of the Miphates. An atmosphere of mystery always surrounded him, which I, as a young girl, found utterly irresistible.

He was six years my senior back when I fell for him. I was just fifteen, and my gods-gift had newly manifested. I don't remember anything of that time. They tell me I experienced a severe reaction to the sudden outpouring of power and collapsed unconscious. When my father's court mages were unable to revive me, he sent for Mage Morthiel, the most powerful Miphato of our time.

Morthiel brought with him a promising acolyte, young Artoris Kelfaren.

I don't know what magic Morthiel used on me. My memories of the aged Miphato consist of cold hands, wrinkled skin, and an unsettlingly deep voice. But Artoris—he was by my side when I first woke from my long sleep. There he remained in the weeks that followed, as my strength slowly returned. And I loved him. Oh, how I loved him! My first love, my only love. He was so wise, so handsome, so dangerous, and so . . . forbidden. I would have given him everything he asked of me.

It was some weeks after my recovery that we were discovered entangled together in my bed, my clothing all in disarray. Father had Artoris dragged out into the yard and bound to a pillory. I begged. I pleaded. I protested that nothing had happened, nothing that *mattered* insofar as the king's ultimate plans for me. Father merely laughed and said he would cut off Artoris's manhood and give it to me as a keepsake. He would have done it too, were it not for Mage Morthiel.

As it was, Morthiel convinced Larongar to give the young man a lashing, then turn him back over to the Miphates. That he succeeded is testimony to the aged Miphato's power and influence with the king. Artoris was given twelve lashes. I was forced to stand and watch each blow as it was delivered, to listen to each cry as it ripped from my lover's lips.

Morthiel left with his acolyte the very next day, never to return. My last glimpse of Artoris was from my bedchamber window where I leaned out as far as I dared, watching as his pain-hunched figure rode out from Beldroth Castle. I hoped he would look back at me just once. He never did.

Since then we've exchanged in secret no more than a handful of letters. Each time Artoris's ink-scrawled words assured me of his ongoing and ardent devotion. With those words, I fed my flame of passion, determined not to let it dim with either time or distance. I would show my father that he couldn't break my spirit, neither with laughter nor with lashes.

Looking up into Artoris's handsome face now, I try to recall some of that burning feeling which had raged so hot in my veins. I know it's him and yet . . . he feels like such a stranger.

"Gods!" he exclaims, his eyes roving over my face. "You're even more beautiful than I remembered." He grabs my hand and draws it reverently to his lips. A shiver runs up my arm, but I don't pull away. "When I received your letter, I set out from the citadel at once to meet you here. Nothing could keep me back."

A nervous laugh escapes my lips. "And what did your master think of that?"

He frowns. "My master?"

"Morthiel. Mage Morthiel."

A shadow seems to pass over his face, darkening his eyes. "I am my own man and make my own choices. When I heard of your impending marriage to the Shadow King, I knew what I must do. I knew I could not leave you to be sold off to a monster."

Still smiling, I glance beyond his shoulder. There the crimson-cloaked figures stand in a row, hands folded, heads bowed. There are so many of them. Surely they could not have ridden from the citadel without Mage Morthiel's knowledge. I look up at Artoris again, my lips parting to question him further.

But suddenly his mouth is on mine. Hard hands grip my upper arms, pulling me to him, then one of his hands slips behind my head, fingers digging in, pulling my prayer veil askew. Shock races through me, but I shake it off, try to lose myself in his kiss like I once did. Something isn't right. His lips are too demanding, too hungry, and his tongue presses between my teeth, filling up my mouth. This feels more like an attack than an embrace.

I push away, gasping for breath, and quickly slip my fingers over his mouth to keep him from lunging at me again. "Careful!" I say with another laugh that doesn't sound like me at all. "Captain Wulfram will see." Where is the captain anyway? He and his whole company of armed men should not be ignoring the sudden arrival of Miphates on the temple grounds. Isn't it their job to protect me?

A deep chuckle rumbles in Artoris's chest. "Not to worry, sweet princess. No one is going to stop us now." With those words, he turns and beckons. One of the crimson cloaks strides forward, leading a chestnut mare. "Quickly now," Artoris says, taking the reins and turning to me. "We ride for Evisar at once."

"Evisar?" I blink, surprised. When I'd dreamed of Artoris coming to whisk me away, I'd certainly not envisioned us returning to the citadel. The Miphates never welcome outsiders into their secret spaces. "Won't Morthiel send me straight back to my father?"

Artoris grins. It's a subtle, rather sly expression, both like and unlike the devilish smile of the young man in my memory. "Morthiel doesn't answer to the king." Before I can parse through this enigmatic statement, he presses a hand to the small of my back, guiding me toward the mare. "We must hurry. I have many enemies, and word of my arrival in these parts will travel quickly. The sooner we are away from here the better."

I'm just opening my mouth to protest, to remind him that I have personal belongings I must gather, to question the wisdom of this plan, which suddenly feels too rushed, too forced.

Before I can utter a sound, however, a voice rings from above: "Ilsie!"

I whirl on heel. My sister descends the shrinehouse stairs. Behind her, priests of Lamruil gather around the dark opening to the chapel. It's too dark by now to see their faces, but I can feel their unwillingness to venture out, to draw any nearer to the mysterious cloaked figures below. Aurae, by contrast, hurries in a billow of white veils, looking ghostly in the light of the pale lanterns hung from poles to light her way. "Ilsie, wait!" she cries.

I pull away from Artoris, trying not to notice the way his hands snatch after me. Hurrying toward my sister, I arrive at the base of the stairs just in time for her to throw herself into my arms. She's trembling, frightened, her gentle eyes wide and fearful. "Ilsevel, what's going on?" She gazes over my shoulder at the cloaked figures, now mounted and waiting. "Who are these people?"

Aurae was only ten years old when Artoris visited Beldroth. She didn't know anything about our relationship at the time, and I never shared with her the secret letters I received or revealed my feelings for the handsome mage. I hardly know how to explain now, especially not with Artoris's eyes burning into the back of my head.

"Aurae," I say instead, taking her hand and squeezing it hard. "You know I can't marry the Shadow King. I just can't."

She glances at Artoris, waiting beside the mare. "What are you saying?" Her voice is tight and low. "Ilsie, you're not . . . you're not leaving with this man, are you?"

I smile. If it's a little forced, I tell myself it's simply because I hate to hurt my sister, hate to leave her in this way. "I love him," I say simply. "I've loved him for seven years now but was forced to keep it secret."

Aurae shakes her head. "You can't be serious. Who is he?"

"It doesn't matter!" I glance back at Artoris, meet his gaze. His face is so hard and stern, it makes my heart drop in my chest. But this is it. This is my only chance to escape. And with time, surely everything I once felt for him will return. Such feelings don't just disappear into thin air. "I love him." If I say the words with enough conviction, I can make them true once more. "And he's here now. I'm leaving with him, and I won't be coming back."

"But the alliance." Aurae reaches out, gripping my forearm as though she can hold me here. "You can't abandon the alliance. You can't abandon our people!"

My stomach knots. "Skewer the alliance," I growl. "Do you really think those trolls are the means to our people's salvation? Do you really think Father intends to use them to stop this infernal war of his? It's only going to get worse. He and the Shadow King will find new excuses to go to battle, and I won't be part of it. I won't be a playing piece in their games."

Aurae stares at me as though she doesn't know me. And she doesn't, not really. No more than I know her. We only know each other in the roles we've been forced to play, in the parts that we've been molded into every day of our lives. Sister, daughter, princess, pawn. The real me, the real her—those are mysteries as yet undiscovered. Perhaps we will never know each other truly.

But I must take this chance to discover my own true self. It might be the only chance I get.

Aurae's lip quivers. Her grip on my arm tightens for a moment. "Ilsie, you won't find freedom by running away."

"I won't find it any better by staying." The sharpness of my answer makes her wince, and I immediately regret my words. "Please, Aurae," I continue in a gentler tone, drawing her toward me. "I cannot spend my life the property of any man."

"Ilsevel." Artoris's voice snaps like a whip behind me. "It's time to go."

I wrench free of my sister's grasp. She utters a little sob and reaches for me, but I spin on heel and hasten to the red mare, accepting Artoris's leg-up into the saddle. Despite my skirts, I swing my leg over the mare's broad back. It feels good to sit astride a horse once more, not carted along in a carriage like precious goods. I cast a last look around the courtyard, still expecting Captain Wulfram and his men to make their appearance, weapons drawn. I see only a handful of priests and novitiates, watching from windows, wordless and unwilling to interfere.

"Stay close to me," Artoris says, mounting his stallion and urging it up beside my beast. "We ride hard through the night.

No turning back now."

He lifts his hand, signaling to his strange, silent companions. Then he spurs his horse into motion, and my mare surges into tandem stride with his. We thunder from the temple yard. I spare only a single glance back to where my sister stands beneath a solitary lamppost. The wind wafts her prayer veil back from her small, pale face. Tears roll in silver trails down her cheeks.

I face forward into the evening gloom and ride on. On to new life. On to freedom.

2

TAAR

A CHILL WIND BLOWS LIKE A WHISPER OF FOREBODING across the twilit valley. I watch it ripple through the tall grasses until at last it reaches me where I sit astride my mount, hidden among the trees. Breathing deep, I scent what information that wind brings: the stench of blood, the sharp sting of incense, carried down from the shrinehouse, which stands on its hill across the valley, directly opposite my current position. The temple of the Dark God dominates this stretch of land, and none but a few lonely shepherds dare dwell in its shadow. I cannot say that I blame them.

I study that shrine, built into the high stone outcropping. I've never understood the desire to worship a god of darkness and death. There is so much of both in this world already; would we not be better spent devoting our prayers to that which brings light and life?

But humans are strange creatures. There's little good to be had trying to fathom their ways. I'm more concerned with what defenses may or may not be established on those steep slopes.

My mount stirs beneath me, excited perhaps at the stench of bloody sacrifice. He shakes his head, and moonlight catches on the lancelike horn protruding from his brow. "Steady, Elydark," I murmur, stroking his massive shoulder beneath a curtain of mane. "We shall have our sport soon enough."

A rumble sounds deep in his throat, followed by a voice of dancing light and shadow, which appears in my head, meaning without words: **Nyathri comes.**

I narrow my eyes, peering out across the valley once more. Sure enough, a rider and steed approach. Almost invisible to the naked eye, the licorneir gallops at full tilt, her head outstretched, her mane and tail flowing like ripples of silk. She is a smaller beast than my own, quicker, nimbler. Ashika, her heart-bound rider, rides low, her body molded to her mount's until they are nearly one. Nyathri is the most sure-footed of her kind, which is why I chose her and Ashika for this reconnaissance mission. At the sight of them, my pulse kicks up a pace. The speed with which they come tells me they bear good news.

A low rattle in my ears heralds the arrival of another rider and beast. Not a licorneir. No, the beast which draws up alongside mine is a long-legged reptant: hoary, bristled, with huge, muscled shoulders and a low-hanging, predatory head. It stands nearly as tall as my powerful steed, but where Elydark is a creature of almost terrifying beauty, this thing is an aberration, repulsive to the senses.

It's rider, by contrast, projects glamours enough to dazzle even my impervious eye. Though beneath those glamours, Lord Lurodos of Noxaur is no doubt a monster equal to his nightmarish mount, in the light of this pale moon, he is the very picture of the seductive fae lover, one who would lure unsuspecting maidens to their doom. He lashes his beast savagely with a razor-edged flail, drawing ribbons of blood in its flesh, then grins at me as he pulls it to a halt. "Is that your girl returning?" he asks, indicating the approaching rider with his flail.

I don't like his tone. Lurodos views my kind as a subclass species and holds us all in contempt. The feeling is mutual—I loathe everything about Lurodos, who is a brute without honor. We would not have chosen to conduct this mission together. In fact I argued vehemently with Prince Ruvaen to let me and my Licornyn riders handle this matter ourselves.

"No," Ruvaen had answered, waving aside my concerns. "If the rumors we've heard are true, this is too great an opportunity to miss. I need both of you on this—your brains, Lurodos's brawn. Between the two of you, I have every confidence you'll bring back our prize."

I shift in my saddle, refusing to answer Lurodos. We've been on this hunt for days now, but never this close to our quarry. I hate leading my men out into the mortal world like this, exposed to this hideously magic-deprived atmosphere. Worse still, our going leaves the Hidden City all but unprotected. I will not feel at ease until I return and see for myself that my people are safe.

It all comes down to what will happen tonight.

Nyathri draws closer. She moves in shadows and silence, but I can feel even from this distance the burning tension in both her and her rider. My hand tightens around the hilt of my sword. Surely Ashika would not urge her licorneir so desperately if she did not bring the information we need.

I turn in my saddle, looking back at my people, gathered among the trees. "Mount up," I command. My words are swiftly carried back through the ranks.

Lurodos chuckles darkly. "You're getting ahead of yourself, Taar, my friend. Maybe you and your Licornyn are more bloodthirsty than I was led to believe."

I cast him a cold glance. "My people are always keen for a fight."

The Noxaurian shrugs. "That's as may be, but never so keen as my own boys." He sweeps back his cloak then, revealing the small crystal vial he keeps tucked at his belt. My eye seems to go straight to it, pulled by some compulsive force I cannot resist. Lurodos sees the look and laughs outright, slipping the vial free and holding it out to me between finger and thumb. Though the cut crystal reflects moonlight, the dark liquid contained within seems to draw all light to itself and swallow it whole.

"Go on, King," Lurodos urges, speaking the title like an insult. "You and your men must take a draught tonight before the fighting begins. Bring out the savage and let it play!"

A hot serpent coils in my gut. Elydark, sensing my tension, shifts nervously on his massive hooves, but I can scarcely hear the warning song of his voice in my head. My pulse throbs too loud. That single vial of dark liquid momentarily takes up the whole of my vision. Behind Lurodos's urging, I can almost hear another voice, a softer voice from memory, whispering: *"Take it, Taar. Take it and save us all . . ."*

Elydark snorts and tosses his head, dragging my awareness back to the present. I draw a sharp breath of thin, magic-starved air through my nostrils and wrench my eyes up to meet Lurodos's mocking gaze. "My people have no need to augment either their courage or their prowess."

The Noxaurian's teeth flash in something between a smile and a snarl. "Is that so? In that case, what would you say to a little wager? Whoever takes the most heads tonight wins, and the loser owes him a prize. A new slave, perhaps. Or a warbride."

"We're attacking a temple," I remind him coldly. "The priests are noncombatants and not to be harmed."

"*Human* priests. Hardly worth the blood spilled from their worthless hearts."

"Servants of Lamruil," I reply. "Am I correct in thinking that you Noxaurians hold the Dark God in special reverence?"

"Not I nor any of mine!" Lurodos hefts his flail, the spikes flashing in the moonlight. "We worship Tanatar, God of War, and don't give two *shakhs* for another deity! And Tanatar likes it when we bring him heads—men, women, children, they all are pleasing in his eye. So my people will take their dose, and we will carve through any who happen to stand in our way, priest or otherwise."

I stare at the man, this maniac over whom I wield no control. While I do not like the idea of unarmed men being cut down like animals, I cannot protect the priests of the shrinehouse from what is coming for them. So I say only: "Just as long as your people remember that our target is to be taken alive."

Lurodos scoffs. "I'll leave that to you, my friend. As you're so hellbent against killing, you can have the fun of trying to capture a death mage. Be my guest."

A chill lances through my veins. I've encountered death mages before and do not relish the prospect of meeting one in battle. But this is the first chance we've had of capturing one of Morthiel's servants in many years. I cannot let this opportunity pass me by.

Ashika draws near now, her shimmering mount carrying her up the rise to where we wait among the trees. Lurodos's reptant recoils from the delicate Nyathri, bristled skin shivering in dread of her spiraled horn. Lurodos strikes it again with the flail, drawing blood from its haunches. I ignore them and lift a hand to greet my scout. "Ashika," I say, clasping her forearm as she draws up beside me. "What news do you bring?"

The Licornyn rider's face splits in a great grin which confirms my every suspicion. "He's here," she declares. "Mage Artoris is here at this very temple. I saw him with my own eyes!"

"And what of his company?" I demand, keeping check on my own excitement. "Are there many with him?"

"I counted ten hooded mages. Their cloaks were red."

My brow tightens. Red cloaks? That means Artoris journeyed from the citadel and left the safety of the waypost roads in the company of mere acolytes, not yet fully-fledged Miphates. That is good news for us, for while acolytes may wield impressive magic, they won't be anywhere near as deadly as Mage Artoris himself. They won't command death magic. But something doesn't seem right here.

"Only ten?" I repeat. "You're sure of this?"

Ashika nods eagerly even as Lurodos whoops in triumph. "The night is won already!" the Noxaurian declares. "Only a Miphato fool would leave the citadel with so small a force. He's begging to be hunted down like a cur."

I shoot him a dark look. "You would be wise not to underestimate our enemy. Even a single death mage can kill a dozen foes with a single spell."

"Aye, but I've got dozens to spare. When his spells have run out, and he's busy trying to scribble down another, we'll take him."

Lurodos turns in his saddle then and barks a harsh command in his own evil language. The reptant riders assembled in the forest behind him answer with a series of barks, snarls, and yodels, teeth flashing, weapons ringing.

"Lurodos," I say, urging Elydark to stand between him and the open valley. "We must plan our strategy."

"Already done, King!" the warlord bellows. "Charge up that hill, kill anyone who screams at the sight of us, throw a sack over the Miphato's head, and drag him back to Ruvaen. Meanwhile . . ." He bites off the top of the vial, his teeth crunching against crystal. A cloud of *viruli* perfume permeates the air, thick and intoxicating. My vision clouds over, and for a moment, my whole attention focuses once more on that little sliver of darkness grasped in Lurodos's hand. Then he tips back his head and downs the lot in a single gulp. "Meanwhile," he finishes, dashing the empty vial to the ground, "we have our fun!"

The swell of virulium comes over him. An abyss opens in each of his eyes, and black blood tears roll down his cheeks. Utter savagery takes hold of his soul. He throws back his head, issuing a bloodcurdling scream that must echo for miles. Then, beating his own steed with that vicious flail, he charges forth from the trees, his men falling in behind him. They've all taken their own doses of virulium and been overcome with madness. Their cries mingle with that of their reptants, fifty monsters mounted on nightmares, sweeping into the valley below the shrine.

"*Luinar.*" My second, Kildorath, urges his licorneir up beside me at the edge of the trees, watching the Noxaurians go. "Are we to follow?" Flames shimmer along the flanks of his beast, and the light gleams in the depths of his eyes. Kildorath also wishes to take the virulium and give into the madness of bloodlust. But my men are strictly forbidden from partaking of that foul brew.

I grind my teeth. "We will circle round behind the shrine. Artoris is no fool. He will try to escape the moment he gets word of the attack—which will be sooner rather than later now, thanks to our friend Lurodos. We must try to head him off." I turn then, gazing back across my eager company of twenty brave souls. "Ride like shadows, my friends. Swift and silent."

They obey without question, following me as I lead them through the forest, around the valley. Our licorneir move like dreams incarnate, navigating the dense foliage as easily as a dancing breeze. Though here and there one flames with eagerness for battle, for the most part, they remain invisible to the naked eye, and their riders blend into them like phantoms, only caught in chance glimpses. We are faster by far than the Noxaurians and reach our destination first. The temple above is still quiet; Lurodos's assault has not yet reached them. Soon enough, however, the night will erupt in fire and terror.

"Fan out," I bark, swinging an arm to indicate my will. "We cannot let this mage slip through our fingers. Form a perimeter, and—"

My voice breaks off in the combined sound of Nyathri's trilling cry and Ashika's excited, "Look, *Luinar.*"

I face forward. There, just reaching the base of the road winding down from the temple hill, is a party of eleven riders. No, twelve—Ashika's initial count was off by one. But they are, as she said, clad in crimson cloaks with the hoods pulled low; my vision, augmented by Elydark's innate power, can discern the color even by moonlight. I pick out the foremost rider as well, swathed in black robes elaborate with red embroidery. The robes of a death mage. Our prey is here and even now approaching our position.

"Quick!" I growl. "Prepare for battle, but keep your mounts subdued until the last. Surprise is our best weapon."

Without word or sound, my Licornyn spread out to form a semi-circle. On the slopes above, the rooftop of a lower temple building goes up in flames, and the first cries echo down from the hillside. Lurodos and his men attack with wild abandon, unaware their prey has already fled. No matter—I'm just as happy for them to drive our quarry straight into our trap.

"Steady," I whisper, more to myself than to Elydark. My licorneir's gaze is fixed upon the approaching mage, as eager as I to take him down. But we both must remember our mission: capture, not kill. Though there are few men whose blood I should like more to spill, too many lives depend on the information I must draw from Mage Artoris's lips. I adjust my grip on my sword, heart thudding, blood pounding, awaiting the right moment.

One of the riders pulls up sharply. It's a woman—her lithe

shape is unmistakable even beneath the folds of her cloak. Unlike the others, she wears blue, not red, and her face is unhooded. She does not look like a Miphates acolyte. Her horse prances uneasily under her, turning in circles, but she masters it well. Her face tilts up, angling in my direction. The silver glow of the moon bathes her features, revealing a much younger woman than I would have expected. Young and—I notice even through the driving urge for battle in my blood—lovely.

Her gaze fixes on the strand of trees where I even now hide. Of course she cannot see us; licorneir are invisible to human eyes save when enflamed. And yet, if I didn't know any better, I would say that she was looking straight at me.

"Luinar?" Kildorath's voice reaches me as though through the misty haze of a trance. "My king, they are close. Do we attack now?"

I don't speak. I'm caught, somehow. Transfixed by those eyes set beneath that stern, moonlit brow. Suddenly the distance between me and the young woman seems almost nothing. I feel as though I could reach out and touch her, try to smooth that puckered line from her forehead with the pad of my finger. What's more, I want to. The impulse is strong, almost irresistible.

What is this? Some enchantment? Some Miphates sorcery?

Elydark growls, a vicious rumble in his chest. It's enough to snap me back into myself, to break whatever spell had come over me. I grit my teeth and lift my sword arm high. I'm not about to let some Miphata mage catch me in her magic. I have a mission to accomplish. I will see it through.

"Licornyn," I bellow, *"forward!"*

Elydark's muscles bunch and surge beneath me. He bursts from the sheltering trees, and as he leaves behind shadows and leaps into moonlight, his body erupts in flames. Those flames sweep over me, burning both my body and soul, an inferno of raw magic. My Licornyn riders take up the battle cry, pouring out from the trees on either side of me, and we sweep down upon our enemies in a crescent arc of doom.

3

ILSEVEL

⟡

I HEAR THE SONG BEFORE I SEE ITS SOURCE.

Only . . . this doesn't feel like *hearing*. It's more than the simple act of sound entering my ears and vibrating inside my skull. It's too great, too terrible, too overwhelming to fit in such a simple understanding. It's more like *color*. Vivid bursts of color in a range far beyond anything my eyes have ever seen. It's heat as well, blazing across my mind with a reality more real than mere physicality.

It's not a song. It's an explosion.

Through the color, heat, and overwhelming awe, beings emerge. One could almost say I *see* them, though I'm not sure my eyes play a part in what is happening to me. It's as though the song itself creates shapes in my head—creatures of flame, four-legged, long-necked, with great shining horns protruding from their foreheads. Bigger than horses, but vaguely horse-shaped, if the comparison weren't so laughable. Fire burns within their souls, all the colors of the rainbow and more.

Unicorns.

The word appears in my head and, with it, a sense of incredulity. I've heard tales of horned creatures, who are said to be beings of pure magic, untamable, deadly, and beautiful beyond description. But no word in any language is big enough to capture the glory of the beasts even now descending on me. Theirs is a beauty that could sear you straight to the heart and leave your hollowed-out husk smoldering in its wake.

It takes me a moment—a long, everlasting, lifetime of a moment—to realize there are riders on their backs. At first their souls are so blended into the songs of their mounts, I cannot discern where beast ends and rider begins. My mind revolts against the idea of such heavenly beings permitting themselves to be ridden, and yet . . . and yet the oneness of mount and rider, of soul and song, is undeniable.

I am frozen at their coming, that onslaught of fire pouring out from the trees. Shadowy figures move in my peripheral vision, creatures of earth and dust that exist on a plain outside of that thunderous song. Somewhere far away I hear voices shouting, Artoris bellowing commands. But it's all so meaningless compared to the glory that descends upon me with such destructive force. I can do nothing but wait to be overwhelmed, consumed, and—

"Ilsevel!"

The sharp sound of my name bellowed into my ear yanks me back into my physical body. I gasp in an agonized breath and latch hold of the pommel of my saddle just as my horse lurches to one side, dragged by a hand on its bridle. My dazzled vision struggles to make sense of the world around me, but Artoris's voice barks again, close at hand. "Ilsevel, stay close to me!"

He's urged his stallion alongside my mare. Crimson cloaks surround us, forming a protective barrier as riders on fiery beings close in. There's a clash of steel in my ears, and a multi-voiced ululating cry surrounds us. It could be music were it not so terrible.

I turn to Artoris, confused, desperate, and see him holding a book in one hand. It looks so incongruous here in the midst of flames and blades. Then I realize what he's doing—calling upon the power of a written spell. His mouth murmurs the dark, secret words, and one hand moves in the air as though kneading. Sparks of red light appear between his fingertips. The glow intensifies, lighting up his face from below in ghoulish highlights. Magic ignites the atmosphere around him.

One of the flaming beings drives toward us, bursting through the defenses of the crimson cloaks. For the first time, I see one of the riders close-up—a man wearing no armor, his muscled torso completely bare save for tongues of fire licking across his flesh. His hair is long, flowing unbound down his back, and a black band is painted across his face from temple to temple, making his brilliant eyes stand out in terrifying relief. He opens his mouth to utter another one of those strange, ululating battle cries, his sword upraised as he charges straight for me. I raise my arm helplessly against the blow that must fall.

But it never does. A stream of writhing red light streaks through the air and hits the man straight in the chest. He falls from his mount, screaming, his body contorting in unnatural ways, all while that light continues to penetrate his chest. I stare down at him, aghast, uncertain what I am seeing.

Only then do I realize: I'm not seeing—I'm hearing. Hearing the dark song of a curse entering his body, dragging his soul forth. I hear the white light struggling to hold on, resisting the pull of that curse. But it's useless. The magic is too great. It rips the man open and yanks out the light of his life, drawing it in a twisting stream of red and white and bursting anti-light. I follow the line of that song, that stream, back to its source. Back to Artoris, who sits astride his stallion, palm-outstretched to receive the life he has stolen. His eyes blaze with curse-light and his lips move, still speaking the secret words of the spell. I watch, I listen, as the soul of the dying man enters Artoris's grasp.

He clenches his fist, and the song cuts off abruptly, leaving behind a shattering silence. I stare at the corpse of the dead man. The man who would have cleaved my head from my shoulders with a single blow of his sword. I stare at him, lying in broken ruin, his body warped with the pain of his death.

A scream erupts in my head: a song so broken, so dissonant, so wrong. I scream as well, dropping my reins and slapping both hands to my ears. My horse startles. There's a moment of weightlessness followed by a painful thud, and I realize I've fallen and landed hard on my shoulder. It hurts, but I can't think about that now, not with that broken song bursting in my head. I scream again, desperate for the sound of my own voice, desperate for anything that might drown out that horrible dissonance.

Twisting where I lie, I search for the source. I see one of the flaming beings. It's skeletal, demonic, wreathed in flame. Riderless. It rears up, knife-sharp hooves tearing at the air. One of the other flaming beings rushes to it, and the rider tries to catch the screaming beast. It eludes capture, however, and races off into the night, carrying its hideous song with it. Only then can I breathe again.

I drag a painful gasp of air into my lungs, realizing suddenly where I am: on the ground in the middle of a battlefield, chaos erupting all around me. There are more death cries, more soul-songs abruptly ended. Some vague part of me realizes that no one else is hearing these terrible songs, no one else is reacting to them. Is this my gods-damned gods-gift at work?

I've got to get out of here. I've got to get away from these flaming beasts.

No one seems to see me, unmounted as I am. I wrap my dark

cloak around me and run. Pounding hooves and lashing flames churn in confusion on every side. I spy a lone tree and race for it like it's the last bastion of defense in a world gone mad. Somehow I reach it and collapse against the trunk. I drag three agonized gulps of air into my lungs. Only then do I raise my gaze to the temple on the hill.

The rooftops are on fire.

Aurae.

A curse spits from my lips. Gods damn me to the deepest hell! I left her up there. Alone. And now the temple is under attack, and why? The answer appears in my head at the same time as the question itself. These creatures, these unicorn-riders, they're fae. Servants of Prince Ruvaen, my father's enemy. Word must have reached them of Larongar's alliance with the troll king. So Ruvaen sent his fae warriors deep into Gavaria, deeper than they've ever penetrated before. To find me. To kill me. To prevent the alliance from taking place. And my sister is caught in the middle of this attack.

Still using the tree for shelter, I search the battlefield, eyes throbbing with the pain of harsh lights and plunging darks and far too many twisting shadows. Then I see her—my mare. By the grace of the gods, she's close. Her reins are snarled in a branch from this very tree, preventing her from galloping away from the mayhem. I dart to her side. She squeals and tries to jerk away from me. Almost unconsciously, a soothing, crooning song pours from my lips. She responds to it, lowering her head, and I'm able to snatch the reins free from the tree's grasp. She's too tall for me to mount on my own, but I drag her alongside an obliging tree root and manage to scramble into the saddle. From this height, I scan the scene before me once more, taking in the dead men on the ground, some bare-skinned, some clad in red.

Only . . . the crimson cloaks begin to stir. Strange, unnatural movements, pushing themselves up from the ground.

I don't wait to see more. Pulling the mare's head around, I bow low over her neck, urging her back up the temple road. She's eager to escape and responds to me at once, breaking into a gallop. Somewhere behind me, Artoris's voice shouts my name above the screams of the dying, but I don't heed him. I shouldn't have left with him in the first place, I shouldn't have abandoned Aurae. Gods, what was I thinking? How could I have been so selfish? I never dreamed the shrine would be attacked. I can only hope Captain Wulfram is prepared to defend the temple against the fae.

By the time I reach the lower buildings, all such hope is extinguished. I see no sign of the captain or his men. Rooftops are on fire, people are screaming. I rein my mare in, my vision dazzled by fiery glare. Priests and novitiates flee from burning buildings even as shadowy figures dart among them. These figures, though man-shaped, don't move like men. They're animals, all brutal shrieks and bloodcurdling roars. Even as I watch, one of them drops its sword and leaps on the back of a screaming priest, biting into his neck with sharp, savage teeth.

But the guest house is not yet ablaze. My heart leaps with foolish hope. I ride to the back of the building where all is still shadowed and eerily quiet. Springing from the mare, I don't pause long enough to secure her, merely trust she'll be there when I return. I burst through the back door into the deep shadows within. "Aurae?" I call, my voice so thin and weak, it scarcely makes a sound. I hasten down the dark passage, stopping to peer into each room as I go. All is empty, echoing, while outside the slaughter rages on. "Aurae, where are you?"

I step into the front room, the assembly hall, with its mosaic floor and tall windows. Light from the burning building opposite this one falls through those windows and illuminates the faces of the dead lying before me: Captain Wulfram and his men. Their bodies sprawled out, their weapons still clasped in death-rigid hands, their eyes staring up at the ceiling.

Their throats have all been cut.

Everything else fades to nothing. I stand there, in a little slice of space and time, as realization washes over me. All thirty men. Every last member of my armed escort, who were charged with my protection on this pilgrimage. Dead. Not slaughtered by the raiders even now rampaging through the temple. No, I know who did this.

I see Artoris in my mind's eye, astride his white horse, just outside the door of this building. *"Is it done?"* he asked as his

58

crimson cloaks filed out.

My stomach heaves. I double over, sickness rising in my throat, whirling in my head, and vomit all over that mosaic floor.

"Ilsie?"

Jerking upright, I wipe my mouth with the back of my hand and peer into the shadows at the very back of the room. There, crouched behind a set of tall-backed chairs, is a small, pale figure in a prayer veil.

"Aurae!" I run to her, stepping over and around dead bodies, and wrap her in my arms. She's trembling so hard, I fear she'll break into pieces. Sobbing, she buries her face in my shoulder. "They're dead!" she chokes. "They're all dead! And outside . . ."

"I know." I draw back and find she's clutching a knife, no doubt taken from one of the dead men. Her hand shakes so hard, she can scarcely grasp it. I take it from her. I have no training, no skill with weapons. It wasn't considered seemly for a princess to be taught what my mother deemed *masculine* arts. Which means my sister and I are little better than a pair of birds in a snare, waiting to have our necks wrung. But I'm not going down without a fight. "Come on, Aurae," I say, taking her hand and pulling her to her feet. "I'm getting you out of here and—"

The door bursts open. I freeze, one hand still holding my sister, the other brandishing the knife. A dark figure steps into the entry room. His harsh breaths sound like low growls. The light from the fires outside silhouettes his sharp, spiked armor, making him look

59

like some sort of spined demon. He drags a cruel sword along the floor, and blood drips from its edge as well as from his mouth.

Aurae catches her breath, stifling a scream. Just that little sound is too much. The creature jerks its head and fastens a predatory gaze on us, its face momentarily illuminated in red light. It is a beautiful face, perfect features, pale and pristine as a carved statue of marble. Black ooze pours from its eye sockets, running like tears down its cheeks. Its lips curve back from long bloody teeth, and it throws back its head, howling like a wolf.

Then, springing over the bodies of Wulfram and his men, this monster, this walking nightmare, hurtles straight at my sister and me.

I move to throw myself in front of Aurae, lifting my knife in feeble defense. Before I can comprehend what is happening, a small hand snatches the knife from my grasp. There's a blur of motion—a graceful arc of a slender arm, deflecting the cleaving blow of that fae blade. A twirl, light as a dancing spring blossom on a breeze, all fluttering veils and skirts.

Then the knife enters the black eye of that ravening beast.

He stands frozen in shock, his gory mouth gaping. A last gurgle bubbles from his throat. A stream of blood mingles with the black tears pouring down his face. He topples, collapsed in ruin, choking out his dying breath.

Aurae stands over him.

My little sister. Graced by the gods with the gift of dance.

She stares down at what she's done. At the blood on her hand from where the knife entered. At the fae monster lying at her feet. Slowly, her eyes rise to meet mine, her expression a mask of horror. "Ilsie?" she says, my name a trembling question on her tongue.

Then her eyes roll back in her head, and she drops to the ground beside the corpse of the fae she's just slain.

A scream chokes in my throat as I fall to my knees beside her. "Aurae!" I call, pulling her into my lap and slapping her face, desperate to rouse her. "Aurae, no, no, no, you've got to wake up! You've got to wake up, darling. We can't stay here."

A shadow falls across us. I don't look up, don't waste that extra, precious second. I simply lunge for the knife protruding from the fallen fae's eye socket, wrench it free, and hold it up in defense over my sister's still form. Only now do I take in the man standing in the doorway. Not another ravening monster.

"Artoris," I breathe.

He scans the room, his gaze flitting over the bodies of the slain guards before it finally lands on me. "Ilsevel," he says, his voice deep and dark, underscoring the screams of the dying priests outside. "What are you doing? You must come with me. Now."

I shake my head. "My sister—"

He strides across the room, ignores the knife in my hand, and grabs my shoulder. "She doesn't matter," he says, wrenching me to my feet. "You're the only one who matters here. Leave her. We can still get out of this."

"No!" I struggle against his hold. When he won't release me, I lash out with the knife, cutting into the thick fabric of his robe but failing to connect with flesh. "I'm not going anywhere without Aurae!"

Artoris turns sharply on me and, without hesitation, slaps me across the face. I double over. The sting of pain is nowhere near the absolute shock of the act itself. Yanking back my head, I stare up at him, one hand pressed to my cheek.

His teeth flash in a grim smile. "No time for a lover's quarrel, Princess. I need to get you out of here." He grabs my arm again and starts to drag me along, little caring how I stumble over the corpses. "You can tell me how much you hate me later if you like, but I'm not going to let anything stop me from saving your life."

We're halfway across the room, making for the open door. Suddenly another shadow fills that space, broad shoulders nearly blocking out the light. There's only enough fireglow from the windows to illuminate the black band of warpaint streaked across his face and eyes which burn with magic fire.

"Artoris Kelfaren," the fae warrior says, raising his sword and pointing it at the mage. His teeth flash like knives. "You're coming with me."

4
TAAR

'VE NEVER STOOD THIS CLOSE TO A DEATH MAGE BEFORE. I've met them in battle many times, but always at a distance. They prefer to remain removed from the melee, casting their vicious curses from afar. It is too easy to think of them as unholy beings, wielding their godlike powers over life and death. Too easy to forget that they are what they are—mere humans.

This man is very human. He is tall for one of his kind and broad as well, but still several inches shorter than any one of my men and most of my women. His black robes are torn, his face streaked with mud and blood. Pale eyes, flashing with mingled fury and fear, blaze into mine. The point of my blade hovers mere inches from his breast. A single lunge, and I could run him through. The temptation is great, especially in light of the deaths this man brought to pass within this very hour.

Take him alive.

Elydark's voice sounds in my head, song without words, but I understand its meaning entirely. I draw a long breath through my clenched teeth.

Take him alive, my licorneir repeats. **We need the knowledge in his head.**

That doesn't mean he needs all his limbs though, does he? I shoot back. Elydark doesn't respond, but I feel the tension communicated from his soul to mine, and I restrain my sword arm.

Artoris shifts on his feet, moving to place himself more firmly in front of the person beside him. That slight movement draws my gaze, first in a brief glance, then a second look, longer, harder. It's her—the young woman from the valley, the one in the blue cloak. I would have thought she'd been cut down in the altercation, but here she is, gazing at me from over the mage's shoulder, her dark eyes round and wide. When my gaze meets hers, she draws a quick breath and steps back. But the death mage has a hard grip on her arm, and he yanks her back beside him. Something tells me that, wherever this man meant to take her, she was not going willingly.

"Let the girl go, mage," I say, shifting my gaze back to him.

Artoris hisses a curse. Abruptly he pushes the woman away, hard enough that she staggers and tumbles to the ground in a heap of skirts and limbs. I don't fall for this minor distraction. When the mage reaches into the front of his robes, going for a spellbook, I step forward and lay the edge of my sword firmly against his throat.

"If you hope to draw another breath," I say, "you'll keep your hands where I can see them." The death mage freezes. His eyes flick sideways to the woman, who is scrambling backwards, trying to put distance between herself and the two of us. "She is not your concern," I growl, and his gaze whips back to mine. "I am. Hands up!"

Slowly Artoris raises his hands. They tremble in the firelight. If he could cast spells via his eyes, I would be blasted to cinders on the spot. "Gods-damned half-breed," he snarls.

His words cut off sharply when I slightly adjust the angle of my blade, twisting it through the chain around his neck. I tug, and a triangular talisman set with a rotating sphere of dark stone appears from under his robes. Spell-writing covers that stone, tiny and intricate cuts.

I grin. With a quick slice of my blade, I cut through the chain and deftly catch the talisman with one hand before it hits the ground. The mage gasps, but I place the edge of my weapon along his jaw once more. "Turn around," I say. "Hands behind your back."

He obeys. Depositing the talisman in the pouch on my belt, I slip free a length of cord. It's risky to lower my sword, even for a moment, but I won't miss this chance to secure my prey. I bind his wrists, then, knowing the peril of spoken spells, gag him as well.

All the while, I'm aware of the woman, though I won't look directly at her. She crawls to the back of the room where a small body lies in the deeper shadows beside a fallen Noxaurian corpse. Another human female. Dead? I can't tell from where I'm standing. A strange urge comes over me to cross to the woman's side, to kneel beside her and offer my assistance; to guide her from this temple, this house of slaughter, and see that she escapes Lurodos and his virulium-maddened horde.

The mission. Elydark's voice sings in my head, speaking truth I cannot afford to forget. I've lost good men tonight, and many more lives depend on the successful apprehension of this mage. I won't let myself be distracted by one human maiden in distress, no matter how lovely her face may be.

I grip Mage Artoris's shoulder tight, pivoting him toward the door. "Almost too easy," I growl. "I would have expected more resistance from a death mage."

I force him to march forward, making for the door. We've scarcely gone two paces before a crimson-cloaked figure lurches into the doorway. Its cloak is spattered with blood and gore, and it breathes in great, rasping gasps, as though its lungs are tattered. Two gloved hands emerge from deep sleeves, gripping the hilts of twin swords. My gaze drops to those swords and fastens on them intently. Those are Licornyn blades. Taken from one of my fallen warriors?

I look up, peering at the face beneath that deep hood. Before I can discern more than the faintest impression of features, the crimson cloak lunges at me, a blur of flashing blades and blows. I release Artoris and raise my own sword in defense, deflecting and riposting in quick succession. One of those swords whirs toward my head, and I escape with the top half of my skull by inches, losing instead a lock of hair.

I see an opening and go for it, only for my strike to be blocked. Again and again I lunge, staying on the offensive, determined to bring this crimson cloak down. Is this a mage? It can't be. The Miphates warriors are dependent on spellcraft, but this person demonstrates pure strength and swordsmanship. If I didn't know any better, I'd say it was Licornyn-trained. Every move I make is anticipated, every blow blocked with almost laughable ease.

I know this style of fighting. The timing, the grace, the last-minute feints and quick thrusts. But it's impossible. My mind is playing tricks on me.

With a roar I propel myself forward, my sword clashing with both of my enemy's weapons, driving the crimson cloak back against the wall. I press close, my superior strength pinning my opponent in place.

A low laugh whispers across my senses, sends a shot of ice through my veins.

I stare down at the edge of that hood. Then the crimson cloak shakes its head, tosses back the heavy fabric, and lifts its eyes to mine. Dead eyes, gray and filmed-over. Staring out from the face of a dead woman. Bloodless, colorless. Decay eats away part of her mouth, and an old wound on the line of her jaw festers with rot.

69

Even in ruin, I would know that face anywhere, in any world. "Shanaera?" I breathe.

Her rotten mouth twists. "Surprise," she whispers, a vicious purr.

Her leg moves, catching me behind the knees. I go over backwards, too stunned, too horrified to react. My head strikes the stone floor; sparks explode across my vision. For a moment I am vulnerable, my defenses gone. I hear Elydark's voice screaming wordlessly inside my head, but I cannot answer. Any second I expect to feel both of those twin blades plunging into my chest and gut.

Instead the apparition leaps over me in a whirl of rippling cloak. I turn, trying to follow her line of movement. With unnatural strength, she catches up the bound and struggling body of Artoris. Slinging him over her shoulders like he weighs no more than a child, she darts from the building out into the raw light of the burning temple grounds.

I drop my head, let the dizziness and darkness overtake me, the sheer madness of it all. Because that's the only explanation—I must be mad. Mad to think that was Shanaera, to think she's come back from the dead. Mad to believe she could be here, and, even if she was, that she would help a Miphato. I must be battle-crazed. Perhaps Lurodos slipped me some virulium after all.

Vellar! Elydark's voice again, singing, roaring. Suddenly he's there, his flaming presence unmistakable. I open my eyes to find my licorneir standing over me, huge and terrible in the confined space of this hall. **Vellar,** he urges, lowering his nose and nudging me hard in the shoulder. **What happened? I felt such fear, such horror in your heart!**

I cannot explain. I will not. Not yet, at least. Not until I've had a chance to consider what I saw. For now I must concentrate on more pressing business.

"Artoris," I growl. "He's getting away." I roll over, heave myself up onto all fours, and nearly collapse again. Elydark bows his head to assist, and I gratefully accept his help getting to my feet. Still leaning on my licorneir, I take three staggering steps toward the door.

A scream rips through the air.

I pivot on heel. Three of Lurodos's men lurch across the room, darkness oozing from their eyes. I shake my head, and my vision clears a little more, enough to see her: the young woman with the stern brow and the flashing eyes. She stands over her fallen friend, a knife in her hand, and lashes wildly at the nearest ravening Noxaurian. They laugh, spitting black bile between their teeth, amused by her ferocious helplessness. One of them smacks her with the flat of his sword, toying with her. Then one lunges, grabs her by the front of her gown, his awful mouth going for her throat.

By then I'm already across the room. I latch onto the Noxaurian by the hair on the back of his head, and he emits a gurgling screech as I wrench him off. The woman collapses, but quickly scrambles to put herself between her enemies and the fallen girl she's so determined to protect. She's no match for any of them with that little knife of hers, which she doesn't even know how to hold properly. Yet she bares her teeth, fierce as a wolf, and I cannot help but admire her tenacity.

I turn the Noxaurian, forcing him to look at me, and snarl into his virulium-stained face. "She is not your enemy."

"She's human!" the Noxaurian hisses. His abyss eyes blink, sending globs of black ooze down his cheeks.

"Human and delicious," one of his fellows agrees and makes a grab for her. I twist and hurl the first man into him, knocking both of them to the ground. Then I swing my sword, rest the edge just under the jaw of the third ravener. His black eyes goggle, and his throat constricts. Otherwise he goes still.

"Stand down, you dogs," I growl. "You've had your fun for one night. If you lay a hand on this girl, you will lose your lives. Is it worth it?"

Were they still in the initial throws of virulium, they would deem it a fine price to pay. The madness of the black venom would drive them to glad death in exchange for just one bite of human flesh. But the first rush has past, and some reason has returned to their twisted minds. They back down, snarling, hissing, cursing. Then, as of one accord, they turn and flee across the room, scrambling over the bodies of the dead men in their haste to reach the door.

When they've gone, I turn to face the woman again. She's got the fallen girl by one arm and struggles to drag her across the floor. Even if she succeeds in getting the two of them out of this building, she'll fall right into the arms of other Noxaurians, who will only too happily tear her limb from limb.

Gods above, what am I supposed to do? I have no time for prisoners. Not while Artoris is even now making good his escape.

Vellar? Elydark snorts and drops his head, his shining horn stained with battle gore. *Vellar, we must go.*

But I can't just leave her.

"*Shakh,*" I curse, and wipe a streak of blood from my eyes.

Then, sheathing my sword, I step toward the girl. She looks up at me, terrified, and when I stretch out a hand to her, she slashes at it ineffectively with her knife. "Don't touch my sister!" she snarls, her eyes wild, reflecting firelight.

A growl in my throat, I lunge, block her next wild blow, catch hold of her arm, and wrench it behind her. Not hard enough to hurt, but the pressure forces her to turn around and drop to her knees. She shrieks with rage, but when she tries to resist, pain shoots through her body. She goes still, panting hard.

Smiling grimly, I slip another length of cord from my belt and swiftly bind her wrist. As I reach for her other hand, however, and the pressure momentarily eases, she twists suddenly and launches up from her knees. Her free hand goes for my eyes, fingers curled.

"Sheathe your claws, wildcat," I snarl, dodging her attack. One nail scratches me across the cheek, a sharp sting. I catch her wrist and drag her to me until her face is inches from mine. "I'm trying to help you."

She looks up at me, her face ablaze with defiance that cannot quite mask her fear. She has spirit, I'll give her that. Outmatched and outnumbered as she is, most would crumble under the pressure of sheer terror. Yet she fights me, knowing she cannot win. Foolish, perhaps. But courageous.

Then, to my absolute surprise, she opens her mouth and begins to sing.

It is probably the last thing in the worlds I expected. The audacity of that simple act startles me so much, I cannot at first react. By the time I realize what's happening, something has changed. Something has . . . caught me. That melody—soft and sweet, a perfect contrast to all the horror, fire, blood, and mayhem surrounding us—yanks me right out of this time and place, hurtles me across the years. I am no longer standing in a death-filled human temple dwelling. I'm in Evisar, the seat of my forefathers, the home of my childhood. The City of Spires, nestled at the foot of the mountains, where *oriqirel* birds wheel overhead, putting on colorful displays with their rainbow wings, and the water sprites laugh in the bubbling river and wave to all who pass over their bridge.

And I'm riding. I'm riding, riding, across the open stretch of land, making for the city with all speed, joy bursting in my heart. It isn't Elydark who gallops across the plains under me—it is Onoril the Black, greatest of all licorneir. I am a child, seated on the great beast's back, my own father just behind me. His arms wrap around my small body, and I am sheltered, safe, protected. All the things I have not been or felt in these many long years.

The song fills me up, threatens to carry me away with it. But suddenly Elydark's voice bursts through the melody, roaring in warning: *Vellar! Beware!*

A shudder—a quake right through my soul. The song's spell over me breaks, and I jolt back into the present, staring down into the eyes of the girl. She looks as surprised as I do, her gaze not on me, but on Elydark, who stands in flaming power with his horn aimed at her heart. Her eyes swivel to me, and her mouth opens again.

Though I may not understand exactly what just happened between us, of one thing I am certain: I cannot risk her uttering another sound.

With a single, swift blow, I strike her across the temple. She falls immobile into my arms.

5

ILSEVEL

I WAKE UP SLOWLY AND IN PAIN. EVERY BONE IN MY BODY is being actively jostled, and there's an awful stench creeping up my nostrils. At first I cannot concentrate on anything else—just the ache in my bones and that putrid, inescapable stink. Slowly, however, other senses return. The dull thud of my pulse in my ears gives way to a chorus of low moans. Then I blink, and my vision clears enough to take in an impression of bodies in front of me, crammed into a too-small space. Groaning, I close my eyes again, unwilling to see more.

"Ilsie?"

My throat tightens. Wrenching my eyes open, I turn my head and peer up into the shadowed obscurity above. Aurae's face appears above me, like an angel in the darkness. Tear tracks score through the blood and grime on her cheeks, and her doe-soft eyes stare out from deep, fearful hollows. But she's here. Alive. Cradling my head in her lap.

"Oh, Ilsie!" she says, her voice rattling strangely. "I feared you wouldn't wake!"

I reach for her, gripping her hands tight, and try to sit up. Lights seem to burst in my head. I grimace. The last thing I remember is that fae man with the dark band of warpaint streaked across his eyes, bowing over me where I fell. His face, all hard, ferocious edges, was highlighted by the strange fire emanating from the horned beast at his side. The unicorn.

Another groan vibrates in my throat. I squeeze my eyes shut, desperate to drive that image from my mind. Then, setting my teeth, I try again to push myself upright, this time succeeding with Aurae's help. Her hands flutter like little birds. "Where are we?" I ask. My mouth feels as though it's stuffed with rags, and my voice sounds thick and heavy.

"I'm not sure," Aurae says. "A cage."

Even as she speaks, there's a tremendous jolt, and we fall into each other. Moans fill the darkness around us, punctuated by whispered snippets of prayer. We're in a cart of some sort—a cage on wheels, rattling over rough terrain. Heavy animal hides cover the bars, allowing in only brief cracks of eerie red light. By this glow I'm able to discern something of our fellow captives: priests and novitiates, all unfamiliar to my eyes. No sign of Captain Wulfram

78

or his men. But then, they're all dead. Lying with their throats cut in the front hall of the guest house. Slain by Artoris's people.

I shudder, pressing my shoulder against Aurae's. How could I have been so foolish? How could I have trusted that man? I've held the memory of him in my heart for so long, I never stopped to question the accuracy of that memory. To ask myself what sort of man Artoris really is. I always dreamed he would one day ride back to rescue me: from my father, from my life, from my future. For a moment it had seemed as though that dream was truly about to come to pass, complete with the hero astride his dashing white stallion.

Almost unconsciously I rub my cheek, bruised from the blow he'd dealt me. Nausea churns in my gut. But I can't be sick, I won't allow it. This little cage stinks so horribly as it is, and I will not add to it. Swallowing back acid, I sit a little straighter, and ask in a clearer voice than before, "How long have I been unconscious?"

Aurae shakes her head. A flash of red light lances between the bars, briefly lighting up her tear-filmed eyes. "I'm not sure. It's been hours. They stopped twice, once to pass food in through the bars. Bread and a little water. I tried to give you some, but you choked, so I gave it to a priest, who was badly wounded. He's dead now." Her voice breaks, but she takes a deep breath and presses on bravely. "They stopped a second time to drag his body out. I don't know what they did with it. We've not stopped since then. I . . . I think it might have been a full day." She stops again, struggling some moments before she can continue. "Oh, Ilsie! I feared they would stop again and pull your body out. I thought . . . I thought . . ."

She begins to weep. Gently I pull her head down to my shoulder, offering her what little shelter I can behind a veil of my own snarled hair. Her body heaves, and occasionally she draws a ragged breath, but otherwise her tears fall in silence. Gods, what am I supposed to do? I'm the older sister, after all. Older, stronger, braver. Whatever strange image of violence I'd thought I'd glimpsed in the mayhem last night—that deft snatching of my dagger, that perfectly performed pirouette, that gush of blood—it wasn't real. It couldn't be. Aurae is delicate as a fawn, innocent as a dove. And she must be protected at all costs. How, I'm not sure; but it's up to me to find a way.

I look around at the faces of our fellow prisoners. Some of them glance our way, but most keep their heads bowed, their hands pressed together in attitudes of prayer. Do they think Lamruil will help us? I certainly don't. If the gods had meant to help us, they would have gifted me with something useful, something I might use to burst this cage and smite our enemies with divine fire. They gave me a pretty voice instead. That's on them.

So I offer no prayers of my own. Instead I try to wrap my mind around what happened. I had assumed the attack was due to my presence at the temple, that my father's enemy, Prince Ruvaen, sent his men to take me prisoner or kill me. But the fae had seemed far more intent on Artoris than me, as though he was their target all along. It's possible they don't know who my sister and I really are. Why else would they throw us in with the rest of the prisoners? This secret might be our only advantage. Not much of an advantage, to be sure. But at least it's something.

Aurae is quiet now. I hope she's fallen asleep. I wish I could slip back into unconsciousness. Oblivion was certainly preferable to this stink, this fear, this cramped and claustrophobic darkness. I strain my ears for some sound from outside our little cage, but the heavy hides block voices, and the rumble and jolt of the wheels make it hard to concentrate on anything else.

"Ilsie," Aurae says suddenly, lifting her head from my shoulder. "Ilsie, will you sing?"

My stomach knots. I don't sing. Not unless I'm forced to. Other than last night, I haven't sung since Father commanded me to perform for the Shadow King. When I set out on my Maiden's Journey, I vowed that I would never sing again, a vow I've broken only once.

I grimace, remembering the moment of sheer desperation when I opened my mouth and sang at that fae warrior. What possessed me to try such a ridiculous thing? Though I must admit, it did work . . . momentarily at least. My voice always has a profound effect on those who hear it. I'm told it sends them back to places of happy memory and fills them with the comfort of home. Not exactly a deadly weapon, but it had certainly stopped that fae in his tracks.

In the end it was useless, however. A useless ploy, a useless gift.

I breathe out a sigh and press my face into the palms of my hands. "I can't sing," I whisper, fairly certain it's true. My throat is raw and parched, in desperate need of water, and fear tightens my vocal cords. I doubt I could utter more than a pathetic croak.

But Aurae presses into my shoulder. "Please," she begs. "Please, what else can we do? What else can we give them?"

Them? I blink in surprise. Even now my sister is more concerned about the well-being of her fellow prisoners than her own plight. She looks at me with such entreaty. Sweet Aurae. She shouldn't be here. It's my fault she is in this situation. If I'd not left her behind, if I'd been with her when the attack began, then maybe . . .

A lump forms in my throat. Not exactly conducive to singing, but I nod. "All right. I'll try."

Dropping my gaze to my own bound hands, I seek to summon up something, anything, from deep inside. Some spark of that divine fire which the gods, in their capriciousness, poured upon me in a flood of power entirely unasked for. I feel nothing. But Aurae is watching me. While I doubt very much that the priests will care for this spontaneous concert, I can't disappoint her.

So I begin to hum, then to softly croon the words of the first song which comes to mind:

"When the nightingale sings,
The wood waxens green,

WARBRIDE

Leaf and grass and blossoms spring
In the morning of the year serene."

My gods-gift begins to glow in the hollow of my chest, warming each word as it rises to my tongue and tumbles free. I feel the difference in the cage around me as the familiar tune of the old lullaby wraps around each suffering soul. I might hate this gift—but I cannot deny its power.

"And love is to my spirit gone
With one spear's thrust so keen.
Night and day my soul rejoices
In the one my heart hath seen."

One by one, all those fearful faces turn toward me, some in shock, some in surprise. A few flash angry grimaces. But as the words emerge haltingly from my throat, those expressions melt away into the same relaxed, far-seeing calm I've witnessed many times on the faces of my listeners. Each man slips away to some place of peace and comfort deep in his memory. Even Aurae utters a little sigh and rests her head once more on my shoulder. I close my eyes and lean my cheek against the top of her head, still singing. This might well be my last song. Let it be a good one, the best I have to offer.

Images appear in my own mind—my sisters and I in the

springtime gardens of Beldroth. Elegant and reserved Faraine, the eldest, always watchful over the rest of us. Gentle and fawnlike Aurae, kneeling to nurture new blossoms or to assist a fallen fledgling. And me—the ill-fitted, in-between sister, who scrambled up trees to lob pinecones at our infuriated nursemaids, and climbed the garden wall just to feel the thrill of that ten foot drop below, to glimpse the wild hope of open spaces beyond. Open spaces I could never quite reach, because I lacked the courage to leap . . .

A terrible jolt, and I nearly swallow my own tongue. All my rapt listeners gasp as though in pain at the song so abruptly ended. One elderly priest curses, his eyes glaring at me in the dark. "Are we not in peril enough, witch, without you casting evil spells upon us?"

I open my mouth to offer a sharp retort, but suddenly many voices erupt outside. Harsh voices, speaking in a language entirely lacking in any songlike cadence. My stomach knots at the sound, but I pull free of Aurae's grasping fingers, turn in place, and fit my hands awkwardly through the cage bars to grip a flap of the animal hide covering. Pulling it back, I peer out into the shadow-filled world beyond.

We seem to have reached some sort of encampment. I can't make much sense of it. There are fires, and figures surrounding these, and peaked shapes that might be tents. We seem to be stopped close to some large stone building, but whether it is a castle, a tower, or merely a big barn, I cannot tell from this angle. There are too many bodies, too many voices, and occasional glimpses of big, hunch-shouldered beasts for which I have no name.

And yet, somehow, my gaze is drawn straight through this confusion to a single point—a platform, crudely constructed, with eight crooked steps leading up to it. My stomach drops. Though I see no sign of pillory or block or hangman's noose, it looks too much like an execution scaffold to be anything else.

I drop the flap and pull my hands back into the cart, heart thudding against my breastbone. "What is it?" Aurae demands, her voice trembling. "What did you see?"

My mouth moves, but no answer will come. I don't want to tell her. I don't want her to know. I find her cold hands with mine, grip her fingers hard. "Aurae—" I begin, uncertain what lie I'm going to tell.

Suddenly the flap at the back of the cage is yanked aside. Three terrifying faces peer through the bars, features marred with black streaks, like old tears. Their eyes are no longer rage-filled pits of inky darkness, however. They are clear, shining, and strangely catlike, all greens and shimmering golds. Under other circumstances, I might say they were beautiful; but their beauty only makes them more horrible.

They fling open the back of the cage. Long arms reach in, catching hold of the nearest priest. He utters a piercing shriek before he is dragged out. A few of his fellows try to hold on to him, futile efforts to prevent their brother from being taken, but the fae beat them back. All sparks of courage extinguished, they huddle into the far end of the cage, pressing against each other to get away from that opening.

The flap of hide drops once more. After that flash of light from outside, the sudden return of shadow is nearly blinding. Aurae weeps softly, clinging to me. "What's happening?" she asks. "What are they going to do to him?"

I can't begin to answer. Will they execute the man in front of that horde of witnesses? But why? He is certainly no valuable prisoner, and his execution will mean nothing. If they were going to kill him, why go through the trouble of tossing him in this cage and carting him across the countryside? Unless . . . unless . . . Sounds of a goat's final bleating struggle fill my head. I see again that trickle of blood slithering across the altar stone, pooling in the gutter below. They say the fae still practice the old ways of worshipping the gods, sacrificing prisoners of war in their honor. Is that why we've been brought here? Fodder for some dark, religious ritual?

I wrap my arms around Aurae and hold on to her. Leaning in, I whisper, "Close your eyes. Listen to my voice." I begin to sing again then, softly, just for her ears.

"Shut up!" the priest crowded nearest to us growls. "Now is the time for prayer, not song." I shoot him a glare and continue singing, trying to drown out the bark of voices outside our cage, trying to drown out my own terror. One voice rises above the others, such a hideous snarl. I close my ears to it, focus on my own melody.

It's the only comfort I can offer Aurae in what may be our final moments. She is still shivering, but her open weeping has ceased for the moment.

A sudden eruption of sound, like a cheer, makes me choke. The next moment the flap is lifted again, and the cage door is flung wide. More reaching arms, more beautiful, black-stained faces. Another priest, a young novitiate, is dragged forth, screaming. Barks of what must be laughter drown out his cries.

Aurae is whispering prayers now, a steady stream of supplication to Nornala, Goddess of Unity. Of all the deities she might pick! If I were to pray, I would call upon Tanatar, God of War, to rain hellfire down on these fiends. I try to keep singing, but my throat simply closes up. Instead I listen intently to the rise and fall of those awful voices, the cruel laughter, the jeers, the shouts. Once I think I hear the young novitiate's voice cry out, but I don't understand his words. He's drowned out almost immediately in another explosion of cheers. Is he dead? Was it quick?

The flap opens. Arms reach in.

Only this time, the priests scramble and push, jostling me and my sister. I lose my grip on her, and she tumbles forward, and those reaching hands grasp her by her hair.

"*Ilsevel!*" she screams as they haul her out. Out of the cage. Out of my reach.

"No! No, Aurae, *no!*" I fling myself forward, scratching, scrabbling, desperate and wild. I grip the bars at the cage opening, blinking against the red glare, trying to see her, trying to make sense of the mayhem.

A beautiful face looms before me and smiles. Then a hand catches me around the throat. "Not your turn yet, pretty one," a silken voice slips through those bared teeth. "You're next. And you can be sure I'll try for you myself!"

A vicious shove, and I fall backwards, landing hard on the cart floor, struggling to catch a breath. By the time I've managed to scramble upright, the cage door is slammed shut. I throw myself at it, trying to get my hands through the bars, to rip aside the heavy hide flap. I scream my sister's name over and over again. Once I think I hear her calling back to me, but the roar of a thousand fae voices drowns her out. No matter how I strain, I cannot hear Aurae anymore.

She's gone.

Gone.

6
TAAR

THE GRIMSPIRE STANDS TALL UPON THE HORIZON, A
shining beacon rising from the mist-wrapped shadows of
Wanfriel Forest. It is a great tower, a wonder to behold—
tall and thin as a needle. One might almost imagine it pierced
heaven itself.

Ruvaen had the spire constructed in the early days of his
campaign into the human world, as a means to channel magic
from Noxaur. Otherwise the atmosphere of the human realm is
too magic-deprived to support fae life, and his warriors would fade
and shrivel. To leave the vicinity of the spire for any great length of
time will cause lasting damage, which is why, after every venture,
his men must return here to replenish their supply.

Elydark lifts his head and trills a glad song from deep in his chest, as I and my company emerge through the trees and come within sight of the Grimspire. The licorneir are beings of pure magic and delight in the proximity to the fae spires. I don't like it. Our bond is more than enough to sustain him, and the last thing I need is for any of our licorneir to become dependent on the fae.

I signal, and my company comes to a standstill. "We make camp here," I declare, looking back across the weary faces of my men and women. Twenty set out from the Hidden City with me to answer Ruvaen's call to arms; only twelve remain. The death mage's spells took three of them in quick succession once the fighting began, but that was not the worst of it.

No, the worst were those crimson cloaks. Those cursed mages, who did not fight like mages at all. Not once did any of them summon a spell but met our attack with swords and ferocious bloodthirst. We cut them down, one after the other, and yet . . . I shudder as the memory plays through my head. They rose up again. Time after time, like waves hitting the shore. And each time they rose, they were quicker, stronger, more deadly. Worse still, they knew our fighting style, knew every secret, anticipated every move. In the end I could do nothing but order my people to retreat . . . even as I, seeing the mage gallop back up the temple road, chased after in hard pursuit. I was determined not to lose him, not to lose the chance to claim that talisman. I was ready and willing to risk everything.

But I was not prepared for what I met within those temple grounds.

A face flashes through my mind's eye: Shanaera. Dead. As dead as she was three years ago, when I drove my own blade through her abdomen and left her in the field of battle. And yet she stood before me. Looked me in the eye.

"Surprise." Her voice whispers once more in the back of my head.

But that couldn't have been real. It must have been some spell, some Miphates enchantment, which caught me and warped my perceptions. Mage Artoris must have whispered an incantation while I was distracted binding his hands. He filled my head with these hideous images. It's the only explanation I can accept.

I grit my teeth, forcing my attention back to the present. "Kildorath," I call to my second in command. "Ashika."

They have already dismounted and begun the process of erecting our field tents. Their licorneir both carry the remains of fallen comrades, sewn into their cloaks for the journey home. They turn at the sound of my call, faces full of old battle wounds and recent loss. Kildorath's expression is fierce, Ashika's solemn.

"Leave your licorneir and come with me," I say, dismounting Elydark. "We will make our report to Ruvaen."

Both riders turn at once to their mounts, reluctant to be parted. Elydark also touches his soft nose to my chest. **Vellar,** he speaks into my head, **let me come with you.**

But I know too well what will happen once he gets near to that spire. The draw of magic will lure him, and though I trust the bond we share, I don't care to have it tested. *Stay, my friend,* I tell him, running a hand down his neck beneath the sheen of his long mane. *Stay and watch over the others. They are suffering and will need your presence to give them confidence.*

Elydark casts his gaze across the remaining licorneir. We managed to catch and subdue three of the heart-torn beasts in hopes they might be saved. The others fled into the night, stricken with grief. Their riders dead, they will not last long in the human world, are likely already faded to whisps of memory and sorrow.

I will care for them, Elydark says and meets my gaze. **You may depend on me.**

His eyes are ageless and endless, windows into the eternity of the realm from which he springs. But they are also familiar. I trust no other in this life as I trust my licorneir. I stroke his nose again, then turn to beckon Kildorath and Ashika. Without another word, we make for the Grimspire.

The grounds surrounding the great white structure are crowded with Noxaurians and mercenary forces from across the Eledrian Realms, whom Prince Ruvaen hired to assist in his ongoing assault on these lands. I and my crew are one such mercenary force, sworn to serve the Prince of Night temporarily, to our mutual benefit. There was a time when the fae would not have treated with my kind. I was more than a little surprised when the prince showed up on the edge of my land one day and proposed the alliance. We quickly discovered a natural alignment of interests, however. Though I am king of my own people, I humbled myself for their sakes and swore service to the prince until such a time as my oath is fulfilled.

I've had plenty of opportunity over the years to regret that oath. While Ruvaen himself has proven a fair and judicious lord, he is too often surrounded by faithless monsters seeking only to further their own rapacious ends. Monsters like Lurodos.

I meet the Noxaurian warlord at the base of the spire. We have avoided each other since last night's attack; I would have been just as happy to never set eyes on the man again, if I'm honest. Streaks of dried virulium still stain his cheeks, his neck, his shoulders. He smiles at the sight of me, showing bloody teeth. "Well now, if it isn't our half-breed king," he says, and offers a mocking bow. "Did your men manage a bit of fun last night, or did my lot hog the choicest pickings?"

His rabble absolutely decimated the temple and left it a pile of burning ruin, a gigantic pyre for the fallen priests' corpses. While I am no friend of humans, the utter brutality of the act leaves me sickened.

Silently vowing to stick my knife in his throat if the gods ever grant me the opportunity, I merely nod and enter the spire, my two warriors swift on my heels. Lurodos chuckles and falls into step behind. We mount the spiral steps to the upper chamber where Ruvaen awaits our report. A human slave, all long face and downcast eyes, opens the door for our entrance, announcing softly: "Master, King Taarthalor and Lord Lurodos have arrived."

Ruvaen stands across the room before a tall window, overlooking the campsite below. His back is to us, and with his long white hair and silvery robes, he might well be a statue standing there in the glow of a single glowing *incantis* orb, which hovers in the center of the high ceiling. The orb light flickers in the depths of vivid violet eyes, when he turns to look at us as we step through the door. Those eyes are sharp, shrewd, never missing any opportunity that might chance to reveal itself. Though Ruvaen is but a prince, he has ruled in Noxaur for many turns of the cycle now. His father is not dead—beyond that, no one knows. Ruvaen keeps his secrets and keeps them well.

He eyes me with interest now, reading truth in my face no matter how carefully I mask each emotion. He waits until I, my two followers, Lurodos, and his three brutes all stand before him before speaking. "So," he says, "after all this—after all the information and resources and outpouring of magic I've provided—the two of you have failed to apprehend Mage Artoris."

Lurodos crosses his arms over his enormous chest. "It's this *ibrildian* king of yours. He was too meek and mild at the last, unwilling to give his men the virulium and take out the mage's defenses in one fell swoop."

Ruvaen turns sharply to me. "Is this true?"

I meet his gaze coldly. "I will not give my people virulium unless I have no other choice."

Lurodos throws back his head and laughs outright. "*Shakh-*

less half-breed! What, are our Noxaurian ways too much for your delicate constitutions? There was a time you Licornyn weren't so squeamish."

My jaw grinds hard enough to shatter stone. It's true—not many years ago, virulium was passed among the ranks of my riders. I was, for the most part, resistant to using it myself, knowing as I did the source from which the venom springs. But I did not prevent others from dosing in the heat of battle, and could not deny the results when we claimed victory after victory. It is possible, if I had allowed my men to use it last night, we would not have lost so many to the death mages.

But I vividly remember what it felt like to drive my sword into Shanaera's gut.

I remember the startled look in her eyes, even through the black madness, even through the streaked tears.

I remember weeping, useless apologies spilling from my lips, even as I lowered her body to the ground in the midst of that battlefield.

She had turned on her own. She was slaughtering our people. The demonic brew got the better of her, and she could no longer discern friend from foe. I had no choice but to take her down. Though in truth, I'd lost her already. Whatever Shanaera once was had been devoured by virulium long before my blade pierced her flesh.

"I would rather die than taste that evil brew again," I declare now, my voice a low growl.

"You certainly will die then," Lurodos replies. "You and all your kind, as Morthiel captures you, one by one, and drags you into his hidden fortress. Who will care for your virtuous abstinence then? Not I. I'll laugh and cheer the gods-damned mortal mages on in their endeavors!"

"Enough, Lurodos," Ruvaen says, his voice soft but quick as a knife. The Noxaurian lord shuts his mouth, though his eyes continue to burn into mine, full of resentful hatred. "Why don't you go see to the auction and pick yourself a likely slave to cheer your spirits?"

Lurodos shrugs. "I have slaves enough."

"Then tend your wounded, count your earnings, or file your reptant's bloody nails for all I care. Just remove yourself from my sight and be quick about it."

The Noxaurian warlord's lip curls, but he holds out his hand and accepts the sack of silver offered by Ruvaen's slave. Half of the sum agreed upon should we successfully bring Mage Artoris in alive—still a generous payment for a mission gone so disastrously awry. Lurodos hefts the sack once, then bows and exits the room, tossing back over his shoulder, "I'm off to count the heads of the priests I collected last night. I'll pick a choice one for you to remember me by, King Half-Breed. Consider it a gift."

I make no response but breathe a little easier when the man is gone. I meet the prince's eye, and he motions with one hand. "Send your people out, Taar. I would have words with you in private."

Kildorath and Ashika turn to me, unwilling to take orders from a Noxaurian. I nod, and they step from the room, silent and wary. They will wait just outside the door, ready to come at my shout. But I am safe enough with the Prince of Night.

The moment my Licornyn are gone, and the slave has shut the door behind them and himself, Ruvaen utters a foul curse and runs a hand down his face. "I swear, Taar, that Lurodos is a fiend incarnate. I'd rather hoped he'd get his soul dragged from his body by that death mage—but men like him are hard to put down."

I offer no response. I have often wondered over the years why Ruvaen doesn't cut Lurodos loose. The man has committed war crimes enough to turn the stomach of even the staunchest human-hater. Time and again he's proven impossible to control. But he's powerfully connected in Noxaur. Even Ruvaen, ruling prince that he is, must watch his step. A prince is not a king, after all.

Ruvaen steps back into the chamber and drops into a chair before an ornate, silver table. There is food and drink aplenty, and he waves a hand in silent invitation to me. I shake my head, and he proceeds to pour himself a glass of sparkling *qeise*. "All right, Taar, my friend," he says, swirling the glass idly and watching how the bubbles dance. "Tell me in your own words what took place. How did the death mage slip through your grasp?"

For the space of a single heartbeat, I'm back in that shadowed room, face-to-face with the apparition of Shanaera, pinned against the wall behind our crossed blades. But that is not a story I care to tell or try to explain, even to myself. I say only, "Lurodos could not maintain control over his horde. A death mage like Artoris Kelfaren will be caught with intelligence, not brute force."

Ruvaen sighs and takes a long pull of *qeise*. "One man," he says, more to himself than to me. "One man against fifty Noxaurian raveners and twenty Licornyn riders. The most ferocious forces seen across the worlds. And yet he got away. One man."

"He was not alone," I admit somewhat reluctantly. "He had ten men with him."

"More death mages?"

I shake my head. Whatever those crimson cloaks were, they weren't Miphates. I don't think they were even human. A terrible suspicion has been growing in my mind in the long hours of our journey to the Grimspire. But I'm not ready to share just yet. I need time and evidence. Besides, part of me still hopes I'm wrong. "I don't know what they were," I admit. "They were skilled in battle and did not seem to be susceptible to our weapons. That is all I can say."

"*Shakh*," Ruvaen groans and leans back in his chair, staring up at the *incantis* orb shimmering overhead. "Do you know, I'd almost believed Evisar Citadel was within our grasp? After all these years."

Silently I study the prince. Sitting there, sprawled in his chair, glass in hand, the front of his robe partially undone, to all appearances, he would seem the picture of the indolent fae lord, careless and cruel, without a worry in the worlds. But this is not the Ruvaen I know.

He has never shared with me why he longs to breach the barriers of Evisar. I myself have reason enough—the simple drive to return to the city of my birth, to reclaim the ancient capitol of my kingdom, to restore Licorna to the glory it knew in the days of my father and grandfather and great-grandfather, back as far as memory can recall and farther. That glory should have continued undimmed for generations to come . . . save that my father foolishly allied himself with humans and permitted Miphates to enter his domain.

Oh yes, I have reasons aplenty to seek the reclamation of my city, my citadel. But Ruvaen's motives remain a mystery.

"All is not entirely lost," I say after a time. Reaching into the pouch at my belt, I withdraw the talisman hidden there—the triangle of dark gold containing the rotating sphere, etched all over with Miphates spell-writing. "I managed to retrieve this off the mage's neck."

Ruvaen holds out his hand to accept the trophy I offer. His eyes flare in the *incantis* light, leaping to meet mine. "Is this what I think it is?"

"The key through the *obscuris* spell surrounding Evisar," I say. "Unfortunately I could not apprehend the mage himself to work the spell, but if you can find yourself another Miphato with the necessary spell-craft . . ."

"Say no more." The prince leaps to his feet, clutching the

talisman in his fist, his face alight with ferocious excitement. "I have Miphates prisoners aplenty—surely one of them is still intact enough to chant a spell or two. Do you realize what this means, Taar?"

I do. It means we are closer than we ever have been to recovering the kingdom I once knew, to purging the land of the dark infestation that has so poisoned it since the final days of my father's rule. "You will muster your forces for an attack on the citadel then?" I ask, trying to keep my own eagerness in check.

"I will," Ruvaen agrees. "It will take some doing. And, of course, we must find a way to work the talisman first. But the time is finally right, my friend. I will honor the oath I made to you on our first meeting. Together, you and I shall drive those Miphates bastards from your realm and reestablish your city under Licornyn rule." He extends his hand, and I do not hesitate to grasp it. "Prepare your warriors to ride when I send the word."

"With pleasure, Prince," I respond.

In that moment a burst of raucous cheering erupts from beyond the window, rising from the gathered crowd. The noise has rumbled in the background of my awareness throughout this interview, though I hardly marked it before this moment. Ruvaen releases my hand and glides to the window to look out on the goings on below. "Ah!" he says, gazing out. "The bidding is well underway, I see. What a sorry specimen that is. It's a wonder any will part with hard-earned silver for him."

Curious, I move to the window and stand at his shoulder. Down below, a ragged priest is dragged up onto a platform surrounded by greedy Noxaurian faces. "What is this?" I ask, my brow furrowing.

Ruvaen shrugs. "The humans Lurodos says you insisted on not killing in cold blood." He casts me a sidelong glance. "It is tradition among Noxaurians to sell off prisoners to the highest bidder."

My blood goes cold. I'd never stopped to consider the fate of those whose lives I spared. "And what will happen to them?"

"Most will be transported back to Noxaur," Ruvaen replies. "Human slaves are valuable, you know. They are generally more malleable than other species and extremely hardworking if properly motivated. A well-treated human slave can last a long while in Eledria. But, ah! What is this?"

Even as he speaks, the priest is dragged from the platform, and the crowd parts to make room for the next captive. She steps into the glow of the three floating *incantis* globes, and my heart seems to lodge between my ribs.

It's her.

It's the girl, the one who sang to me in the temple, freezing me in place. The ferocious young woman who fought so hard to defend her fallen sister. I'd sent them to be gathered with the other captives, hoping to keep them from being slaughtered and burned with the rest of the temple inhabitants. In truth I've not thought of her since; my mind has been plagued by too many other concerns. But there she is, standing under that glaring spell-light, her shoulders back, her head high. Even clad in tattered, blood-stained garments, her hair snarled around her shoulders, she looks fierce and proud. Like a queen.

"Well, this is certainly unexpected," Ruvaen says. "I thought you said it was a temple full of moldering old priests? How did this lovely flower end up in the fray? A little nun, perhaps?"

My mind flashes back to the vicious way she went at me with both knife and nails. "I think not."

Ruvaen grunts. "No matter. Nun or not, underneath all that grime is a trophy indeed. She'll make a fine warbride."

"A what?" I turn to the prince sharply, studying the side of his face.

He offers me a small, mirthless smile. "Did you not know? Any female captives are sold as brides, not slaves. The men get lonely on these long campaigns, you see. It's a way to keep their spirits up and might encourage a *little* less random slaughter of the peaceful populace along the way." At my horrified expression, he lifts an eyebrow. "A brutish practice, I know. What would you have me do? I maintain control here by a thread. I am not king, after all."

"What happens to these warbrides?" I demand, my throat tight, my mouth hard.

Ruvaen grunts. "It's best not to ask."

I stare down at that horrible scene—the red lights, the leering shadows, the hungry faces of the Noxaurian warriors, still stained with *virulium* residue. I know what will happen to the girl. I know what her fate will be this night and, should she live to see them, all the nights to follow, for the rest of her life.

The bidding has begun. Harsh voices sing out in quick succession, eager to claim this choice prize. The auction master grows agitated, clearly not hearing the sum he seeks. He barks at the crowd, even throws a knife into their midst. They back away slightly, looking at each other, and for a moment, the bidding ceases.

Then a stir of movement in the back of the throng. I rip my gaze away from the upright little figure under the lights, trying to see who has come. To my horror, Lurodos strides to the base of the platform, his leering face bathed in *incantis* glow.

"Fifty silver heds!" he declares, his voice carrying up to the spire window. "Fifty," he repeats, and licks his lips, "for this toothsome human morsel."

7

ILSEVEL

＊───◦❀◦───＊

AS I STAND HERE ON THIS AUCTION BLOCK AND LISTEN
to these hideous voices bidding for my life and body, I
find myself wishing suddenly—distantly, stupidly—that
I'd understood before what the alliance with the Shadow King
meant: a shield. To stand between me and all the evil forces of
the fae realm. For who among these monsters could match the
monster bridegroom my father picked for me? He could hew any
one of them in two with a single swing of his right arm. I, and all
Gavaria, might have been spared, as the troll king and his terrible
horde sent these creatures howling back to whatever dark realm
would claim them.

I may not have loved my intended husband. But perhaps he
would have offered me that protection I never received from

any man in my life. Not my father—his only protection was to keep me unsullied to serve his ultimate purpose. Certainly not Artoris. He sought to claim me, to possess me, and I mistook it for something else entirely.

Now I stand unprotected before this teeming mass. No father, no lover, no husband to shield me. I have nothing but my own tattered courage between me and the horrors this night will bring. In a few moments one of these monsters will drag me away into the dark, and then . . .

"Come on, you gremlin scat-stains!" the taloned man standing behind me rumbles, rolling his eyes in mock disgust at the crowd. He waves a hand at me, a sweeping gesture that curves to mimic the lines of my body, no longer hidden beneath my cloak. "Twelve, fifteen, twenty heds . . . Is that the best you can dredge up from your miserable asses for this lithe and lovely female? Or do you want me to put her aside and bring out another priestling instead?"

"Twenty-five!" someone shouts at once.

The auction master groans and flings something sharp into the crowd. Monsters part ways, whooping with laughter, as a nasty, curved blade vibrates in the ground beside the boot of the offending bidder. "Let me hear fifty, or I'll send the next one through your eye!" the auction master cries. "Do I hear fifty? Fifty heds, or I send her back to the cage."

The staring eyes blink up at me, the leering mouths murmuring to one another, but no one answers the auction master's demand. For a moment hope swells. Sure, the cage is not exactly freedom, but it's better than the alternative, isn't it? Perhaps I can work out some means of escape, find Aurae, and—Oh gods. Was Aurae sold as a bride as well? No, I can't think about that now. I've got to be sharp, got to watch for my chance and be ready to take it. I've got to—

"Fifty silver heds!"

A ripple of movement stirs the shadowy mass before my eyes. I blink against the glare of light overhead, struggling to see. A new figure appears among the rest, dwarfing the others with a bulk that is absolutely staggering. Long hair of pure, shining silver flows to his waist, and his skin is dark with a strange, purple sheen under the otherworldly glow of those orbs. Muscles bulge across every exposed inch of him, from his thick neck to his powerful calves. It's almost grotesque, yet I find it impossible to look away from him. Perhaps it's glamour.

But there are those telltale streaks of black tears marring his cheeks, just like the rest. I know the moment I set eyes on him that it was he who led the attack on Ashryn Shrine.

"Fifty," he says again, drawing close to the edge of the platform. He's so tall, his head is almost on a level with my feet. He smiles up at me, a hungry expression. "For this toothsome human morsel."

My stomach drops. My knees turn to water. Of all the monsters who might claim me, somehow I know this is the worst. If he takes me, I will surely die . . . but not tonight and not soon. I see it in his eyes, like a promise, like a vow. He will keep me alive for a long, long while, and, when death finally comes, I will praise the gods for even the most painful release.

Silence captures the whole of that noisy throng. The fae look at one another, trying to decide who among them is brave enough to bid against this man. He throws back his head and utters a laugh like a wolf's howl straight to the stars above. "Will none of you test me?" he demands, opening wide his arms and turning slowly in place. "Have none of you the courage? Come! Bid on! See how high you can drive the price."

He goes on taunting, but switches back to that snarling tongue which I do not understand. When he happens to catch my eye, he laughs again and points at me. "Hurry up, Ralnor!" he demands of the auction master. "These fools would rather *shakh* themselves than throw in their lot against me. Take my bid and hand over my prize. She's eager for her wedding night to begin—look at that lusty face!"

At this the throng begins to laugh again, calling out suggestions of what I might do to please my new husband in the hours before dawn. The auction master laughs loudest of all and, though perhaps disappointed he could not drive the price harder still, begins the countdown. "Lord Lurodos takes the warbride at fifty silver heds! Going once . . . going twice . . ."

"Fifty-one."

A sudden intake of breath gusts through the crowd.

"Who said that?" the fae—Lord Lurodos—demands, whirling with a smile that's close to a snarl. "Who dares come between me and this sweet human flesh? Show yourself!"

My lungs are too tight to manage even a gasp. Breathless and lightheaded, I can do nothing but shift my gaze to the back of the horde, where yet another path is being made and yet another figure approaches at a rapid stride. He steps into the glow of the suspended orbs, and I feel as though I've been punched in the gut. Because I know him: the man who took me captive, who struck me and left me in that cage. The band of black warpaint across his temples is gone, as is the fiery magic which had burned deep in his eyes. But I know him. That face will haunt my nightmares to the end of my days.

And did he . . . did he just bid on me? Against this massive monster?

He comes to a stop eight feet from Lurodos, and no man dares stand between them. It's as though some powerful force propels the other fae back, so that the two of them stand in a clear space before the platform, beneath the orb light. They are an interesting contrast—both massive and muscled, but while the one is swollen to the point of distortion, this new man is well-proportioned, sculpted rather than bulky. He projects no glamour that I can discern, though it may be that his magic is simply better disguised. His long black hair is tightly braided back from his face and falls in thick waves past his shoulders. A beard shapes his jaw in clean, strong lines, unexpected on the face of a fae man. He might be the only man or monster in this entire gathering to sport facial hair.

The newcomer folds his arms, muscles moving in the light in a way that makes me lightheaded. He wears nothing on his torso save pauldrons. The leather straps crisscross over his chest, emphasizing its breadth and definition. He looks straight at Lord Lurodos and states again in a loud voice which rumbles across the murmuring crowd of onlookers: "Fifty-one silver heds for the warbride."

Lurodos barks with laughter, slapping his knees as though this is the greatest joke. "What is this? Does the little half-breed have a spine of bone after all?" Though his lips twist back to show each and every bloody tooth, there's no mirth in his eyes. He turns to the auction master again and bellows: "Sixty heds. Call it, man, and hand her over."

Shaking so hard my breath rattles, I turn my head to see the auction master's uneasy gaze darting back and forth between the two fae warlords. He does not like that this new man has arrived. His attitude implies he believes things will go badly for him personally. In a rush he starts to say: "To Lord Lurodos and sixty heds, going once—"

"Sixty-one."

My eyes shoot back to the second warlord. He doesn't look at me but keeps his gaze focused on Lurodos, as though sighting prey. Though he does not touch them, he wears twin knives on his belt, and I get the impression that he's loosened them in their sheaths, ready to draw at need. The gold jewels set in their hilts catch the orb light like winking embers.

Lurodos doesn't laugh this time. He takes a single step toward his nemesis, then whirls and barks, "Seventy—"

"Seventy-one," the newcomer inserts.

The fae monsters draw back still farther, exchanging eager glances and murmuring in their excitement. By their gestures, they seem to think the two bidders will soon come to blows. And they might. The tension in the atmosphere between them is palpable. A single spark, and it will combust. And where will I be then? Could it be the distraction I need? Perhaps the sight of these two brutal warlords trying to gut each other will be absorbing enough that I might slip away over the back end of the platform and vanish into the forest of tents and shadows beyond.

I grip my ragged skirts, heart thudding so hard, I cannot comprehend the auction master's words when he calls out behind me. He must be trying to make light of the situation though, for a ripple of laughter carries through the onlookers. Lord Lurodos draws a breath through flared nostrils, but steps back half a pace, turns to the auction master and says: "Very well. No human is worth the price, but I'm a sporting man. One hundred silver heds." He pulls a sack of coin from his belt and tosses it lightly. The metallic *clink-clink* inside seems to echo in my ears.

My gaze flicks back to the second man, the second monster.

Will he answer the bid? Do I want him to? Of the two men, I can't say which I fear most. Is there ever a good choice between the bear and the tiger? Both will rip my flesh from my bones in the end. I find myself staring at those twin knives once more. I set my teeth. Whatever happens, I'm not going down without a fight.

"What's this, Taar?" Lurodos goads, hefting the little sack once more. "Had enough already? I thought you were a man of—"

"One hundred and one."

The second warlord's voice rings loud in the emptiness of the first man's unspoken words. For a moment they stare at one another. Then Lurodos, all amusement gone from his face, strides forward with such purpose, I think they will actually collide, possibly even kill each other. I brace, ready to make my mad dash for freedom, little caring for the fact that a sea of monsters surrounds me on all sides. The second warlord—Taar—holds out his arms as though daring the first to take his shot. Lurodos stops. Some of his glamour flickers and fades, revealing a glimpse of the truth beneath—a gaunt, ghastly visage, all hollow-eyed and hollow-cheeked. More cadaver than man, with long blackened teeth.

The next instant the glamour pulls back into place, radiating beauty so potent, I turn my face away, lifting a hand to shield my eyes. "I am done," he says. "I will offer no more. But I give you this chance, my friend. Are you sure you want to pay so much?" His growling voice is suddenly soft and sly, but still carries up to me where I stand. "Is that not the total sum of your earnings from our little venture? Don't give up the price of your dead just for the chance to *shakh* a human. It's not worth it, I assure you. They never last long."

The dark-haired warlord holds his gaze for a long, silent moment. Then he turns to the auction master and says again in a voice of steel: "One hundred and one silver heds. For the warbride."

"Going once," the auction master bellows, painfully eager to see the end of this bidding war. "Going twice. *Sold.*"

A great cheer bursts from that crowd. My ears roar with the sound, this chorus singing the victory of the warlord and my own impending doom. I hear the threats and the violence, the longing and the craving reverberating from each and every throat.

Lurodos sneers and reties his money sack to his belt. He tips his head and sweeps an arm in my direction, as though giving his blessing to his enemy. The dark man ignores him but grips the edge of the platform and pulls himself up with apparent ease, muscles constricting and relaxing in a hypnotic rhythm of grace and power. He stands tall before me. Gods spare me, my eyes are on the same level as his clavicle! He takes a step, holding out one hand.

I stagger back from him, painfully aware of all the edges around me, of all the hungry eyes and leering mouths crowding in close once more. "Don't touch me," I snarl, pulling myself up straight. My voice shakes, but I infuse it with all the fire I can summon.

The warlord shakes his head. "Come, *zylnala*," he says, holding out one hand. "I will take you away from these creatures. Believe me, they have worse in mind for you than I. Come with me, and I'll see you survive the night."

Am I mad, or is that truth I see glimmering in his eyes? No, it cannot be. He is fae and full of trickery. But I'm not about to be taken in by glamours. I hold very still, let him approach one step at a time.

Then I dart for his belt and slip free one of those two gleaming knives. Quick as a flash, I whip it to his throat and freeze. Caught in the intensity of his stare. Caught in that space between life and death, knowing that I, with this feeble blade clutched in my hand, boast no power over either.

The crowd roars with laughter. Jeers and taunts in many languages split the night, and Lurodos's bellow nearly drowns out all others. My hand trembles. I stare into my captor's eyes—black eyes, so dark the pupils are utterly lost. Long, thick lashes fan his cheeks as he blinks solemnly, waiting for me to do something. Anything. Testing my mettle.

I've never killed a man. I'm not sure how. It should be simple: a vicious slice, a gush of hot blood. Of course if I kill him, there are a thousand more to take his place. But at least I'll die with the knowledge I didn't go quietly. That must be worth something.

A wordless cry on my lips, I begin to move my stolen knife. The blade never makes contact with his skin. Long fingers close around my wrist, twisting painfully. The next moment I'm pivoted on my feet, and a powerful arm locks around my chest, yanking me back hard against that muscled torso.

"I don't want to humiliate you in front of these witnesses." His voice is a threat of distant thunder rumbling in my head. "I will help you. I will save your life. But you must not fight me."

"Skewer you!" I snarl and throw my head back, trying to break his nose. He anticipates me and avoids the blow, still maintaining that grip on my wrist, my arm wrenched up behind my back so that I can do nothing but whimper in his grasp.

"Steady now, *zylnala*," he murmurs. "Steady."

With those words he marches me to the top of the stairs, where the auction master still stands. There's nothing I can do but go where he forces me.

8

TAAR

⟨ornamental divider⟩

WHAT IN THE NINE HELLS HAVE I DONE?

The Noxaurian auction master hisses with delight as I drop the sack of coin into his hand. It is, as Lurodos guessed, the entirety of my payment from Ruvaen. For a moment, as I watch the man heft that sack, as I listen to the *clink* of those silver heds, I see the faces of my dead: six men and two women, all of whom I've known since childhood. Warriors with whom I've bled, suffered, wept, and rejoiced over years of hard-won existence in the ruins of what was once our homeland. They gave their lives last night, but for what? A little pouch of silver to increase our feeble standing among the lords and ladies of Eledria?

No. They fought and they died for the hope of reclaiming Evisar. Nothing more; nothing less.

So I watch that sack of silver disappear into the auction master's tunic, and I suppose it is coin well spent. Might as well buy the life of this woman rather than let the silver molder in some forgotten corner of my *dakath*. Though I'm not sure my people will see the situation in quite the same light.

"Her cloak," I say, holding out my hand to the auction master.

He drapes the stained and tattered garment across my arm and grins, lifting his eyebrows suggestively. "Have a most excellent night, your lordship."

The muscles in the girl's arm tense beneath my grasp. Gods damn the man, is she not frightened enough as it is? I flash my teeth in a snarl but make no answer as I guide her down from the platform. She goes unwillingly, resisting even when doing so sends new shots of pain up her arm and shoulder. Where does she think she'll go if she breaks free?

Halfway down, however, she goes suddenly still then shrinks back into me. I look beyond her to where Lurodos stands, waiting to greet us at the base of the stairs. His gaze rakes slowly over her body, appraising every curve and angle. Finally he flicks that gaze to meet mine.

"Well, Taar, my friend," he says, speaking in growling Noxaurian. "I hope you plan to ride her and ride her hard. If not, come dawn, she is mine. In fact . . ." He takes out his own sack of silver, payment from Ruvaen, and sets it down on the edge of the platform, just at the feet of the auction master. "Payment in advance—testimony of my confidence. You're not man enough to do what you must to keep her from me." He turns his attention back to the girl. Though she stands three steps up from the ground, her head is just about level with his. "My appetite will only be whetted with suspense," he purrs, shifting his words to common Eledrian, which she will understand in her own tongue. "I look forward to getting to know you better. Meanwhile, sleep well and dream of me."

I push from behind. The girl staggers forward, tripping down the last few steps. Only my grip on her arm keeps her upright, but I shift my hold slightly so as not to cause her pain. "Back off, Lurodos," I snarl. "Go find some other poor soul to torment. This one is mine."

"For the moment," he replies, eyes half-lidded as he backs away slowly. "For the moment, yes."

I hasten into the crowd, which parts to make room for us as we go. Blood pounds in my ears. I'm not familiar with Noxaurian customs, but I do know the fae are rigid when it comes to rules and rites. What sorts of laws govern the buying and selling of warbrides? Is there any truth in what Lurodos is claiming, or is he only trying to unnerve me?

If it is true . . . I may have bought this woman only a few hours' reprieve.

The crowd laughs and makes crude remarks as we pass, but otherwise loses interest in us as the next human prisoner is dragged onto that platform, and the bidding begins once more. Just as we reach the end of the mob, however, I find myself face-to-face with Ruvaen. He stands with his arms crossed, a bemused expression on his face. "Well!" he says, grinning broadly from me to the girl and back again. "That was spectacular, I must say. I do enjoy seeing Lurodos taken down a notch or two." He lifts an eyebrow and tips his head a little to one side. "I only hope you have the necessary follow-through."

I meet his gaze, silent.

The prince chuckles, shoulders heaving with mirth. "Come, man, didn't you know? The law of warbrides requires a wedding ceremony immediately upon purchase followed by a consummation, which must take place before dawn. If either of these requirements is unmet, the next highest bidder may claim his winnings at first light." He tips his chin, looking at me from beneath the ledge of his brow. "You have until dawn, my friend." He turns to the girl once more and looks her up and down. "There's a pretty creature under all that grime. I trust you won't find the task too onerous."

It feels as though all the wind has been driven from my lungs. This was not what I'd anticipated, not in the least. I'd thought I'd pay the fee, get her away from the spire, away from Lurodos and his monsters, and just . . . turn her loose. If there's one thing I need even less than a slave, it's a bride. Particularly an unwilling, murderously hateful bride.

My throat is tight. I force my next words out in a painful rasp.

"What sort of ceremony? For the wedding, I mean."

"It doesn't matter," the prince replies easily. "Whatever is suitable for your own people."

I look down at the girl, who's staring determinedly at the ground, her jaw clenched tight. She's a pathetic sight, her gown torn, her skin stained with mud and blood, her hair pulled free from its pins and falling in snarls about her shoulders. Still beautiful, though. Undeniably beautiful, though I curse myself for noticing. Beauty or not, she is a human and, therefore, my natural enemy. Not the woman I would have chosen to take as my wife under any circumstances.

I open my mouth, prepared to tell the prince I've changed my mind and will not accept her. But then I see Lurodos's leering face in my mind's eye. He will take her and break her within the hour, laughing as he does so. She may be human, but I do feel some degree of responsibility for her plight. After all it was I who took her captive, I who put her in that cage. Now her life is once more in my hands, as though the gods themselves have placed her here. Can I, in good conscience, abandon her to certain doom?

No one, not even my worst enemy, deserves to be turned over to the likes of Lurodos.

"So be it," I say, my words clipped and final. Maneuvering the girl, I begin to march her away from the crowd and the spire in the direction of the Licornyn encampment.

"Taar!" Ruvaen calls after me.

I look back, eyes narrow.

"I'll send some of my people to freshen her up a little. Just to help matters along." He smiles, his eyes flashing in the glow of the nearest *incantis* orb. "And you may have use of my personal pavilion for tonight. If you require it."

My gut knots, but I offer a single nod. Then, grimacing, I steer the girl onward. Neither of us speaks, but occasionally she pulls against my hold, determined to break free, though there's nowhere for her to run. "Stop struggling," I growl at last. "You'll only cause yourself pain."

As though in response, she yanks hard enough that I risk breaking her arm if I hold on. Instantly I release my grip. She wrenches away from me, staggers back, turning to face me as though to meet my attack. Her hair tumbles over her face, but she throws it back, and I'm met with a pair of flashing dark eyes, limned with pain. For a moment she stands there, four paces from me, breathing hard.

Then she turns and takes three running strides. And stops. Before her stretches miles of Noxaurian encampment, full of monsters and flickering fires. She backs up, then turns and takes three more steps in the opposite direction. More monsters, more shadows, more glaring red flames. She looks like a hare, foot caught in a snare, running in circles. Not yet willing to accept the inevitable.

Finally she turns and looks at me again. Her full lips are parted and colorless, but a red stain brightens her pale cheeks. Defiance dances in the depths of her eyes even now, despite the hopelessness of her circumstances.

I fold my arms, meeting her gaze firmly, calmly. "You can come along quietly," I say, my voice pitched low and, I hope, nonthreatening, "or you can run. I'll not stop you again. But if you run, you lose my protection henceforth."

"Protection?" Her lip curls. "What protection?"

Even in just those few syllables, her low, throaty voice calls to mind the song she sang in the heat of battle and terror. The naturally melodic quality is intoxicating, no matter how viciously she spits the words. But I must be wary. I must not forget how she transfixed me, rendering me helpless for those few moments in the heat of battle. And Elydark is not here now to break the spell should she try it again.

I take a step toward her. She flinches, but when she doesn't flee, I take another step and another, until I stand mere inches from her. A glare of red light from a nearby campfire dances across her delicate features. She has a dark mark on one cheekbone, a blemish some might say. Not worth the price of a hundred silver heds. Any fae would glamour it away in a heartbeat, unwilling to look upon such a spot. And yet that slight imperfection adds an undeniable interest to her face in defiance of the laws of conventional beauty. It suits her somehow. She is defiance personified.

Many Noxaurian warriors surround us, some eyeing us with

more than casual interest, waiting like hounds to see if my prisoner will make a break for it and give them an excuse to give chase. Aware of their interest, I drop my voice low so that no ears but hers might hear: "As long as you are with me, you are safe. No man, woman or creature in this whole encampment will dare lay a finger on anything that belongs to me."

She bares her teeth. "I don't *belong* to you."

I lift one brow. "I just paid a hundred silver heds for you."

"I thought it was a hundred and one?"

"Exactly. Which means, in the eyes of all you see around you, you are my property."

She draws a long breath through flared nostrils. Then, with a vicious, "Skewer you!" she lunges at me with both hands, pushing as though to throw me off balance. She succeeds only in jarring her bones; I don't move an inch. Her wide eyes flare, staring me up and down, at last returning to my face. With a little, "Oh!" huffed through parted lips, she turns and takes two steps.

A pack of horned kobolds, each standing as high as her waist and leering with lascivious attention, block her way. They stretch out their three-fingered hands, long black tongues lashing from wide-opened jaws. The girl stifles a scream and staggers backwards until she bumps into me. The temptation to wrap my arm around her, to pin her against me, is strong. But I resist. I merely glare at the kobolds until they retreat, then smooth my brow into a mild expression when the girl turns. She's so close. She puts her hands up and presses them to my chest to keep a little distance between us. For a moment she can only stare at those hands, white against my sun-browned skin.

Finally she lifts her big eyes to mine. I hold her gaze, determined that she should see the truth in my face. "I will not harm you. You have my word."

She presses her lips into a tight line. Then she holds up her wrist, rolling back her sleeve to reveal the dark bruises dotting her skin. "You've already harmed me. More than once, I might add."

"True. Though I would like to point out that, in those instances, had I not exerted some force, you would have landed yourself in situations far more deadly. Do you deny it?"

She can't deny it. But that doesn't stop the hatred burning in her soul. There's little enough I can do to douse that flame. Gods, how can I persuade her? How can I assuage both her fears and her suspicions? She does not yet know the true depths of her peril . . . or all that this night holds for the two of us.

At this thought, fire, low but insistent, stirs in my veins. But no. I'm not going to think about tonight or Ruvaen's offer of his pavilion. Nor am I going to consider the possibility of simply handing this girl over to Lurodos here and now. There must be some alternative as yet unexplored. But for the moment . . .

I cross my arms, as much to keep myself from grabbing her again as anything. "While neither of us may care for the situation in which we find ourselves," I say, my voice level, "I believe I can get you out of this in one piece and—eventually—return you to your own people. But you'll have to trust me."

"*Trust* you?"

I breathe out a short sigh, almost a curse. "Or don't. It makes no difference. But follow my lead and stay close. Is that too much to ask?"

The girl says nothing. She swallows hard, the muscles of her slender throat constricting. While she doesn't answer me, neither does she turn and make yet another hopeless attempt to escape. I'll take that for what it's worth.

She shivers suddenly, a whole-body spasm. Not from cold, I think, but it reminds me that I'm holding her cloak still. "Here," I say and shake out the stained folds before wrapping the garment around her slender shoulders. "This is yours, I believe."

She huddles into the fabric, gripping it tightly at the throat like it's the last shield between her and all the shocks of this brutal world. She shivers again, closes her eyes. Then, very softly: "My sister. She was . . . she was sold before me."

My brow tightens. "Did you see who bought her?"

The girl shakes her head. "I didn't see anything. Not from the cage."

A dart of pity shoots through my heart. I saw last night how determinedly she sought to defend the fallen maiden. To be parted from her now, knowing she was likely sold as a warbride as well . . . I can imagine the horror churning in this girl's heart. However, there's nothing I can do for her. Not yet at least.

"We must secure our own situation," I say firmly. "Once you are properly sealed under my protection, then we will make inquiries after your sister. I swear it." It will probably be too late for the other girl. But if I don't lay claim to my warbride at once, I wouldn't put it past Lurodos to make a play for her before the dawn deadline. We have a long night ahead of us. I'm not sure that I can truly save her life, or if she'll even let me try. But I've made it this far.

I take a few steps in the direction of my camp, then pause and look back at her. Her expression is conflicted, torn between her unwillingness to leave behind her sister and knowledge of her own helpless state. I don't touch her, nor do I command. I need her to come with me willingly. If she won't come this time, I will walk away and leave her to face whatever consequences come.

At last, with a little sigh, she nods. Huddled in that cloak, she steps to my side, and we walk together through the Noxaurian encampment. I feel the moment when we step beyond the radius of the spire's magic. Here my own people have pitched camp among the trees on the fringes of Wanfriel Forest. The small *dakath* tents, huddled together around campfires, look like a miniature of the Hidden City. A little slice of home in this foreign land.

Kildorath sees us coming. I had sent him and Ashika back to the camp, barking the command even as I sped from the spire and hastened out to the auction on my impulsive rescue mission. They gave me strange looks but did not question my orders, having learned over the years to trust my leadership.

But my second does not hold back his questions now.

"*Luinar,*" Kildorath cries. His eyes fasten on the girl with disgust. He plants himself between her and the Licornyn camp, as though to prevent her from entering. "*Luinar,* why have you brought this creature here?"

He speaks in Licornyn at least, which the girl does not understand. His tone, however, is clearly hostile. She draws a half-step nearer to me, eyeing him warily, her small fists clenched as though for a fight.

"It's a long story, my friend," I answer with a heavy sigh and a shake of my head. "The short version is this: I seem to have purchased myself a warbride."

"You've *what?*" This exclamation comes from Ashika. She and her licorneir draw near. Ashika gapes quite openly at the ragged little figure at my side. Nyathri, by contrast, narrows her intelligent, otherworldly gaze. Her pointed ears cup forward, and her nostrils flare. Something about the human intrigues her . . . possibly the fact that she is looking directly at the beast. Which should be impossible: licorneir are invisible to mortal vision save when enflamed in battle. But the girl at my side cannot seem to take her eyes off delicate Nyathri.

I haven't time to marvel at this phenomenon just now, however. As though finally coming to grips with what I've said, Ashika utters a great whoop of laughter. "I should have known it would come to this! Everyone has been saying you must take a bride and start making little heirs. Would no one back home have you? Is this how you resort to getting yourself a queen?"

"Peace, Ashika," I growl, aware of the curious stares from the other men and women in our party. They all close in on us now, riders and licorneir alike. Gods help me, the last thing I need is an audience for my discomfort. Most of them, at least, are more confused than anything. They assail me with a storm of questions which I am hard pressed to answer to anyone's satisfaction. In the end Ashika is still laughing in great, gulping guffaws, Nyathri is still eyeing the girl with silent intensity, and everyone else looks somewhere between baffled, amused, and disgusted.

Except for Kildorath. He looks ready to slit the girl's throat. When I finish my convoluted little tale, he turns to me, the muscle in his cheek ticking with tension, and hisses, "Have you forgotten Shanaera so soon?"

He could not have delivered a better-aimed blow. My chest tightens, and I drop my voice an octave. "Your sister and I were through long ago. Long before her death."

Kildorath's eyes spark with pain. He knows the story of his sister's brutal end—of the virulium coursing through her body and soul, of the madness that sent her ravaging her own friends. He knows I put her down. That I carry the burden and the pain of that single act with me every single day of my life.

I loved Shanaera—and I knew her better than anyone, better even than her own brother. Which is why I knew as well that she could never be my wife, Queen of the Licornyn. The darkness in her soul ran too deep. I could not love her and not love that darkness equally. And that was a risk I dared not take.

Perhaps I was wrong. Perhaps if I had believed in her more, she would never have turned to virulium. Perhaps if I had followed my heart and not my head, none of us would be in this situation now. But what good can come of this vain wondering? It is done. Shanaera is dead—and that apparition I believed I'd seen last night wasn't her. It couldn't be. I don't believe it. I won't.

I hold Kildorath's gaze, watch the play of emotions flicker in his eyes. He curses at last and shakes his head. "Please, Taar," he says, foregoing my title and appealing to me as a man. "Please, do not go through with this. Do not take this human as your bride."

"And what would you have me do?" I demand, stepping closer to speak my words to him so no one else can hear. "Would you have me discard her like some unwanted animal? Would you have me throw her to the wolves?"

"Yes," he answers at once, without hesitation. "I would."

I draw back from him. While all the Licornyn share a distrust of humans, Kildorath hates them more than any man I know. He blames them for Shanaera's ultimate demise. But I will not heap condemnation on the head of this one young woman simply for being the same race as our enemies. She herself is not responsible for the atrocities committed by her kind.

Refusing to answer my second, I turn from him to Ashika and

say only, "Where is Onor Vamir? Bring him to me."

In short order the young priest is pushed to the forefront of the throng. Though only eighteen summers old and no warrior, he rides with our company, for we need someone on hand to perform initial death rites over our fallen—to write the runes on their flesh and see to it that their souls are properly guided from their broken bodies. This is Vamir's first mission beyond the borders of our realm, and he's as wide-eyed and nervous as one would expect. But he's performed his part admirably, and for that, he has earned my respect.

He goes down on his knees before me. His too-large cassock billows about him, secured at his waist by a *nornil* belt of many complex knots, all unique, all sacred to the Goddess of Unity. His hair is likewise bound with complex knotted wire and braids, symbols of his devotion to his goddess. He bows low, the ends of his long braids nearly brushing the ground. "How may I be of service, *Luinar?*" he asks, his voice slightly quavering.

"Onor," I say. It feels odd to address this boy as *father,* though it is the correct term for a priest of his standing, regardless of age. "You are qualified to perform the *vellar* ceremony between a man and a woman, are you not?"

His gaze shifts from me to the human girl, who has stood silently all this while, watching and listening. She narrows her eyes at Vamir, and the young priest hastily looks away. "Y—yes, *Luinar,*" he stammers. "The initial binding is simple enough. I can perform it now. But," he adds, his brow puckering with concern, "the second ceremony is more complicated. It will have to be performed on *silmael*, which is nearly a month from now, and—"

"That will not be a concern." I have no intention of dragging this unwanted bride along with me for a month. I need only buy us a little time while I decide what's best to be done. Nothing more.

"In that case, my king, I am ready to perform the service," Vamir says and, with assistance from Ashika, scrambles back to his feet. "For the initial binding, you must take her hand and hold it up between you."

I turn to the girl and extend my right hand, palm upturned. She looks at it then at me. "What?" she demands, in her own language. It's the first time she's spoken since our arrival in camp. My people hastily draw back several paces, like she's a snake and might strike at any moment.

"Just take it," I say in her own language. "This must happen."

"What must happen, exactly?"

I hesitate. Ruvaen's caution and Lurodos's threats ring in my ears. But now is not the time to explain. "We must seal the bond of protection between us," I say instead. It is the truth at least, if not the whole truth.

She studies me, the line of her brow drawn tight. Slowly, cautiously, as though extending her hand to stroke the head of a rabid dog, she places her fingers in mine. I grasp them tight and lift our hands up as the priest bade.

"Not like that." Young Vamir frowns and reaches out to adjust our grip. The girl's eyes flash. For a moment I fear she will yank away or even lunge at the priest.

"Look at me," I growl. Her gaze darts to mine. "Look only at me."

She grimaces. But she obeys, much to my relief, and allows the priest to interlace our fingers, arms upraised, forearms pressed together. He begins the prayer:

> *"The night of silence has ended.*
> *Now is the morning of song.*
> *The days of rain are over.*
> *Now is the time of shelter.*
> *Cold shall not enter your bones,*
> *For, to each other, you shall be warmth.*
> *Let the fires join and be one flame.*
> *Let the bodies join and be one flesh."*

As he speaks, the ancient Licornyn prayer flowing in melodic stream from his tongue, the licorneir surrounding us bow their heads. A wordless hum, a swelling song, emanates from their centers, burning through the long, multi-hued coils of their horns. The voice of the priest and the soul-song of the licorneir blend into a perfect harmony as the blessing of the Goddess of Unity is called down from heaven.

The girl's arm tenses, her fingers tightening in my grasp. Her gaze shifts to the licorneir around us. Because she can see them. Or sense them at least, though her mortal perceptions should be entirely blind to their presence. This is a mystery I cannot fathom. Is she not human as I have assumed? But what else could she be?

"Look at me," I murmur again softly. Her eyes snap back to mine. She does not understand the young priest's words, but she must sense something of the importance of this moment. As for me? Guilt twists my gut. This ceremony, this prayer, this song, is sacred to my people. I have borne witness to it many times over the years, and believed I should stand in the center of this song myself one day. There was a time when I thought it would be Shanaera's hand I clasped, her forearm pressed against mine. Not a stranger. Not a captive who cannot meet my gaze without trembling.

Onor Vamir slips a silken skein of *velra* from his belt. As the words of the binding song continue to flow from his throat, he begins to wrap the golden cord around our arms. The girl catches her breath. She tries to pull away, and only my grip on her hand keeps her in place. "Stop!" she says, shaking her head. "Stop. Whatever is happening here, I don't want it."

"It is the only way, *zylnala*." I try to soften the roughness of my voice. "You must stand still. It will be over soon."

Ragged breaths blow through her parted lips. "I know what this is," she growls. "It's a handfasting. My people have a similar custom."

I neither acknowledge nor deny it. I merely look at her, watch the understanding war with resistance in her eyes. She does not trust me. Perhaps she never will. But she is without options, without allies. Even my own people, the tall warriors surrounding us, would rather see her dead. Kildorath's face, hovering on the periphery, looks positively murderous. I will have to deal with him later. For now I keep my gaze focused on the girl.

"Gods-damn," she hisses at last. "I thought I'd seen the last of this nonsense."

Then, grinding her teeth, she clasps my hand firmly and presses her forearm against mine once more. She meets my eye and does not waver when Vamir binds our arms with the *velra* cord, nor when he inscribes the sacred rune of the Goddess on my breast and hers. The *ruehnar* ink burns the skin, and she flinches, but does not pull away.

"Now," Vamir says, stepping back from us, the bottle of *ruehnar* still in his hand. "Now it is time, Taarthalor Ragnataarthane. You must speak your troth to your bride. If your vows prove true, come *silmael*, she will speak them back to you. Thus is the will of the Goddess."

"The will of the Goddess," my watching riders murmur in response. All except Kildorath, who stands with his arms folded, his expression stone. Ignoring him, ignoring all of them, I focus on this young woman before me. It seems strange to speak these sacred words, knowing even as I say them that I have no intention of living them out beyond a few hours at most. I can only hope the Goddess will see the intention of my heart and forgive me

this sacrilege performed in her name. At least the girl does not understand what I say:

> *"With my faith will I honor you.*
> *With my body will I protect you.*
> *With my arms will I shelter you.*
> *With my heart will I warm you.*
> *From this day forth, my mouth, my lips, my tongue,*
> *My every waking breath,*
> *Are dedicated to your pleasure and delight.*
> *My life is yours,*
> *And, should you require it,*
> *My death."*

The words, though spoken, become song when combined with the ongoing hum of the licorneir surrounding us. As I speak, as the song swells, the girl's tight brow relaxes, and her eyes soften somewhat. A faraway look comes over her, as though she hears voices calling from a great distance. Her eyes are still on mine, but she seems to see into another realm entirely.

When my song is done, my vows declared, she blinks and snaps back to the present. "What was that?"

I'm not about to interpret those sacred words. I say only, "I have now sealed you under my protection."

"Am I supposed to say something?"

"You are not required to. Not tonight."

But something has happened. Something has changed inside of me now that those sacred words have fallen from my lips. I feel a strange sense of . . . connection. A draw, a bond, to this girl, this stranger, whose name I do not know. Is this the Goddess's work in me? One does not speak her holy words, one does not sing her sacred songs, without becoming essentially changed.

More to reassure myself than her, I lean in close to the girl and whisper in her ear: "I vow this to you, *zylnala,* above all other vows: I will return you to your own people, safe and whole." This vow may not be infused with holy solemnity, but I mean it with my whole heart.

She swallows, her eyes very dark in her pale face. Then she nods.

Vamir steps forward, ending the ceremony with a final prayer: "United by the will of the Goddess," he intones, and my people respond: "Blessed be the Goddess."

As he speaks, the *velra* cord wrapped round our forearms vanishes suddenly. The girl gasps. "What the—? Where did it go?"

"Nowhere," I reply. "It is still there." It is strange to have to explain this part of the ceremony to my own bride. I've grown up observing many such moments; it's easy to forget that every culture and every race has different practices to celebrate their bondings.

She stares hard at her own arm, trying to discern what cannot be seen. "So . . ." she says slowly, "is my hand permanently stuck to yours now?"

A chuckle threatens in the back of my throat. I swallow it back and answer simply by releasing her hand and taking a step away. She sucks in a relieved breath. But when I move my arm, the faintest glimmer of gold flashes in the air. "It is *velra*," I tell her, "woven from the roots of the *ilsevel* blossom, which is sacred to my people. The influence does not last more than a few hours, but it temporarily binds us to one another."

Her eyes flash, confusion mingled with something like shock. "What did you say?" she demands.

"It is old magic," I begin, but she shakes her head.

"No, that . . . that name. Was it . . . ? Did you say *ilsevel?*"

I blink down at her. She looks truly unsettled, though I cannot fathom why. Before I can offer any answer, however, Ashika murmurs, "What do *they* want?"

I turn from my bride to see three tall, solemn figures approaching. My own people part to make room for them, and the licorneir retreat, unwilling to be seen by strangers. The newcomers pay them no heed but proceed straight to me and bow. They are women—cold, cruel, and beautiful Noxaurian women, ladies of the prince's court. Their hair is black as night and bound back from their faces with bands of onyx and jet. Their skin is the dusky purple of twilight.

"Prince Ruvaen sends his compliments," the foremost of them says, her voice deep and rich. "We are to prepare your bride for you."

My bride, as they call her, eyes the women nervously, her

expression tight. I cannot imagine explaining to her what they intend, not with all my own people watching. I say only, "Go with these women. They will take you somewhere safe where you may bathe. They'll find you fresh clothing as well."

She pulls her cloak a little closer. "You said you would help me find my sister."

"And I will. But for now you must do as I bid. Let these women help you, let them see to your wounds. I will be along shortly." She narrows her eyes, looking from me to them and back again, trying to decide whom she fears the least. "You are under my protection," I say, hoping my voice is reassuring. "No man, woman, or creature in this whole encampment will dare lay a finger on you now." For tonight at least.

The girl holds my gaze for a long moment. Then, with a short nod, she turns to the three women. They place her in their midst and guide her away, towering creatures, at least a head taller than she. But she lifts her chin imperiously, and though she is ragged and terribly mortal compared to their immortal beauty, still . . . I cannot explain it, but my eye is drawn to her. In a crowd of women, no matter how powerful their glamours, no matter how exquisitely crafted their perfections, I suspect I should still find myself seeking this girl's face and form.

Grimacing, I glance down at my forearm, now bare to the naked eye. But I feel the constricting coils of the *velra* cord, tighter and more painful than I expected. It urges me to follow after her, to not let the girl out of sight. Only by sheer will do I refuse.

The moment the three women have disappeared with my bride, Kildorath turns on me. He steps in close, his shoulder against mine, and hisses through clenched teeth, "You're a fool, Taar."

"Careful, Kildorath," Ashika warns with a dry chuckle. "Fool or not, he is your king."

"What do I care?" Kildorath throws up his arm, turning to her and the others watching. "Our king should remember his duty to his people! He should not go buying himself a little human distraction while our companions' remains have not yet been laid to rest with their forebearers." He whirls on me once more. "You make a mockery of our sacred rites, you spit in the face of the Goddess, you—"

"Have done, Kildorath." My voice is swift and final as a descending blade. "Speak no more or suffer your king's wrath."

He stares at me, breathing hard. Until this moment I would have said I could trust him with my life. Even when word of Shanaera's death reached him, Kildorath sought me out, knelt before me, and swore his loyalty all over again, though I never asked it of him. He has been my faithful second and my friend for as long as I can remember. But this perceived betrayal may have pushed him too far.

Before anything dire can happen, Ashika steps between us. "What I should like to know," she says, addressing me and planting her back firmly to Kildorath, turning herself into a living barrier, "is what you plan to do with the human. You cannot bring her home to the Hidden City. Humans are forbidden to enter there."

I am well aware of the laws of our people. And I have no intention of bringing that girl anywhere near my city. "That is my concern, not yours," I say. "For now I want all of you to gather your things and set out for Cruor tonight. Go to the Luin Stone and await me there for one day but no longer. If I do not join you, you are to proceed to the Hidden City. Our people have been undefended for too long."

Kildorath looks as though he will fight. I wouldn't put it past him to challenge me for the kingship itself, so intense is his wrath. In the end, however, he turns away and sets to work disassembling his *dakath*. His licorneir, Miramenor, a strong beast with a golden hide which shimmers with inner fire, approaches and bumps his shoulder, offering comfort. Kildorath pushes it away and refuses to meet its eye.

With a sigh, I turn to find Elydark approaching. He hung back throughout the ceremony, not joining the other licorneir in song. No doubt he disapproves of my recent choices as well. And no doubt I'm about to hear of it.

Vellar, he says, his eyes solemn, his song a rumble in my soul. *What have you done?*

I don't know exactly. I run a hand down my face. *I'm still trying to figure it out.*

The velra bonds are divinely ordained. You cannot break

143

them without severe consequence.

It's nothing I don't already know. But I can't very well back down now. *I'm not sure how sacred this bond is, made under duress.*

My licorneir shakes his mane, the sharp blade of his horn flashing in the firelight. **The ways of the Mother Goddess are strange. Even my kind sometimes struggle to understand.**

That's not terribly encouraging, brother-soul.

Perhaps not. But it is the truth.

9

ILSEVEL

———❦———

THE LAST THING—*THE VERY LAST THING*—I WANT IS to cling to the terrifying man who bought me and beg him not to send me from his presence. Something tells me that would give decidedly the wrong impression.

Besides, when it comes down to it, who do I fear more: these tall, solemn-faced ladies? Or the battle-scarred warlord who, in recent history, has struck me unconscious, tossed me in a cage, bought me with silver, and performed some sort of unnerving handfasting ceremony with me entirely without my consent? The answer should be self-evident.

Nevertheless, I find myself oddly reluctant to step in among that trio of dusky-skinned, yellow-eyed beauties. There's something indescribably deadly about them: like they might know how to draw out an excruciating death by hours or days. Even years if they wished.

But I'm not about to make a fool of myself. If they're going to march me off to devour me with a side of blood wine, I'll at least make a show of courage. I don't know how much I believe the warlord's insistence that no one will dare touch me. He seems confident enough, but the fae are tricky bastards. For all I know, this is part of some elaborate game, luring me into false security. I'll stay on my guard. And the moment I see an opportunity, I'll escape.

Wait for me, Aurae, I silently plea, like a prayer. Let any good angel that might linger in this place carry my voice to my sister. *I'm going to find you, just . . . wait for me.*

The world has somehow grown darker since the warlord took me out of the main encampment. More of the fires have burned down low, but none of the shapes surrounding them seem to be idling toward sleep. There's an air of increased excitement and impending mayhem everywhere I turn. Thankfully the three women provide a sort of living shield around me. I only catch stray glimpses between their tall, robed forms—a leering mouth, a flash of tooth, a pair of forms contorted in strange, violent configurations.

We come to a small, stone building set a little apart from the tents. Figures come and go through its open door, but, at a single word from the tallest of my three escorts, everyone inside vacates at once. The women strip me of my stinking, torn clothes and make me stand in a pool of cold water, right there in the middle of the stone chamber. Streams of water summoned as though by magic pour from various pipes along the ceiling and douse me in an icy flood. It bites, and I yelp. Then I lean into it, welcoming both the pain and the discomfort. At least it's a distraction from the faraway scream in the back of my head.

Ungentle and vigorous, the women set to work scrubbing me down with pumice stones and rough cloths. I utter a mewling protest, but they give me such looks, I immediately shut my mouth, hold out my arms, and submit to their ministrations. They are agonizingly thorough. I'm raw and half-frozen by the time they pull me from the water and apply soft towels to my skin. Then they set to work on other parts of my body—my ragged nails, my snarled hair, my feet, my neck.

When they pay special attention to my loins, suspicion rises, a cold knot in my throat. I swallow it down, let it burn up in the furnace of fury roiling in my breast. In my mind's eye, I see again that dark warlord. His handsome face, so chiseled and fine, seems to fill the whole of my vision. I feel again the strength of his hand clasping mine as he made those solemn vows.

I hate him. This man who bought me. This man who claims me as his possession, his prize. He is everything I have fought against, everything I have spent my entire life resisting. Master and monster. *Husband.*

I won't give in to him. I don't care what price was paid or to whom. I will not be possessed. I will not submit.

And yet . . . How many times did I rage like this against Father? How many times did I tell myself I would not let him make me sing again? How many times did I boldly declare that I should not be married off to whomever he wished? I vowed not to marry the Shadow King, only for all my efforts to land me in a worse situation by far. As though it is my god-ordained destiny to be someone's captive.

The women begin to dress me next. If I cherished any lingering doubts as to where this night is going, those vanish in an instant as they wrap me in gauzy folds of translucent white. To call it a gown is laughable—it is merely a flimsy bit of fabric, the softest I've ever felt. I cannot fathom what it is made of. It's like wearing flower petals. It wraps my body loosely, secured only by a little belt at the waist. Easy to tear away. Even when the belt is secured, the plunging neckline exposes most of my bosom, and the fabric is so sheer, only a few doubled-up folds offer anything resembling modesty.

The fae women inspect their work, smoothing my hair, pinching my cheeks. One speaks to the others in a rapid language I cannot understand. Her sisters shake their heads as though to say this is the best they can manage. I hate them. If I had a dagger on me, I would plunge it straight into the tallest woman's black heart and damn the consequences.

But I have no weapon. No recourse, no allies. So I clench my fists and tell myself that I am not submitting. I am merely biding my time. It's a lie; and I know it. I'm just not willing to admit it.

They drape a heavy cloak over my shoulders. Not my cloak—that has disappeared along with all my other garments. This one is lush velvet, black but with a purple weft that catches the light. It is warm and shielding, and I despise myself for the gratitude I feel as I huddle into it. The trio leads me from the bathing chamber back out into the night. Hundreds of eyes turn to me, all reflecting the red light of their fires, individual faces obscured. I duck my head, afraid to meet those hungry gazes, and hasten to keep pace with the women's long strides.

A figure steps suddenly in front of us, blocking our path. The women stop abruptly. One of them places an unyielding hand on my shoulder, fingers pinching deep. The tallest of the three speaks sharply, a note of command in her voice. The figure—a great fae man—does not move. He turns his head to me, and the glow of the nearest fire illuminates his face.

I catch my breath. It's him. The other fae who bid on me, the massive man with the silver hair. He smiles slowly, his gaze roving over me, as though he can see right through the velvet cloak. Then he meets my eyes.

"Well, little morsel," he says, "think of me throughout the long hours of this night. You can bet I'll be dreaming of you and looking forward to getting to know you better come dawn." With those words, he licks his lips, revealing a dark purple tongue and the glitter of sharp teeth.

My body starts to tremble harder than before. I feel myself ready to fall to pieces with terror, with hopelessness. With weakness. Instead, I channel it all into pure, burning rage.

"The next time you see me, sir," I say, speaking loud and clear, "you will surely die."

There's little hope of my following through on such a threat. But I infuse my voice with absolute conviction and even let the smallest trace of my gods-gift, a hint of song, deepen my tone so that the meaning plunges deeper than mere words can penetrate.

The fae lord's smile falters. He draws his head back somewhat, surprised. For a moment his glamour flickers, and a shadow of concern falls across his brow. Then he laughs. And in that laugh, I hear the echo of my father's laugh—mocking and dismissive. Confident in his own mastery over me, both body and soul.

The foremost of the women speaks sharply again. This time there's a glint of steel, and I wonder if she and the fae lord are about to come to blows. But he steps aside, still laughing, and sweeps a hand to let us pass. I refuse to look back at him, though I feel his eyes watching me as I trot to keep up with my escort.

Ahead of me looms a large pavilion. It dwarfs the smaller, rougher tents dotting the landscape around it. My heart lurches at the sight, but the women sweep back the flap opening, and usher me inside. A warm, luxurious space meets my eyes. If I didn't know any better, I'd think I'd stepped into a royal palace. Lush tapestries line the walls, providing both beauty and insulation from the elements. Two elegant chairs with scrollwork arms and legs of gold sit opposite each other before a central fire. This burns bright, and the smoke funnels up through a gap in the pavilion peak so precisely that it must be ensorcelled. Layers of fur rugs disguise any hint of hard ground, and burning braziers both illuminate the space and offer a delicate note of incense to tempt the senses.

But what dominates my vision is the bed. It's massive—big enough to hold a small giant. It reminds me, in a strange way, of the sacrificial altar slab at Ashryn Shrine. Only, rather than blood, it's draped in red velvet and white furs. Two great posts at the head of the bed support a canopy of shimmering silk embroidered in starburst patterns.

I cannot look away. Suddenly it seems very important to hold on to my rage, to grasp it with everything I've got. Before this wave of terror douses it, and I'm left shivering and helpless in its wake.

Without a word or look at me, two of the fae women glide across the room, navigating around the fire and the chairs. They approach the bed and, in almost perfect synchronization, affix a golden cord to each of the posts. I know at once what they intend to do.

"Oh, hells no!" I growl and whirl to plunge right back out of the pavilion, heedless of the monsters waiting on the other side. I smack into the third and tallest fae woman. She looks coldly down at me. "No!" I say, shaking my head ferociously. Then, before I can stop it, my voice shifts to pleading. "I beg of you, don't do this. Don't truss me up like a sacrifice!" It's too much, too horrible. Being bought, sold, owned, possessed . . . and now the sheer shame and indignity of those ropes? I can't bear it.

The fae woman reaches for me, but I'm just quick enough to elude her grasp, staggering back almost into the fire. The other two women close in behind me. *"No!"* I scream, and dart to escape them. Not fast enough. They move like cats, quick and lithe, their otherworldly grace more than a match for my frenzied fear. They catch me, drag me back to the bed, utterly deaf to the abuse I screech at them.

It takes the three of them to pin me down, raise my arms over my head, and fasten the silken cuffs securely around my wrists. They pull so tight, it hurts. I wrench against them, and they only tighten more. Kicking, snarling, I thrash on the bed. The taste of copper blooms in my mouth, and I think for a moment I've managed to snap one of their hands, only to realize I've bitten my own tongue.

"You monsters!" I cry, spitting blood. "Witches! May the gods cast you to the deepest of the nine hells for this! May the demons suck the marrow of your bones!"

They stand silent, one on each side of the bed, one at the foot. The lefthand woman, the tallest and most severe, reaches out to smooth the hair back from my head. The woman on my right quietly dabs blood from my lips and blots it from the sheer fabric draped across my panting bosom.

Then she leans in a little closer and whispers: "Despair not, mortal. There is a knife under the cushion. Use it wisely."

Her voice is so soft, for a moment I wonder if I imagined it. She straightens, and all three women back away, solemn, silent. They slip from the pavilion one after the other, leaving me to my fate.

I go still, heart thundering with panic. Then I scream again and yank at the bindings. While I doubt very much that I'll find a knife under any of these cushions, what good would it do me anyway, bound as I am? Damn, damn, damn it all to the nine hells! Rage pulses in my veins, and I let out a scream, as loud and long as I can summon.

Finally exhausted, I fall back on the soft furs and stare up at the embroidered canopy overhead. All those delicate stars, wrought in shimmering threads. It's beautiful work, I notice dimly. Expert craftsmanship. Not fae-made, of course—everyone knows the fae can work no craft of their own but must steal from other races. I wonder who made this particular piece. Some dwarf or gnome. Or a human slave, perhaps.

Closing my eyes, I breathe out a shuddering sigh. My sister's face appears in my head. Aurae—is she out there somewhere in the night in a similar position? Sold as a bride, forced into the bed of some monster? Oh, gods, no. Spare her that much at least. She doesn't deserve to suffer for . . . for my mistake.

Because this is all my doing. I can see it now. If I had never written to Artoris, if I had never told him where I would be, he wouldn't have come. He wouldn't have killed poor Captain Wulfram and his men. Then, when the fae set upon us, we wouldn't have been defenseless. Good people are dead—the men of my escort, the priests. Maybe my sister as well. And all for what? Because I didn't want to be married off to a stranger.

The bitter irony burns in my belly.

Opening my eyes, I twist my arms again, determined to get free. The silk cuffs dig into my skin, but my right hand—it seems to be making progress. I concentrate on that one, contorting, tugging, relaxing, and tugging again. Suddenly my wrist pulls free, and my fingers slip through the silk. I gasp and close my eyes, momentarily so flooded with relief, I can't think or move. Was it just luck that someone didn't fasten this cuff as tight as she should? Or did that fae woman purposefully loosen it, just to give me a chance? It doesn't matter. One hand free isn't enough. Drawing a deep breath, I reach for the lefthand cuff. Triumph swiftly turns to frustrated disappointment. I cannot seem to pull it free; the strap simply will not give. I'm no better off than I was before, except . . .

Wait a minute. What about that knife? Slipping my hand under the pile of cushions, I feel around cautiously. And there, there! Cold metal, just at my fingertips. I grip a thin hilt and pull out the small weapon, so tiny and delicate. So deadly. And right here, in my hand.

My mouth goes dry. I stare at that knife like it's the key to freedom. This time, when opportunity presents itself, I won't hesitate. This time I will plunge the blade straight into my captor's throat.

Footsteps sound at the pavilion entrance. My heart leaps. I have a split second in which to decide what to do. Then I'm shoving the knife back under the pillow and reaching out to grasp the cuff from which I've just freed myself. My only real weapon here is surprise.

So let him see me as he expects to: bound and helpless. Just how he wants me no doubt. But I'll show him. Very soon now.

The tent flap rustles then pulls to one side. My bridegroom steps through.

He stands on the far side of the fire, so I cannot see him clearly. Just an impression of his wide-shouldered frame and the glitter in the depths of his black eyes. Those eyes fasten on me, lying on the bed. In all my writhing and twisting, my already flimsy garment has become twisted around my legs, revealing my calves, knees, most of my thighs. One breast is all but escaped, the sheer fabric only just clinging to the peak of my nipple. But this is good. Isn't it? Distracted by the sight of so much bare flesh, perhaps he won't notice that one of my hands is free.

I've forgotten how to breathe. I can only lie here, gripping the binding cords with both hands. Staring at this man who has somehow, in the last few hours, become my husband.

The warlord passes a hand over his face. *"Shakh,"* he growls. It sounds like a curse. Then he shakes his head and begins to stalk around the fire toward the bed. He's washed himself since last I saw him. His armor is gone, and his torso is naked, every finely-tuned muscle gleaming in the fire light. A wide leather belt spans his waist, and I note the two knives sheathed there, both much larger than my own secret weapon.

I can't help scrambling as he draws near. It's a reflex, this need to put space between us. I kick, and my flimsy gown hikes up even higher than before. He stops short, his expression stern. "Please, little one," he says and holds up both hands. "I mean you no harm. I vowed to protect you. To shelter you. I should bring terrible dishonor down on my head if I betrayed those vows now."

I draw a long breath through clenched teeth. "Easy enough for you to say. You're not the one tied naked to a bed."

He looks away, the muscle in his jaw tense. Then, reaching for one of the velvet blankets, he picks it up and, much to my surprise, drapes it over my body. There's something tender, almost reverent in the way he does it. As though I'm something to be cared for, something precious. The fire in my belly churns. How dare he? How dare he behave with this mock chivalry, when it's his fault I'm here to begin with?

The warlord takes a step back from the bed, his gaze flicking to my bound hands then swiftly bouncing away again. If I didn't know any better, I'd say he was nervous. Which makes no sense, under the circumstances. "I'm going to release you," he says, "if you will permit me."

He waits a beat, as though expecting me to give my permission. I say nothing; I only glare at him. At last, with a slight tilt of his head to one side, he draws closer, reaches for the cuff around my left wrist. This is it: my one and only chance.

Dropping hold of the righthand rope, I dart my hand under the pillow, whip out the knife, and lunge straight for his throat.

He catches my wrist.

He moves with such fluid grace, he doesn't even seem fast. It's too easy, the way he takes in what I do, anticipates where my blow will fall, and simply prevents it. As though he expected as much all along.

Without apparent surprise or discomfort, he turns my wrist and studies the blade still gripped tight in my white-knuckled fingers. "Lurodos," he says, and his brow darkens. His eyes flash back to meet mine. "Who gave you this knife?"

I don't answer. I grind my teeth and stare at him, daring him to do his worst. He'll punish me—of course he will. I just tried to kill him, after all. He'll punish me, he'll hurt me, and I won't let him know how much I fear him and the pain he's about to inflict. I must hold onto my rage at all costs.

He grimaces. Firelight flashes off sharp canines. "This knife bears the sigil of House Uldreyin, of which Lord Lurodos is head. He must have bribed one of Ruvaen's servants to slip it to you. Did she loosen that manacle as well?" When I hold my tongue, he squeezes my wrist ever so slightly. My fingers splay; the knife drops. He releases his grip on me and catches it, all in one deft motion. Sitting on the edge of the bed, he tests the balance of the blade across his fingers. "This is a fine weapon," he says softly.

Then, quicker than thought, he slashes out. The other cuff falls free.

I don't know how long I sit on that bed. Staring at that broken bit of rope, that silk restraint. At the dark warlord seated beside me, my knife still in his hand. It feels like hours. Hours before my

"WHO GAVE YOU THIS KNIFE?"

lungs finally remember how to draw breath.

Suddenly I'm scrambling out from under that blanket, half-falling to the floor. I pull myself upright, clad in nothing but that sheer gown, feeling the glow of the fire against my cold skin. I wrap my arms around myself, trying in vain to cover my nakedness.

The warlord simply averts his eyes. He tosses the knife, catches it by the point of the blade. Then he hurls it. I let out a gasp, but the knife lands harmlessly in the soft rug at my feet.

"Pick it up," the warlord says.

I hesitate only for a moment. Then I whip that knife off the ground and hold it between us, ignoring the way the little blade trembles in my grasp. He watches me for a moment, still sitting there on the edge of the bed. Finally he breathes a heavy sigh, plants his hands on his knees, and stands up. Gods, he's so huge! Earlier, when I'd compared him to the other fae man, I'd said he wasn't as big or bulky, but I must have taken one too many knocks to the head. Just now, standing here in this pavilion, I cannot imagine anyone taller, broader, more powerfully built. Yet nothing about him is gratuitous. Each muscle is so perfectly honed, like a work of art labored over for many years.

He approaches me. I back away, but he keeps coming, until I hit one of the supporting tent poles. My heart races wildly, and my chest heaves as I struggle to breathe. He looms over me, firelight playing across his beautiful features. The line of his jaw is sharp enough to shatter marble. Hair as black as a raven's wing flows over his shoulders, and I suddenly have the inexplicable urge to reach out and touch it, to discover if it is as thick and glossy as it looks.

Hastily I drop my gaze to the knife blade between us. For the space of five breaths, neither of us moves.

Then one of his big, scarred hands wraps around mine. My heart sticks in my throat. He turns my wrist, angling the blade, and presses it up against his bare torso. "Here," he says, his voice a deep rumble. "Right here. Thrust up, and if you put enough force into it, you may just strike the heart. Then I will fall before you, my death's blood pooling at your feet. You will be free of me."

I stare down at that point which even now makes a small indentation into his flesh. *Do it,* I tell myself. *Go on! This is your chance, your only chance.* But I'm frozen.

"I would suggest, however," he continues softly, "that you wait until I tell you the whole truth of your situation. A truth I myself did not know until . . . recently."

I glare up at him. "Fine. Speak your piece while you yet have breath."

Though I know exactly how foolish, how pathetic I sound, he doesn't laugh. It's strange; I'm so used to being mocked for any displays of defiance. My father loved to provoke me to lash out just so he could delight in my futile rebellions.

But this man only nods. He draws a long breath. "The buying and selling of warbrides is not practiced by my own people," he continues at last in that low rumble of his. "It is a Noxaurian custom. Do you understand this?"

I blink once. Then shake my head.

"The fae who dwell in the Realm of Noxaur are a strange, dark brood who honor strange, dark laws. I am told they commonly sell captive women to the highest bidder as brides. Spoils of war. This is what they intended for you before I intervened."

"Right." I'd gathered that much already. "So I am your *bride* then?" I push the bitter word past the lump in my throat.

"You are. But only because I did not realize the full extent of the Noxaurian law. My intention was simply to win the bid and return you to your own kind at the next convenient opportunity."

Hope surges inside me, almost too painful to be borne. "And will you? Return me to my people, I mean?"

He closes his eyes, breathes out through his nostrils. And still that knife hovers between us, the tip resting in that indentation just below his sternum. "When I paid the price, I entered into Noxaurian law," he says at last. "It may not be the law of my own people, but it is binding, nonetheless. I must abide by it or accept the consequences."

"What consequences?"

"If I deny you as my warbride, you will, by law, pass into the possession of the next highest bidder. In this instance Lord Lurodos Uldreyin of Noxaur."

Ah. I nod slowly and lick my dry lips. So that is what the fae man who met me outside the pavilion meant. He expects this warlord to give me up. My stomach coils. As much as I fear this man, I fear

Lord Lurodos more. Something tells me if he had been the one to enter this tent, I would still be bound to that bed. I might never have risen from it again.

I begin to shake. My grip on the knife weakens, and I fear I will drop it. I straighten my spine, firm my hold, and stare up into the warlord's black eyes. "All right then, I understand. You took me as your bride and must maintain appearances for the time being. But there is no reason, is there, that you should not follow through on your original plan?"

He looks down at me. There's compassion in his gaze, which unnerves me more than I like to admit. It makes me want to trust him. Which is the last thing I need.

Then he speaks his next words, and all chance of trust scatters to the four winds: "If we do not consummate this marriage before dawn, the law of Noxaur states you must be handed over to Lurodos."

I stare at him. His words resound inside my head, a hollow echo without meaning. I don't seem to be connected to my body anymore. When my knees buckle, it seems to be happening to someone else. The knife starts to slip from my fingers.

Swiftly the warlord takes the blade. The next thing I know, his strong arm is around me, and he's helping me away from the tent pole back into the middle of the pavilion. For a wild moment I think he's taking me to the bed, and I don't even have the strength to fight. Instead he leads me to one of the little scrollwork chairs by the fire. With unexpected gentlemanliness, he sits me down, then sets the knife in my lap and places my hand over the hilt. Rising, he leaves me and crosses the room to a tall, upright chest. I hear the slide of drawers, the clink of crystal, the sound of liquid pouring.

He returns to me with a delicate silver cup in one hand. "Here," he says, kneeling and holding the cup to my lips. "Take a sip. Just one—it's strong."

I obey. It burns all the way down my throat. I cough but manage to keep it down. The warlord sets the cup aside and remains kneeling there, watching me as I pull myself together. The brew, whatever it was, has a strengthening effect. It takes the fire of fury in my chest and seems to diffuse it through the rest of my body.

Placing my hand to my breast, I look into the warlord's face. His eyes are a little above mine, though he is kneeling. "Let me see if I've got this right," I say in a voice of unnatural serenity. "You must ravage me. For my own good. Is that what you're saying . . . *husband?*"

He turns his head, his face shielded by the thick curtain of his hair. After several long breaths, he looks at me again, and I'm struck all over by the absolute beauty of his face edged in firelight. "Little *zylnala*," he says, "I swore an oath to protect you. I know I am a rough man, a man of war. But I am also a man of honor. I would never touch a woman without her consent. Whatever happens between us tonight, it will be your decision."

"Oh, how nice." I laugh, my head whirling with the aftereffects of that drink. "So I get to choose between being ravaged by you or by your rival. How gentlemanly of you to leave the decision up to me! You should be decorated for your chivalry."

He takes another deep breath through his nostrils. Then he stands and backs away from me, his expression solemn. "I wish the circumstances were other than they are."

"They might be," I snarl, "if you hadn't taken me captive in the first place. If you hadn't manhandled me and knocked me senseless and left me in that cage on wheels."

"My only intention in the moment was to save your life."

"And I'm supposed to believe that? You attack a temple, slaughter the priests, kidnap me and my sister, but oh! You never meant any harm by it. Perhaps I ought to thank you for the courtesy of not disemboweling me on the spot."

He turns away. His powerful shoulders are stiff and set. Is he angry? At me? Good. I would rather meet him wrath-for-wrath than deal with one moment more of his gods-damned gentleness. It's too much, too much! And the whole time I'm sitting here, chatting with him over a cup of fae wine, Aurae is . . . *Aurae is . . .*

I leap from the seat. Knife clutched in my hand, I sprint across the room. Heedless of the fact that I'm wearing practically nothing, I grab the tent flap, push it aside.

A sea of darkness spreads before me, punctuated by points of red light. I am blind, stupid, standing there in that opening with my mouth gaping. Then the voices start.

"Did that half-breed fail to fill ya, girl?"

"Are you running to find yourself a real man?"

"Come play with me, my sweet! I'll give you a proper *shakhing* in short order!"

This and more, far cruder, floods my ears. My night-stunned vision clears somewhat, just enough for me to take in the leering faces, so beautiful, so terrible. And there stands the silver-haired Lurodos, arms crossed, looming large above the others. He catches my eye, and a cruel grin twists his lips.

I leap back, heart thudding, and yank the tent flap down into place. Immediately silence drowns out those voices. There's probably some spell on the pavilion, some glamour to keep out unwanted noises. I stand here in this glamoured space, gaze fixed on the flap. It might as well be a wall of stone ten feet thick.

So. After everything—after all that death and destruction, the suffering of all those innocent men, the burning of the sacred temple—here I am, right back where I started. I've only exchanged one stranger's bed for another.

Slowly I tip my head down, stare at my own bare, carefully manicured feet. Will I do it? Will I let this warlord have his way with me in hopes that he will honor his word and set me free?

Maybe this is all for the best. After all, were I wed to the Shadow King, there'd be no chance of freedom following my wedding night. Whatever indignities I suffered then would have to be suffered again and again, for the rest of my life. This is just one night. I can endure one night.

And when it's all over? This man doesn't know my name. He doesn't know who my people are or where I belong. Perhaps I can convince him to drop me at the Gavarian border. In the end I'll escape my father, my marriage, my prison . . . all of it.

Yes, this is better. Surely this is better.

Dread knots my stomach.

Grimacing, I turn at last to face the warlord. He stands by the fire, watching me. His gaze rakes down my body just for an instant before coming back to my face. I resist the urge to try to cover myself and instead look him in the eye. "How long . . ." I swallow. "How long do I have to decide?"

"Dawn," he responds. "Or rather, a little sooner. We will need time to—"

"Yes." I draw a shuddering breath. "I understand. Just . . . just give me a moment."

"Take your time, *zylnala*. Only remember, if you make no choice, the choice will be made for you. You will belong to him. And there is nothing I can do to prevent it."

10

TAAR

———⚜———

I RAID RUVAEN'S STORES FOR BOTH FOOD AND DRINK.
Something tells me the prisoners were provided with little of
either during the journey through Wanfriel Forest to the spire.
While the girl has not complained, she must be famished.

Most Noxaurian food would be dangerous for a human to eat.
The last thing I want is to get her half-crazed on fae fruit or fae
wine. Whatever happens in the next few hours, she must be clear-
headed and certain of her decisions. But I find a bottle of pure
river water which tastes of the mortal realm. There's baked bread
as well—bunyi bread, with a strong, earthy flavor made from root
flour. It should be acceptable for her palate.

I place the bread on a plate, pour water into another one of
Ruvaen's silver cups, and cross the room to where the girl sits by

the fire. Goddess spare me! I have to brace myself every time I look at her, dressed in that little bit of absolute nothing which Ruvaen provided for her. Damn the man. It's all but impossible to keep my gaze from roving, searching for tantalizing glimpses beneath those folds of sheer cloth. There is little enough left to the imagination, but what little there is could set a man's imagination ablaze.

I must not let such heat consume me. Not tonight. Not with her.

She is so young. I'd noticed it before, but seeing her in this gentle light, all the dirt and mud scrubbed from her face, the truth strikes me full force. Too young for the likes of me, inexperienced and frightened. I feel like a beast, especially when the sight of her enflames me so. But I am no beast. I can and will control my urges, no matter how potent the temptation.

And if she requires abstinence the whole night through, what then? Will I turn her over to Lurodos come dawn? The idea galls me more than I like to admit.

Shaking this thought from my head, I set the food down on a small table beside her chair. "Come," I say. "Eat." She looks at the plate then up at me. "It's not enchanted," I assure her.

"That sounds like something a fae trying to trick me into eating enchanted food would say."

"I am not fae. And if I were, I'm sure I could find more subtle ways to deceive you."

"You are not fae?" Her brow puckers slightly as her gaze flicks over me, taking in my proportions. "What are you then?"

"I am Licornyn," I answer shortly and turn away. I must tear my gaze from her before the burning in my loins drives me insane. Gods above, I don't even know this woman! I've never been the kind of man to lie with a stranger, to share intimacy with someone for whom I did not feel deeply. Yet the vows I made this night draw me to her more profoundly than I would have expected. I can still feel the place on my forearm where the *velra* cord secured us to one another. It's tight, uncomfortable, and yet, in some inexplicable way . . . delightful.

"What is your name?" Her voice is abrupt, as though she's just worked up the courage to speak.

I look over my shoulder to find her twisted in her seat, leaning over the back of it and studying me. I take care not to let my eyes wander. "You may call me Taar."

She snorts. "See? You *are* fae. Everyone knows that particular trick. *You may call me* is not the same as *my name is.*"

A small smile pulls at the corner of my mouth. "My name is Taarthalor Ragnataarthane." She blinks as the syllables, spoken in a strong Licornyn accent, spill smoothly from my lips. It must sound strange to her human ear. "But," I add, "you may call me Taar."

Pursing her lips, she looks down at the bread on the plate, resting in her lap. As though suddenly decided that it probably is neither poisoned nor enchanted, she takes a bite. I wait until she has chewed and swallowed before asking, "And you? What may I call you?"

She glances up at me. I can see the calculation in her eyes. "Lyria," she says.

"But that is not your name, is it?"

Her expression tightens. She unconsciously squeezes the bread in her fingers.

"You may tell me the truth," I continue. "As I said, I am not fae. I cannot use your name to manipulate or control you."

She nods, looks down at her mangled piece of bread. Takes a bite. Chews. Swallows. Then: "I do not want to tell you."

That's honest at least. I nod. "Very well. I shall continue to call you *zylnala*. It suits you well enough."

"And what does . . . what does *zyl-nala* mean?"

"Songbird."

To my surprise, her eyes flash as though I've just said something deeply offensive. She pushes the plate of bread aside, heedless of how it knocks over her cup of water, and gets to her feet. Once more I'm faced with all her flesh displayed through the folds of that nothing gown. Heat pools in my gut. I turn away sharply, even as she marches to the far side of the tent. There's an opening in one of the upper pavilion panels which offers a glimpse of the night sky. From the tail of my eye, I see her standing with her head tilted back.

Once I am sure I have my body under control, I allow myself to glance her way once more. She gazes out at the stars high above. There's a look of such intense longing in her eyes—soft and gentle on her fierce little face. A sad expression which moves my heart unexpectedly. I find myself wishing that I could do something about that sadness. That I might somehow satisfy her longing, at least in part.

But I am not that man. I am a stranger, her captor. Her enemy.

"Why did you do it?"

Her voice is so soft, I almost miss it. Then I frown. Does she mean the auction? Does she want to know why I paid that ridiculous sum to save her? I'm not sure how to explain it, not sure if I can. Even to myself.

But she turns to me again, her arms defensively wrapped across her breast. A little shiver ripples down her spine. "Why did you attack Ashryn Shrine?"

Ah. A good question, and one that must weigh heavily on her mind. Not exactly conducive to a night of passion. Still, if these are the answers she needs from me, I owe her the truth. "You mean, why did I lead a violent assault on a temple full of elderly priests?" I grimace. "My men were under strict orders not to harm the denizens of the shrine. We were there to find someone."

Her eyes narrow. "Who?"

Does she think we went through all that trouble to capture her? I suppose it's not an outlandish suspicion. She and her sister are obviously highborn ladies. Perhaps they would be worth some ransom; perhaps that's why she will not tell me her name.

"Mage Artoris Kelfaren," I answer without hesitation. After all, if this little conversation is about earning trust, my best course is to be as truthful as possible.

Her features tighten subtly. She lifts her chin. "I see."

It comes to me then that I saw her in company with the death mage twice: first on the field outside the temple grounds, then again in the building where all the dead men lay. The mage had seemed determined to hold on to her, even against her will. There's something there. Something she's not telling me.

"You know him," I say. Not a question.

She swallows and looks down at her feet. Then: "I thought I did."

Something knots in my gut; something fiery and twisted that I will not name. But my next words come out a little darker than I intend: "Are you and he . . . ?"

"What?" The girl's head shoots up, eyes wide. "No! That is . . . no." She licks her lips as though trying to decide what to say next. "I knew him when he was an apprentice mage visiting my father's household. We met again by . . . by chance. At the temple."

Lies. Human lies, exhaled from her lips as naturally as breath. I saw the way he gripped her arm. I remember as well seeing her among the Miphates who rode out from the temple. Her sister was not with her at that time. Which means either the Miphates were taking her by force, or she was running away with them. With *him*.

Every instinct urges me to press her for information. But what good will that do either of us just now? The moments are slipping away, leading us ever nearer to dawn. I must focus on the task at hand. On earning her trust. On saving her life. I can question her later, but only if I keep her from Lurodos's clutches.

So I nod as though accepting her story. "I see." Slowly, careful not to startle her, I approach the fire and take a seat in one of the two chairs, then wave a hand to indicate the other. She stands her ground, arms still folded tight. Stretching my feet out toward the blaze, I assume a more relaxed, unthreatening pose. "We received word that Mage Artoris was seen entering the temple grounds. We have been hunting him for some time now. He was in possession of a certain talisman vital to our efforts."

"Your efforts to subdue all Gavaria under fae rule?" she asks darkly.

I raise an eyebrow. "Is that what you believe?"

"It's the truth, isn't it?"

I interlace my fingers, regarding her for a long, silent moment. Then: "While I cannot speak for the fae, that is certainly not *my* goal."

Her eyes burn with suspicion. Not exactly conducive to either trust or intimacy. I sigh and choose honesty. After all, what do I have to lose? "This talisman is wrought with magic spells that can open the secret paths to the Citadel of Evisar, where certain of my people have been taken captive."

She tilts her head slightly. "And it required an entire ravening horde of berserker fae to take on *one* Miphato and steal this talisman?"

I smile grimly. "But this man is not just any Miphato. He is a *necroliphon*—a death mage. He wields magic far more terrible than anything known to the fae. And he is but a student of those dark arts. His master, Morthiel, is more powerful by far. It is believed he has delved into the Rift to summon magic directly from Ashtarath herself."

That name—that demonic utterance, never intended to be spoken, but meant to be felt like a shadow, a shiver of dread in the darkest corners of the soul—seems to dim the fire and darken the whole chamber. Suddenly this little sphere of life in which I and the girl exist feels as though it's cut off from the rest of the living worlds and sits poised on the brink of doom. One wrong breath will send us pitching into darkness unending.

The moment passes. Whether real or imagined, the fire brightens once more, and the shadows retreat to the deepest corners of the room. I blink mildly at the girl, who stares at me with a mixture of horror and confusion. Gods above, this is not exactly wooing language! The incongruity of our situation is almost laughable: her in that gown, in this room, with the incense of seduction burning in our nostrils—while I sit here rattling on about necromancy and demon magic. But how do I prove myself worthy of her trust if I do not speak plainly and answer her questions with truth?

We are silent for some while. I watch the dancing flames, ensorcelled, naturally, to last the whole night through. But my attention is entirely focused on her, still standing across the pavilion under that open sky-flap. I feel her gaze upon me, her scrutiny intense enough to burn.

Finally she moves. I don't look up as she crosses the pavilion and takes a seat in the chair across from me. She perches there, very upright and proper despite the indecency of her gown. Her water is spilled, but she picks up the cup of fae wine I'd given her earlier and takes a sip. Immediately she coughs and sputters.

"Here," I say, rising and stepping around the fire. She flinches away from me, but I pretend not to notice and simply fetch the spilled water cup. I return to Ruvaen's cabinet, refill the cup with fresh water, which I offer to her. She accepts without a word.

I take my seat again. The fire crackles between us, the only sound in an atmosphere suddenly heavy with unspoken tension. Will this night ever end? The truth is, every time I'm near her, the desire grows to touch her, to hold her. To taste her. She's like a note of discord in the song of my soul, driving me wild in both mind and body. I can withstand this temptation. I will not touch her without permission, but . . . I don't know if I can bear to turn her over to Lurodos in the morning.

"Do you serve Prince Ruvaen?"

Her question is abrupt and a little unnerving. I'm forced to look at her again, to study that stern line of her brow as she watches me intently, awaiting my answer. "I have sworn allegiance to the prince under certain conditions," I answer carefully. "Should those conditions fail to be met, we will part ways. Until then we share a common goal. Not," I add with emphasis, "the subjugation of Gavaria."

"And the burned villages of my people? The razed towns, the

decimated crops?"

"I am unaware of such things."

"Oh, really? And what about my—what about Princess Faraine's convoy? That was you, wasn't it? They say she was journeying from the convent in the Ettrian Mountains when a party of riders on flaming unicorns attacked their company."

Her eyes blaze with such indignation, I have to wonder why she should care so much about the human princess. Perhaps they know one another—it would not surprise me to learn this girl had spent time at the court of King Larongar.

I reach out, take the scarcely touched cup of wine from the table, swirl it, and sip. Honesty. I must give her honesty—though it may not be convenient just now. "My people were sent to take the princess hostage," I say, watching the way the wine moves in a small maelstrom within the cup. "Rumor reached us that King Larongar intends to form an alliance with the Shadow King of Mythanar, an alliance we very much wished to prevent. But the Shadow King himself showed up to defend the princess." Though the fire dances brightly, my own vision seems to darken. "We lost good riders and licorneir that night."

I see their faces—each of the brave riders and steeds who rode out on the mission and never returned. I was not with them; I'd argued against sending them at all. Ruvaen insisted, however, and I was compelled by the allegiance I'd sworn to honor his wishes. I sigh and take another draught from the cup. It is a perilous business, going to war with humans. Though physically weaker, they have devised such methods for war as would make my forefathers shake their heads in dismay. And allied with trolls? I don't like to think of what consequences that will bring.

"War is not a pretty thing," I speak into the silence at last. "But sometimes it is a necessary evil."

She sniffs and flashes me a bitter glance. "An easy answer for a warlord such as yourself."

"I did not choose the life of warlord. My people were thrust into this conflict when I was still a child. If I had not grown into the warrior they needed, the Licornyn would have been wiped out long ago. Ours is a perilous existence." Looking up, I find the girl studying me intently. "I will always speak truth to you, *zylnala*," I say, my fingers tight around the silver cup. "That doesn't mean I will sit here and justify the choices I've been forced to make for the last many long years. You know nothing of my people, nothing of my world, nothing of my life or the necessities which drive me."

Leaning forward, I set the cup back down again then remain with my elbows resting on my knees, my head inclined toward hers across the dancing flames. "But I swear to you, had I my way, the Licornyn would live in peace from this day forth. We would erect our *dakath*, and they would take root and flourish into cities once more. The rivers would run free, and the wild creatures would drink from their waters and not be corrupted. The *oriqirel* would fill the skies with their colors, while the licorneir raced freely across the open plains, their song echoing in the hearts of every man, woman, and child. Licorna would be as it once was in the days of my grandfathers."

She holds her tongue while I speak. I do not know if she hears me, if she cares for anything I say. Her gaze is fixed on the flames, her expression far-off and contemplative. Time is slipping away from us. For a few hours our separate stories have been drawn strangely together; how long now before the dawn that inevitably rips us apart? How long before she must enter into the fate Lurodos plans for her? Perhaps it would have been kinder for me to let the raveners kill her in the first place.

Breathing a sigh, I lean back in my chair and lay my arms along the rests. I tilt my head back, close my eyes. I'm so tired suddenly. Tired of always trying to achieve the impossible—to save my people, to break the dark hold the Miphates wield on our land. And now this girl. Somehow, foolishly, I've assumed responsibility for her life. As though I needed one more burden weighing on my shoulders! I was a fool to make that bid; I'm a fool to sit here with her now.

So I don't. I send my mind as far away as I can—back to those images of childhood which the girl's singing had awakened in me last night. I see myself astride my father's great licorneir, Onoril the Black. His flowing mane whips in my face, and his powerful song reverberates in my soul. I am one with him and the open sky above us and the great stretch of land before us.

Together we ride for the City of Spires, and the citadel gleams like a beacon, guiding us home—

"Stop that."

I tip my head and open one eye. The girl sits with hands clenched, scowling at me. "Stop what?"

"That song. Stop humming it. Please."

I blink. Only then do I realize that I've been softly humming some remnant of the tune she'd sung last night. "Is it not your own song, little *zylnala*?"

She presses her lips together. Then: "I am no songbird."

"I would beg to differ. Even in the midst of battle, your voice stopped me in my tracks. If I didn't know any better, I would have thought it magic." I tip my head, looking at her from under my brows. "Is it magic?"

She shrugs, but otherwise, does not answer. The silver knife with which she'd tried to cut my throat in bed lies on the table beside her. She picks it up, toying with it absently.

"I'll take that as a yes. And are you a Miphata then?"

"No!" Her protest is sharp. "I am no part of the Miphates order. Not now. Not ever."

I nod slowly. I believe her. Though there was power in her song, it was nothing like the written spells of the Miphates which I have encountered many times over the years. There's a certain acrid aftershock to those bursts of stolen magic. Everything about this girl's voice was natural and sweet, utterly unforced. "I have never heard such music from the lips of man or woman," I muse, more to myself than to her. "Though it is strange to say it, the nearest likeness I have ever heard is the song of the licorneir."

"What does that mean?"

I cross my feet at the ankles, adjusting my seat to a more comfortable angle. "The licorneir are said to be the children of the Goddess of Unity. They sing the unifying song of the stars. Legend has it that, if they so chose, they could join their voices into one great song of absolute beauty and destruction." I shrug. "I have never witnessed this. Licorneir sing together only for holy ceremonies, and then only a few at a time. Otherwise they join their songs with those of their heart-bound riders. Each song is unique and only shared between rider and beast."

The girl frowns. Something I've said has confused her. But she asks no questions, so I continue: "Your voice made me think of that legend: a song, multitudinous even in wholeness. I've never heard anything like it, certainly not from the mouth of a woman." I eye her. "Will you tell me about it? This talent of yours?"

"There's nothing to tell." She looks down at the knife in her hand, turning it around and rubbing the end of the silver hilt. "I can sing; I choose not to."

"So if I ask, you would not sing for me now?"

"Gods, no!"

I'm more disappointed than I like to admit. Part of me had hoped music might be a way through to her. I'm starting to think there isn't any route past her prickling defenses. She is so frightened, and her walls are so high. And there simply isn't time.

The girl gasps suddenly, dropping the knife she's been toying with. I turn my head sharply and, in the same instant, smell blood. Red, human blood which wells from a cut along the fleshy part of her palm and drips in her lap.

Instantly I leap to my feet and hasten to the bed. Without regard for Ruvaen's finery, I whip out a knife, cut a swath off the soft silk canopy, and return to the girl's side. She's grasping her wounded hand, shuddering with shock as she stares at the oozing red drip down her wrist. "Allow me," I say, kneeling before her.

Though reluctant, she permits me to take her hand. I'm suddenly aware, as I wasn't before, how soft her skin is. I'd already assumed she was a highborn lady based on her air and manner of speaking. These soft hands only confirm that belief— the hands of a woman who has never pursued hard labor in her life. Her fingers try to curl, as though to clench down on the pain. "No, no," I say softly, and smooth them open, heedless of the dripping blood. "Like this." Turning her hand, I inspect the slice. It's thin but surprisingly deep—Lurodos's blade boasts a deadly bite. Carefully I press the torn flesh back together, even as more blood wells. She sucks in a sharp breath at the pain. "Easy," I whisper. "It will be over soon."

Then I begin to sing.

It's an ancient song, wordless—sound full of meaning more

profound than language. It begins soft and low, a rumble in the back of my throat. As the first few low notes vibrate in the air, I feel my connection to Elydark awaken. My licorneir, somewhere out there in the night, away from the main encampment, remains nonetheless bound to me, soul entwined with soul. My song calls to him, and he responds, sending a pulse of song back to me. It fills my chest, deepens my voice. I draw on the pure, raw magic of the licorneir as I sing, and a soft glow—not seen so much as felt—suffuses the air around her hand resting in mine.

The cut begins to knit. The blood-flow staunches, the flesh draws back together, becoming as it wishes to be: whole and healed.

The girl stares, her mouth open, her eyes wide. She doesn't seem to draw breath until I use the cut silk to mop up the remaining blood, revealing a small white scar beneath the stain. "How . . . how did you do that?" she manages at last.

"My people aren't just warriors," I reply, the last reverberations of Elydark's song still in the back of my throat. "We used to be singers, artisans, craftsmen. But above all, we were healers." I turn her hand gently around, inspecting my work. The fire's glow plays across her skin, the elegant bones of her wrist and long, tapered fingers. I run a thumb along that new pale scar. She shivers, her breath catching. "The Goddess of Unity is alive in the song of the licorneir. That song, when channeled correctly, may remind split flesh what it means to be whole. It takes years to master, and in truth," I admit with a sigh, "we do not sing as we once did. Not since the Rift."

The girl's eyes are fastened on me. I become aware suddenly of how close we are, of how her tight breath brushes against my skin. Though kneeling, I am taller than her when seated. She is obliged to look up into my face. I cannot bring myself to look anywhere but at her hand . . . and even that is a great temptation, so delicate, so finely made. I want to raise those fingers to my lips, to kiss them, to gently bite them, to . . .

"You have a lovely voice."

Heat steals unexpectedly up my cheeks. I let go of her hand, rise, and back away to my side of the fire. "Coming from you, *zylnala*," I say, "that is a great compliment."

Gods, what is wrong with me? I thought I'd mastered the worst of my urges but, here I am, fighting the same battle all over again—fighting to keep myself from grabbing her arms, yanking her from that chair, and burying my face in the curve of her neck and shoulder. From losing myself beneath the waves of her soft, scented hair. I take a seat across from her and stare into the fire. Neither of us speaks for some while, with nothing but the crackle and snap of embers to punctuate the silence. Finally I run a hand down my face. My breath is coming hard and fast, and I know we cannot go on like this for much longer.

"I do not wish to frighten you," I say after what feels like hours, "but you must know our time is slipping away. If I am to help you, if I am to save you, a choice must be made."

"Choice." She whispers the word bitterly.

"There are more choices than one here," I continue as though I did not hear her. "I swore to protect you. If you ask it of me, I will take you from this encampment now. I will summon my licorneir, put you on his back, and we will ride out together, facing whatever foes stand in our way."

Even as I say it, the hopelessness of the proposal hits me like a wave. Elydark and I are formidable together, but against the entire Noxaurian host, urged on by Lurodos and driven mad on virulium? We don't stand a chance.

The girl watches me, her dark eyes shadowed despite the firelight. Reading my expression, she asks softly, "How far do you think we'd make it before they cut us down?"

"Possibly to the forest's edge. Then my bowels would be spilt upon the ground and my head raised on a stake. My licorneir would erupt in flame, killing all within range before going out once and for all. And you? Should you survive the altercation . . ."

She doesn't answer. She knows the unspoken truth well enough. Huddled back in her chair, she looks down at her once-wounded hand, at the little white scar, now healed. Her expression is intent, her brow furrowed in that line which is already becoming familiar.

"Why do you care?" she asks at last. "Why go through all this trouble, this risk?" When I don't answer at once, she continues, "If it were just for a chance to lie with me, you could have done so by now. It's not like I could stop you. Is it because you want me willing? Do you not like it when your victims struggle? Or is it . . . is it possible you really are as noble and self-sacrificing as you pretend to be?"

I am not noble. I am not self-sacrificing. Not in this instance at least. The truth burns in my gut, deep down where I can no longer refuse to acknowledge it. I simply could not let a monster like Lurodos have her. Not this fiery creature, who fought so hard to defend her fallen sister, even against foes far beyond her scope. Not once has she backed down, not once has she let fear be her master. Courage burns through her veins like song, lighting up her very soul.

Looking down at my right forearm, I feel again the invisible cord wrapped there. The sacred *velra* bond, which cannot last for us, as we are not meant for this lifetime union. But I feel it nonetheless, stronger than I like to admit. How can I be so drawn to, so compelled by, a woman I do not know? A human woman no less. Gods, I don't even know her name!

"I promised to tell you no lies," I say at last, not lifting my gaze from my arm. "But in this instance, I can tell you no truth either, for . . . I do not know the answer to your question. All I know is, when I saw you up there on that scaffold, surrounded by those bloodthirsty brutes, I could not leave you there."

I look at her then, careful to meet her eyes and let my gaze stray nowhere else. "This bond we share may be only temporary. But so long as you are under my protection, I will do as I vowed: I will guard you, shelter you, and, insofar as it is in my power, I will strive to give you both pleasure and delight." Sighing heavily, I offer a half-smile. "I wish we had more time. Time for me to prove myself, to earn your trust. Such is not the fate the gods have ordained for us, however. So I ask for your trust unearned. Give me this chance to prove myself worthy of the asking."

She lowers her gaze, studying the fire between us. She cannot be aware of how the skirt of her gown has parted, revealing much of her long, lithe legs. I have seen many beautiful women in my lifetime; it's not as though this sight is anything new. Yet somehow these tantalizing glimpses are a revelation. Everything about her is new, thrilling, with the promise of further discoveries waiting to be made. My body goes hot and cold, and I grip the arms of my chair tight with both hands.

Finally, after what feels like an endless interval, she rises, pressing her scarred hand to her breast. She comes toward me, rounding the fire, and I stand as well, towering over her. I wait to meet her, my pulse racing, filled with uncertain hope and dread. The moment has come, but I do not yet know what that moment may be. Her eyes are downcast, and I cannot seem to tear my gaze away from those soft lashes fanning her cheeks.

She comes to a stop within arms' reach of me. I wait, my breath held tight in my chest.

"When it is over," she whispers, her voice only just audible over the crackle of the fire, "when the law is satisfied . . . you will help me find my sister."

"I will."

"And you will free us both?"

"Yes. I will see you safely delivered wherever you wish and provide you with any necessary supplies."

She nods. A long, shuddering breath eases through her parted lips. I watch the delicate flutter of her pulse in her throat, the play of light across her features. Then she lifts her dark lashes and gazes up at me from eyes like two deep forest pools.

"Very well, warlord," she says softly. "Do what you must. Save my life."

11

ILSEVEL

❧※❧

I DON'T KNOW WHAT I EXPECT TO HAPPEN NEXT. NOT EXACTLY.
My heart throbs so fast, I fear it will make an audible boom
in my breast. My body shivers as though cold, though the heat
from the nearby fire is almost oppressive against my skin. I stare up
at this massive, terrifying man. This warlord. This brute. Red glare
highlights every chiseled edge of his body, even as it did when I first
saw him, surrounded by screams and blood and terror. Looking at
him now, that's all I can remember—not the gentle touch when he
tended my hand, or the low, rumbling croon of his voice when he
sang. He is nothing but a stranger to me. My enemy.

And yet I just told him to do as he willed with my body. All in
the desperate hope that he might turn out to be a man of his word.

Run, my mind tells me, a scream in the back of my head.

Run, get out of here!

But I won't. I meet his gaze, hold it without shrinking.

When I was fifteen and I invited Artoris into my chambers, the door was scarcely shut before he was on me. Will it be the same with this man? My experience with such matters is limited to that desperate moment of gasping, grasping, and groping seven years ago. Of being pushed onto the bed, of my clothes ripped and my body pinched, and everything moving too fast. I told myself it was all right to be frightened. It's love; love is frightening. I told myself the sick churning in my gut was excitement, that the way my skin shivered at the touch of his hands was a thrill. And when I whispered, "Wait, wait, wait!" into his ear—and he answered, "I cannot. You are too much for me. I cannot resist you"—I reminded myself that I was the one to invite him into my chambers. I knew what I was getting myself into. Didn't I?

So when I screamed—when the guards down the hall burst into the room and pulled him off me, hitting him in the gut so that he doubled over—when he was dragged out to the pillory and shamed before the whole of my father's court—I knew it was my fault. I did this to him. Every lash he took seared my conscience even as it ripped his flesh. And I vowed I would love him forever, despite anything my father did, despite how every force in the worlds seemed determined to tear us apart.

Those memories flash through my mind now, one after another, as vivid as though freshly lived. And with them, the memory of Captain Wulfram and his men. Piled up dead on the floor of that hall, their throats slit. That is the kind of man Artoris is—a man who will kill any who get in his way. A man who will not take no for an answer. The only way to survive such men is to show no fear. I've learned that lesson well over the years, living in my father's court. Any trace of weakness will be exploited, so one must always stand firm. And when courage fails, fake it. Fake it until you yourself believe it.

My body is stiff. Dread churns in my gut as I gaze up into the warlord's eyes. Taar—a harsh name, like the tearing of claws through flesh. It suits him. I wonder, will he tear my flesh as he takes his pleasure from me? Before I set out on my Maiden's Journey, my father's favorite mistress, Fyndra, was brought to my chambers to instruct me on the arts of the bedroom. She told me what I could expect from my wedding night. Every word that fell from her laughing mouth filled me with horror.

This may not have been the bridal chamber I'd expected nor the bridegroom I'd anticipated. And yet, somehow, here I am. As though it was always my fate to end up in the arms of some ravenous stranger. But if I can just endure for one night . . . if I can get through the next few minutes . . .

Taar moves.

I try not to flinch. He merely extends his hand a little, after all. He stops, his fingers hovering inches from mine, not yet touching me. I stare down at them, noting all the little details. Innumerable white scars across the knuckles. Calluses from riding and wielding weapons. A big hand, strong and unexpectedly graceful, with deep nailbeds, pale against his sun-darkened skin. His forearm is corded with sinewy muscle, the kind of muscle developed from long hours of combat training. How easily could he snap my neck?

"*Zylnala.*"

I catch my breath and force my gaze up to his. Those black eyes, like windows to the night sky, seem to take up the whole scope of my vision.

"*Zylnala.*" The word falls from his lips so gently, I scarcely believe that voice can belong to this great, solid, stone-carved man. "I will not harm you. Not now. Not ever. Will you let me take your hand?"

What is this? I frown. Didn't I just give him permission to plunder my body for the sake of satisfying some fae law? Now he's going to *ask* to hold my hand? Still, it's not as though I can tell him *no*. Mouth dry, I nod my head. Once. Short.

He reaches a little farther. His large fingers dwarf mine as they close around them. His skin is hot, while mine is like ice, despite the near fire. He stands for a moment, pressing my fingers firmly but without pain. Then he draws my hand toward him. I tense, uncertain and suddenly afraid. Is he going to . . . to *place* my hand somewhere? Fyndra told me about this, about how a woman can please her man. Of where to grasp, where to tug, how to apply just enough teasing pressure. I've never done anything like it. What if I can't manage correctly? What if I fail to satisfy him? He might refuse to consummate our strange marriage and toss me out into the night, into the grasping arms of all those waiting, hungry monsters.

But Taar simply places his other hand atop mine. "Look at me," he says.

I swallow hard. Then I glance up as commanded.

"Have you had any experience with a man?"

Heat floods my cheeks. Which makes me angry . . . angry that I should suddenly feel so vulnerable, so foolish. But I won't let him get the better of me. Holding his gaze, I nod again firmly.

He tilts his chin, studying me closely. "It would be best, under the circumstances, if we were entirely honest with one another. If you prefer not to tell me, that is your choice. I ask only that you do not lie."

My throat feels tight, my mouth dry. I draw a short breath and will my voice not to tremble. "I've had . . . some. Experience, that is."

He nods solemnly. "And was it pleasant for you?"

Unable to hold his gaze, I turn to stare at the dancing fire. Then, because I cannot see how withholding the truth will help in this instance, I shake my head.

"I see." Taar is silent for a long moment. His thumb rubs gently across the top of my hand, a lazy back and forth. I'm keenly aware of that touch, that pressure. I scarcely focus on anything else. "And are you yet a maiden?" he asks at last.

I flash him a quick, sidelong glance. Then nod again.

"I thought as much. You are able to see the licorneir—I noticed the way you looked at Nyathri back at the encampment. Ordinarily humans cannot see the licorneir when they are not burning. Only those who are yet innocent."

"Innocent?" The word bites through my teeth. "I am not *innocent*." Would an innocent girl be caught in bed with a man six years her senior? Would she send him to the pillory because she could not stifle her screams? Would she write to that same man years later, somehow still believing the fantasy she'd invented of a hero on a white horse and, in so doing, bring death upon both her own entourage and the priests who had offered her hospitality?

I am not innocent. Not by a long shot.

Taar does not answer at once. When he does at last, it is merely to whisper, "I see."

"Oh, do you?" I snap. His black eyes study my face intently. I don't like it. I want to snatch my hand from his grasp and wrap my arms around myself again. But I'm committed to this course, aren't I? I'm not going to show cowardice at the moment of crisis. "Well, spare me any further study of my character or virtue. Why don't you simply get on with it? Rip off this gown, spread my legs. Have your way with me. I told you to do it, didn't I?"

I'm shivering now with rage as much as anticipated pain. No doubt I seem pathetic to a creature like him—like a fluffy lapdog yapping at the heels of a wolf.

His expression is neither disgusted nor amused, however.

Merely thoughtful. He waits until I've finished speaking, until I'm standing with my breath coming in short gasps, my chest heaving under these flimsy folds of nothing that make up my gown. Then he speaks again in a low rumble that stirs heat in my gut: "Tell me, *zylnala,* do you know how I may best please you?"

"What?" I'm not sure if he could have asked anything more unexpected. To my knowledge, the couplings of men and women have never been about what she wants, what pleases her. I remember too vividly how my father would publicly grope and paw at my mother and, when she fended him off, would turn those same attentions on his mistress. All done in the presence of witnesses on purpose to demonstrate his ownership. Though Fyndra laughed and my mother sneered, both subtly communicated their helplessness against my father's lusts. What did their pleasure or comfort matter?

Mine certainly hadn't mattered to Artoris when he pushed me onto that bed. He simply took what he wanted, his mouth rough and hot, his hands hard and grasping. "You love this, you dirty little minx," he breathed into my ear, and I told myself that he must be right. How would I know any different?

"A woman's pleasure in the bedroom," Fyndra told me at the end of her instruction, *"has everything to do with the power she may derive from pleasing her man. If a powerful man likes you—if he needs you, if he craves you—you will always have security in this dangerous world."*

I stare at Taar. This husband whom I do not intend to keep. How could he ever please me? The idea is simply unfathomable.

"I . . ." I shake my head, hating the way my voice trembles despite my best efforts to keep it low and measured. "I'm not sure I . . . am capable of . . . pleasure. Under the circumstances."

The warlord nods and looks down at my hand once more. He draws a long breath and exhales it slowly. "We will try," he says at last. "We will go slowly." With that he lifts my hand to his mouth. His breath is warm against my frigid skin. His lips hover for a moment, and he looks down at me, his eyes deep and knowing and terrifying. "This will be a night of discovery," he says softly. "For both of us."

It occurs to me for the first time that this might not be an easy situation for him. Despite his prowess, his power, his dominance . . . perhaps this is not what he expected to happen. He said he did not know the laws of Noxaur when he bid on me. For all I know, he might not want me. Not like *that*, anyway. Not like Artoris did. I am human, after all, and he is . . . well, he may not be fae, but he is certainly not human. I may very well be entirely undesirable to his eye.

Why does that idea displease me? It ought to be a relief, yet part of me is disappointed. That small, dangerous, almost-suppressed part of me which knows I am meant to be hungered for, and to feel that hunger in return.

Taar lowers his mouth to my hand and kisses me for the first time. His lips are warm and soft. It's not a simple peck or salute. He lingers for a moment while his eyes hold mine.

My heart tightens and performs a little flip. This is unexpected. There's something in that touch, something in that way he looks at me. A promise of sorts, simple and yet profound enough to stir something deep inside me. A fire in my gut that no longer feels quite like rage.

He lifts his head again. His hand still grips mine, and I feel where his mouth had been. The flesh burns, and streaks of warmth radiate up my arm. He takes one step back, then another. He's leading me, I realize. Away from the fire, away from the two chairs. Into the softer light which bathes that great bed. My stomach knots. I feel again as though I'm standing on top of the garden wall back home, and a strong wind blows. That rush—that thrill of terror. That sense of an imminent plunge just waiting to claim me, coupled with a strange, unnatural hope that maybe, just maybe, if I stepped out into the empty air, I wouldn't plummet, but fly.

Taar sits down on the edge of the bed. Gods, even seated, his head is still level with my own! This man is huge, truly huge. How will I ever . . . that is, I am supposed to receive him inside me, and yet . . . I don't think I can. He's got to be very large down there.

Damn it, I'm starting to tremble all over again.

"Now, now, *zylnala*," he says. Ever so gently, he runs his knuckle along the curve of my cheek. "I vowed to let no harm come to you. Remember? Allow me to prove myself here and now. You will suffer no pain at my hand."

A likely story. But I nod and steel my spine. "Do it then," I say. My voice sounds harsh in this space of firelight and softness. "I am ready."

He shakes his head. "I think not. What I must do, I cannot do without your trust. You must be willing to place yourself wholly into my care and keeping. Only then can we achieve what we must together."

I shake my head. I've had about enough of all this foolish talk. "I'm not an idiot," I growl. "I've seen horses coupling."

Taar blinks. "Horses?"

"Yes. And cats. And dogs."

His brow puckers, confused. His hand withdraws from my cheek.

"I'm saying that I may not have much experience of my own, but I know the basics of what must be done. It doesn't involve anything you're describing, none of this *trust* and *protection* nonsense. None of this *achievement*. What is there to achieve about it? Unless you're expecting something from me beyond the basics of coupling."

His eyes rove across my face, his brow drawn tight. He's much older than I had initially thought. Now that I'm close and not in fear of imminent death, I can take in finer details than I had before. There are the trace beginnings of lines at the corners of his eyes, which I would not have expected to see. A fae certainly would have glamoured them away. Perhaps he isn't fae after all. But whatever he is, he is unnaturally beautiful—breathtakingly, terrifyingly beautiful. Beautiful and old, not in years, but in experience. In life lived and suffering endured. The depth in his eyes might well be endless.

He blinks slowly, his black lashes thick and curled. "Ah!" he says at length. "Of course, I had heard tell that other peoples practice different bridal customs." He looks down. His gaze strays briefly across my exposed body but focuses on my hand once more. He lowers his other hand, pressing my palm firmly between both of his. "Among the Licornyn, the wedding night proceeds thusly—the man must prove to his bride that she may trust his vows, including the vow to bring her pleasure and delight all the days of their shared life." He looks up again, catching my gaze with his. "It is *your* pleasure that matters here tonight. Our marriage will be consummated when we have discovered together the fullness of your delight here on our marriage bed."

I stare at him. What am I supposed to make of this? "So . . . so you're not going to . . . ?"

"If a man fails to please his wife, she may choose to end the marriage the next morning. Or she may give him more time, depending on the extent of his efforts. But if he were to take his pleasure from her without having first seen to her satisfaction, that would be the sign of an oathbreaker. She would be well within her rights to demand *vel-rhoar*. A sundering of their bond."

My mouth opens and closes. Divorce. He's talking about divorce. Initiated by the wife for her husband's failure to . . . to *please* her?

The only divorces I've ever heard of—and there've been few enough, that's for certain—were always the same situation: a husband, tired of his wife and seeking to make a more advantageous match, inventing some excuse to convince the priestesses of Nornala to grant a sundering of their union. The wife never puts up any fight; after all, if divorce is not granted, her husband might turn to more lethal means to end his marriage.

But what Taar has just described . . . the concept is so utterly foreign. I don't know what to make of it. "Surely you're joking."

"I assure you, I am not." My warlord husband reaches out once more and brushes my cheek with the tips of his fingers. "If we are to seal our marriage tonight according to the custom of my people, it is my duty and my honor to find what pleases you. What brings you release and satisfaction."

Blood throbs in my veins, pulsing through every limb and stirring in my stomach. I shake my head, trying to break the force of his gaze. "Can I not . . . can I not simply declare myself satisfied? Can we not shake hands and be done with it?"

A smile tilts his mouth. That sudden flash of white teeth through full lips and beard shocks me and sends the pulsing throb in my gut even lower, deeper. "Unfortunately, no. That is not the satisfaction this particular oath requires of me."

"What then?"

"You do not know?"

I swallow. Then shake my head.

"Ah! You truly are an innocent then."

My teeth grind, and my hand, still caught in his, clenches into a fist. "I am not."

But he shakes his head hastily. "I mean no offence. *Innocent* seems to me a kindlier word than *ignorant*."

"I'm not ignorant either."

"In this matter you are," he persists. "You have neither the knowledge nor the experience to understand of what I speak. So, if you do not care for *innocence*, you must accept your *ignorance*. And allow me to instruct you."

The fire at my back seems suddenly much too hot, and the pressure of his hand gripping mine too firm. But his fingers trace the line of my jaw, so unlike any touch I've ever felt from a man. Artoris was all hard grasping, painful and hot. This is gentle, and I find I am keenly aware of the texture of his calloused fingertips, the warmth of his skin. The awareness is so acute, I don't know if it's pleasant, only that . . . I don't hate it.

"Very well." My breath catches on the words, but I force them out regardless. "Instruct me then. Teach me what my own pleasure means."

His smile flashes once more. "It is very simple," he says. "I will touch you. You will tell me if you like it. If you do, I will continue. If you do not, I will try something else. Agreed?"

I can't quite find words to answer, for his touch has strayed from my jaw to my throat. His fingers could encircle my neck quite easily. There's so much raw power in that hand, so much brutality barely contained. Little pinprick sparks break out across my skin. I draw a shuddering breath.

"Do you like that?" he asks, his voice low.

"Well . . ." I whisper, determined not to be easily won. "I don't dislike it."

He nods. "We have our beginning." His fingers trail up and down my throat several times, his thumb pressing gently into the hollow of my collarbone. My heart gallops. "And that, *zylnala?* How does that feel?"

"I . . . I'm not sure."

"Fair enough." He continues to trace my collarbone, featherlight touches that seem to awaken my trembling skin. He lets his fingers play along the thin shoulder strap of the gown, then runs a line of fire along my shoulder blade. His eyes, however, remain on my face even as his hand performs this delicate tracery. He studies me, reading any information my expression may offer. Is he enjoying himself? I don't know. I don't understand what he's gaining from any of this—no physical pleasure, no power, no advantage. And if he knew who I am, if he knew I am King Larongar's daughter? He would probably kill me on the spot.

"Now, now," he says abruptly withdrawing his hand from my skin. "I see fear creeping into your eyes. What is it?"

I blink, snapped out of a semi-daze, and struggle to focus on his face. "I'm . . . I'm just . . ."

"Tell me," he says. "You're slipping away from me. I should like to draw you back again."

I flush and glance off to one side, focusing on the wafting silk of the canopy. I need something to look at, anywhere other than his face. "I don't understand why. Why you're here, why you're doing this. If you don't mean to . . . to exercise your husbandly rights, as it were, why go through with it at all?"

He does not answer right away. Other than my hand, which he holds, he does not touch me. He simply looks at me, considering what I have asked. "I have never cared to treat a woman's body like a receptacle for my passion," he says at long last, as though it's the first time he's tried to articulate the concept in words. "There are men who do, but that is not who I am. If the enjoyment is not mutual, it is not enjoyable for me."

I nod, pressing my lips together. Then: "You haven't answered my question."

"I know." He shakes his head, his brow puckering slightly. "The truth is, I'm not certain what answer I can give. None of this was my plan or intention, and yet . . . I do know that right here, right now, I'm glad to be in this place. With you."

"Glad?" I bite out the word.

"Forgive me," he says. "That was poorly spoken. Let me try again. It is my honor to offer you whatever assistance I may. I expect nothing of you, neither payment nor gratitude. I certainly do not expect you to give me more of your body than you will. If you ask it of me this moment, I will never touch you again." He takes hold of my chin then, pulling my face up so that I must look once more into his eyes. "But if you choose to continue, I should like to keep you here. Focused on my touch and your own responses. Do not let your thoughts wander. Stay here with me."

My breath is so tight, my chest seems ready to cave in. "I'm not sure I can."

He nods, understanding in his gaze. "But will you try?"

"Yes," I whisper.

"Good. Now let us try something else."

He slips his hand around the back of my head, his fingers tangling in my hair. My heart kicks up a notch. He's going to kiss me. And, gods spare me, but I don't know if I like kissing! How mad is that? But when I remember how recently Artoris mashed his lips against mine, assaulting my mouth with his tongue, the muscles in my shoulders start to lock up tight. I brace myself, preparing for the worst.

"There's so much tension in your body," Taar says softly. "Will you give me permission to proceed?"

What choice do I have? I nod.

He looks me in the eye. "I won't if you do not wish it."

"No. Do." The words come out in little bursts, and only when I hear them do I realize how contradictory they sound. I clear my throat and try again. "Do what you must."

He nods. Then he leans forward, closes his eyes, and plants

a kiss on my brow.

I catch my breath. I wasn't expecting that. That pressure of his mouth against my skin, a salute of honor. Nothing grasping or greedy. Simple and yet . . . not simple at all. I don't know how to describe it; I don't know how to feel. I know only that my heart leaps to my throat, and when it thuds back into place, it's pounding faster than before. Warmth spreads from that point of contact between us, as though he is imparting his own body heat into my cold frame.

The fire in my belly flares. Suddenly, to my surprise, I find I want more. I want to feel how those lips of his will make other parts of my body respond. I want to feel them pressed against mine, because maybe kissing could be more than just mouths mangling and tongues tangling. Maybe . . .

He draws back slowly, breathing against my forehead. "Did you like that?"

I nod. It's the first time I've answered without hesitation.

His fingers still on my chin, he tips my head back farther. He sits on the edge of the bed, and I stand between his legs, but our bodies still feel miles apart. What would happen if I dared cross that gulf? If I dared make the leap?

He leans forward, closing his eyes once more. This time he brushes my lips with his, a breathtaking whisper of touch. Something inside me ignites, something I wasn't expecting at all. Not here, not with him. Not ever, if I'm honest.

Once more he withdraws. I suck in a breath, leaning toward him as though to catch and hold his kiss. But he puts a little space between us, his mouth so near I can still almost feel the shape of it. His breath is warm and sweet as it mingles with mine. "And?" he asks, his voice a deep vibration in my chest. "What did you think of that?"

I cannot find words. My hand, which has been stiff and clenched at my side, rises as though of its own volition to touch my parted lips. They seem to burn. I flick my gaze up to his. "Kiss me again?" I breathe.

He smiles. "At your pleasure."

He presses his lips to mine more firmly this time. His hand in my hair pulls me toward him, while his other hand slips around my waist, applying pressure to the small of my back so that I have no choice but to step into him. I press my palms against his bare torso, his skin flaming to my touch. I like that as well—I like the hardness of him, the muscular size and strength of him. I slide my hands gently over his chest up to his broad shoulders. He groans deep, like a growl. The sound shocks me, and I startle. Instantly he pulls back, his eyes still closed. "Oh, *zylnala*," he says. "Do you—"

Before he can ask that gods-damned question again, I dart forward and kiss him myself. My lips are awkward and uncertain. I've always been on the receiving end of kisses, never the initiator. But Taar responds at once, his mouth moving against mine, his lips playing, molding, teasing. A little uncertainly, I open my mouth, inviting him in. He flicks his tongue against my upper lip, and I gasp, but do not break away. He does not fill my mouth like Artoris did, however. His restraint is admirable. And maddening.

He breaks away at last and presses his forehead against mine as we both pant for breath. "If I had my way," he says, "I should like to kiss you like that all night long."

"Can you not?" I answer, the words low and a little guttural. "I . . . I like it. It pleases me."

He smiles. I feel it rather than see it, for my eyes are still closed as I rest my brow on his. "It is a pleasure, a great pleasure indeed," he replies. "But we must keep searching for a pleasure greater still."

I'm not sure there is a greater pleasure, not for me in any case. But, as much as I hate to admit it, I *am* ignorant when it comes to such matters. "What would you suggest then?"

"How about this?"

He kisses me again, but when I try to catch and hold his kiss, he moves his mouth away from mine, exploring my cheek, my jaw, my ear, nibbling and teasing my sensitive skin. And I like it, oh, yes, I like it! I like as well the warm strength of his hands, the one still firmly gripping my head, the other planted at the small of my back. I think those hands could possibly do more, though I'm not sure what.

As though reading my mind, Taar loosens his grip on my hair and lets his hand trail down my neck, more of those gentle, exploratory strokes with which he began this experiment. I like that too, more than I did before. I moan softly, which seems to excite him. The hand at my back tenses, fingers curling into the sheer folds of my nothing gown.

Before I can catch my breath, he spins me abruptly around. I utter a little squeak and fall back against his chest. He catches me, his hand splayed across my abdomen. The other hand moves aside long locks of my hair. His mouth, which had been teasing my ear, now moves down the column of my neck to the curve of my shoulder. And that I like very much indeed. Those kisses send ripples of lightning across my skin. It's almost more than I can bear. I squirm in his grasp.

Hardness wells up against my buttocks, a large, solid swelling, much bigger and more insistent than I anticipated. My heart jolts, and my body tenses once more.

"Have no fear," Taar murmurs, aware of my reaction. "This night is about your pleasure alone. I shall do nothing that causes you pain."

"Are . . . are you sure?" I whisper. Because he feels very urgent, pressed up against me like that.

"Yes," he replies, his breath tickling my skin. "I want you. I can't pretend to deny it. But I am master of myself. I will do nothing you do not ask for." He nibbles the shell of my ear, and I shiver in delicious response. "Tell me now, little bird, what would you ask of me next?"

I don't know. I don't know what to ask. This is all so new. I roll my shoulder, turning my head to one side, and try to catch a glimpse of his face from the corner of my eye. "Kiss me again," I say, as the strap of my gown slips from my shoulder down my upper arm. "There. And . . ." I gasp as his mouth creates more sensation exploding across my skin. "And there, and . . . and . . . *oh.*"

I lose all ability to speak. Because his hand is now sliding up my stomach, slowly, slowly. His thumb traces the lower curve of my breast, slipping beneath the folds of cloth to explore the delicate skin. That thumb trails up along the curve until it finds the nipple. He flicks me delicately, and fire roars straight to my loins. "Do you like that, *zylnala?*"

"Yes." I lean my head back against his shoulder, eyes half-closed, and whimper. "Yes, warlord. Yes, yes."

His other hand slips around to my front until he cups me firmly with both hands, massaging and teasing, toying with me. "And what do you make of that?" he whispers.

I whimper again and press into him, no longer concerned with the hardness against my buttocks. I arch my back, gasping for breath. My own hands slide up to grasp his shoulders and twine in his long dark hair.

"If you like that," he murmurs, "there's something else I want to try. Shall I?"

I don't want him to stop what he's doing, but . . . I'm also curious. He seems to know so much more about my body and its mysteries than I do. Unable to form words, I nod.

He pushes me away from him. I start to protest, but he stands up behind me and turns me to face him. For a moment he simply looks down at me, his gaze holding mine hard. He's so tall—in those moments when he sat with me between his legs, I'd almost forgotten how toweringly huge he is. I feel quite dizzy staring up at him, though that may be due to my sudden inability to draw a full breath.

His eyes slowly, slowly lower, taking in the sight of my mostly-exposed bosom. With exquisite care, he slides the other strap from my shoulder, smooths back the fabric, until the gown simply drops to my waist, and I am bare before him. Heat roars to my cheeks. I've never been so exposed to a man's gaze. It's one thing for his hands to be on me, another entirely to face him, to be looked at with such hunger. Part of me wants to wrap my arms across my chest, to hide myself.

But I also like it. I like that look. I like the craving in his gaze, and I don't fear it. Or perhaps I do a little, but it's a delicious sort of fear, a thrill, a curiosity. His touch thus far has awakened such things inside me as I never believed possible. What more might he do? What more might we discover if I give into fear just a little more?

Red light from the fire flares in the depths of his black eyes. He takes hold of my waist, turns me to the bed. "Lie back," he commands.

I obey. All sense of control slips through my fingers, but I like that too, oddly enough. I sit on the bed, lean on my elbows. He bends over me, massive, dark, and dangerous. With the light of the fire behind him, I can scarcely see his face beyond the shine of his eyes. I lift my mouth to his, and he kisses me again. Kisses me and presses me into the bed, while his hand traces the line of my breast, and his calloused thumb plays with my nipple. I moan, opening my mouth to receive him more deeply. This time his tongue dances across mine. Emboldened, I extend my tongue, teasing his upper lip. Then, impulsively, I take his lower lip between my teeth and bite.

He draws back, grinning wolfishly. "Careful," he growls, teeth flashing. "Two can play at that game." He touches my lower lip with his thumb, pulling at the plump softness. "But not tonight, for I vowed not to hurt you."

"I made no such vow," I point out and catch his thumb with my teeth, holding it there with just the barest pressure.

"No," he agrees. "You did not. If you would like to bite me again, I will not stop you."

But I don't. Not just now. I want to kiss him again, and I want his mouth on other parts of my body as well. So I release his thumb, prop back up on my elbows, and tip my head to one side. "Have you more instruction for me, warlord? What else do you think I would like?"

"So many things. This for example." He bends forward and kisses my neck down to my collarbone, my sternum. I drop my head back, giving him more access. His mouth finds my breast, his lips claiming my nipple. His tongue dances and plays, and I like it, oh so very much! My breathing increases, and the fire in my belly deepens and roars.

Sudden worry shivers up my spine. What if this is it? What if this is the pleasure he spoke of? What if this is the end of his commitment to me? I should be glad if so; I didn't choose any of this. I should be eager to finish, to claim my freedom, to get away from this place as soon as possible.

But if he stops now, something inside me will scream. I don't even know what I need, only that I need, need, *need*.

"Oh gods!" I gasp as he moves from one breast to the other. "Oh gods, help me!"

He draws away again, and the sudden loss of his mouth on my skin is an agony. His lips are swollen and parted, and he stares down at me, breathing hard. "Did you not like that?"

I shake my head and push hair out of my face with one hand. Beads of perspiration dot my brow. "I did!" I gasp. "I do! But . . . but oh! What is this? What is happening?" I could almost sob with ache, with longing. "Can you help me?" I gaze up at him. Desperation claws up my throat, choking out all words. I don't even know what I'm asking for.

But Taar smiles again, that dangerous flash of teeth. My heart turns over. "I can help," he says. "And I will. But you must trust me. You must give yourself fully into my hands. Can you do that?"

I don't know if I can. I don't know if I should. But if I don't, what then? Will this ache in me go unfulfilled? I cannot bear that.

"I trust you," I breathe, damning the consequences. "Do what you must."

He smiles then. His hand, which had been tracing small circles around my stomach, slides down to my knee then up my thigh. His fingers play along the sensitive skin of my inner thigh, exploring farther, higher.

My eyes widen. "Are you . . . ?"

"Hush," he says. "You have no need to fear. Just tell me: do you like this?" He parts my soft folds and flips his thumb across my hot, throbbing center. Stars burst in my head. My head drops back, my neck long, my arms quaking as they hold my torso partially upright. "I'll take that as a yes," he murmurs. "And this?"

His fingers explore down to my wet opening. He slips the tip of one finger gently inside, just to the first knuckle. His fingers are large, however, and I am unused to such intrusion. I bite my lip. "I . . . I'm not sure."

"Perhaps not tonight," he says. His breathing is heavy, keeping time with my own ragged gasps. "But you like this?" He moves a little upward again, back to that sensitive place at the crest. His finger massages me in a quick, circular motion.

"Oh, yes," I breathe. "Oh . . . oh . . ." He continues to toy with me, and that maddening heat intensifies. It is pleasure—it is great pleasure indeed. But it is torture as well, without relief, without release. "Gods!" I cry. "Please, I can't bear it!"

He pulls his hand back. "You do not like it?"

I want to scream, to grab his hand and push it back to where it was. "I do!" I whip my head up, glaring at him fiercely. "I do, I do like it, but . . . but it's too much! Can you not . . . can you . . . ?"

What? I don't know what to ask for, don't know what I need. Groaning, I sink back onto the soft blankets and cover my face with both hands. I might cry. Or screech like a harpy—I haven't decided which.

But Taar catches hold of my wrists, his grip strong and firm. He pulls my hands away from my face and smiles down at me even as I scowl back at him. He bends down, his long hair a curtain on either side of my face, and kisses me softly on my angry, trembling lips. "I think I know what you need," he says.

He kisses me again and again, opening my mouth, enflaming my hunger. I wrap my arms around his neck, pulling him to me as though I might consume him. He is not to be consumed, however. His kisses once more escape my mouth and run down my neck, my breasts, all while his finger continues to toy with me, to torment me. His mouth ventures lower and lower, down to my navel.

Then he slides from the bed and kneels between my bent knees. His large hands grip me firmly by the hips and pull me down to the edge of the bed. He slings one of my legs over his shoulder, and when I push up on my elbows to glare at him again, he grins. I feel suddenly so exposed, so vulnerable. My heart throbs, but that need in my belly throbs harder. I feel as though I will explode if that pressure isn't somehow eased.

"Do you trust me?" he asks.

I shouldn't. And yet . . .

"I do," I whisper.

"Then tell me," he says, turning to kiss the inside of my knee, "is this to your liking?"

My throat tightens. I nod once and bite my lower lip.

His kisses travel up farther. His tongue dances across my soft inner thigh.

"I like that." I moan, my fingers tightening around the velvet blanket. "I like that, warlord."

"Good," he says. Then he leans forward, breathing hot against my most secret places. "And this?" He kisses me, his lips lingering.

I shake my head, another moan in my throat. Hair falls across my damp face. I feel I shall never draw a full breath again. He pulls back, uncertain how to interpret my reaction. Desperately I reach out, grab hold of his head, tangling my fingers in his hair. "Please. More."

"Well in that case . . ."

He pulls me to him, his mouth enveloping me, devouring me. As though I am the one giving him the great pleasure, as though he cannot get enough of me. His tongue plays back and forth, and I fall, my arms suddenly too weak to support me. Reaching overhead, I grip the furs and blankets, moaning as the heat in my core intensifies tenfold, a hundred, a thousand! More maddening, more torturous, more exquisite than ever before. I am completely at his mercy, and I should not like it, but I do. I like it so much, too much.

Something bursts inside me. With it, a cry escapes my lips, a song, a melody such as I have never before uttered. It springs from that deepest well inside me, as all that pent-up tension escapes at last in wave after wave of pleasure.

So this is what the warlord sought. This is the elusive mystery, the secret, the revelation. I understand now what he wanted to teach me, the truth of what my body is capable of achieving—absolute and ecstatic *release*.

12

TAAR

———❧❦❧———

THE SONG OF HER BLISS IS SWEET IN MY EARS.
This is a song I should like to hear again and again, sung
with such passion. Her whole body vibrates in response to
the music I call to life inside her. It seems to catch me up in its
swell and carry me away with her to the very heights of heaven. It's
intoxicating and terrifying by turns and, for the moment, I simply
let myself experience the sensation to the fullest, here in this little
slice of existence. With her.

When at last her ecstasy subsides, she lies trembling and
whimpering softly on the bed. I gently untangle myself from her
legs. My breath comes hard, and my body is fully awake to the
need she's aroused in me. I straighten and look down at her, still
lying on the bed, bared before me, and . . . Oh gods, how easily I

could lose myself in her! I want to enter her, to claim her. To make her truly my wife.

But that isn't what this moment is about.

So I lean forward and allow myself no more than a chaste kiss on that patch of bare skin just above her navel. Her breasts heave, her nipples standing out dark and hard. I know the taste of them now. I know the taste of *her*. And she is sweet, delicate, all things delightful, and . . .

None of this is real.

I stand up and quickly take a step back, aware of the fire behind me. Even more I'm aware of my own urgent body, swollen and painful. Vulnerable. Hastily I put my back to the girl. If I don't, the compulsion to find release might overcome me. But I am master of myself.

"Taar?"

Her voice is soft, still trembling with the aftershocks of the pleasure I gave her, like an echo of the song she sang. I've always thought my name a harsh one, suited to the harsh life I've been forced to lead. On her lips, it becomes something else—something strong and shining.

"Yes, *zylnala?*" I say without turning around. Squeezing my eyes tightly shut, I resist the urge to grab myself and seek immediate relief. Somehow that feels dishonorable. I did not bring her here for my own sake; I won't do anything to make her think otherwise.

She is silent for a long moment, as though choosing her words.

Then: "Is that . . . is that enough? Do we not need to . . . ?"

I shake my head. The question in her voice sounds almost like an offer, and it would be all too easy to let myself interpret it as such. But the truth is, she did not ask for any of this. She did not even ask me to save her. Every moment we have shared was coerced by circumstance beyond her control. I cannot pretend otherwise.

So I won't take her virgin body. I won't plant my seed in her or let her bear the risk of a life she is unprepared to carry. I won't dishonor her or myself, no matter how sweet and plaintive that musical voice of hers is. No matter the hard swelling of my cock.

"By the customs of my people," I say quickly, "the consummation of our marriage is now complete." My voice sounds rough and abrupt in my own ears. I continue ruthlessly even so. "The law is satisfied."

"Oh." She lets out a little shuddering breath. I hear movement, the rustle of fabric. "What happens now?"

I won't turn around. I won't let her see what she's done to me, though I suspect she knows. "We wait for dawn," I say. "Then I will do as I promised and help you find your sister. If it is in my power, I will help you reclaim her and escort you both safely back to your own people. Our association will be over."

She is silent again for such a long time, I begin to wonder if she's dozed off. But at last she whispers, "And . . . what of the other vows you made?"

Shakh me, if I didn't know any better, I'd think she was

225

trying to lure me back into that bed. Grimacing, I bow my head and run a hand down my face. What is wrong with me? We've shared no more than a few short hours together. And yes, those hours involved some of the most intimate, passionate moments I've ever known with a woman. I don't know how it could be, given the fact we know nothing of each other. Maybe it's simply the reality of the vows themselves—the holiness instilled in the marriage bond, which makes me feel as though our connection is much deeper than it is.

But I won't be a fool. Gods, I don't even know her real name! I know nothing about her save that she loves her sister. That she's ferocious in the face of terror. That she has the voice of an angel, a voice instilled with strange magic. That's it. The sum total of my knowledge of this girl.

Or perhaps not.

After all I also know the little mewling sound she makes when I kiss that sensitive place at the curve of her neck. I know how her body shivers when I glide my hands from her hipbones up her abdomen, when I cup her soft breasts. I know her scent, her taste. I know the song of her release.

I know things about her no other living man has ever known.

But she is not mine. Not truly.

"The Goddess, in her infinite wisdom, must understand that such vows, made under coercion, cannot be binding." I turn slightly, just enough to cast her a look over my shoulder. Not enough that she should see how I still swell for her. "As long as you are in my care, you can expect my protection. But I will not touch you again. You will carry your maidenhead with you to give to the man of your choosing."

The girl sits upright, pulling that filmy gown back up onto her shoulders, crossing the gauzy fabric over her breasts. Then she grasps one of the fur blankets and pulls it around herself, though the interior of this pavilion is warm. I cannot help a twinge of regret. I should have liked to dwell on her lovely form a little longer. But this is selfish. So I say nothing.

"What if . . . ?" she begins and stops.

I wait. And part of me hopes. But for what? That she will say I am the man she chooses? That she will ask to remain with me as my wife? That she will invite me back to her bed here and now so that we may spend the rest of the night exploring each other more deeply and face the coming dawn hand-in-hand?

Fool that I am. Even if she wanted it, I could never return to the Hidden City with a human wife in tow. My people would not accept her; some would surely call for her death. No, our story must end tonight. And it will not end with me defiling her. Even if she asks me to.

"Go to sleep," I say at last when her silence does not break. "Take the bed. By my estimation we still have two hours until dawn. You will need what sleep you can get before we set out to find your sister."

"And . . . what about you? Where will you sleep?" She hesitates, then her voice drops an octave. "There is room enough for two here."

Oh gods! Is she trying to break me? "I will stand watch," I declare firmly and, with those words, march to the deepest, darkest part of the tent, out of the firelight. There I drop my head into my hands, breathing roughly in and out. Why is this so much harder than I thought it would be? Not just resisting the temptation she poses, but . . . tomorrow. Everything that must happen tomorrow, when I will carry her out to the human world, leave her somewhere, and then ride away, never looking back. Why is the very idea like a knife to my chest?

"This was a mistake," I groan. Even as I speak the words, the invisible *velra* cord tightens painfully around my forearm.

Somehow I manage to doze off sitting upright in that dark corner. The exhaustion of the last few days simply washes over me in a wave, and I bow my head to my chest and let everything else cease. At first there is nothing but darkness, peace.

But then . . . the dreams.

The girl is there, her voice in my head. I feel her soft body quivering under my palms. I breathe her musk as I nuzzle into her secret places, and she moans. Ah! such a sweet, sweet sound. My body awakens, roused once more with the excitement of pleasing her. I increase my tempo, my breath short in my nostrils, and—

"Taar!"

The harsh bark breaks through the gauzy film of dreams like a dash of cold water. I startle awake in my chair, confused, aroused, and bleary as nine hells. Shaking my head, I rub both hands down my face, struggling to rub some sense back into my head.

"Taar!" that same voice bellows again, loud enough to penetrate all the muting spells surrounding Ruvaen's personal pavilion. "Get your arse out here and bring the human girl's arse while you're at it!"

Lurodos. Recognition hits me with a jolt. I push hair out of my face and look across to the bed, where the girl has also startled awake. The blanket she'd pulled around her last night falls away from her shoulders, revealing her lovely bare skin. Trapped as I am between sleep and wakefulness, between erotic dream and cold reality, I cannot help the sudden surge of fire that courses through my veins at the sight. My mouth goes dry, and I stare, open-mouthed, even as her wide, terrified eyes seek me out in my shadowed hiding place.

"Come on, Taar! By now the girl must be crying for a proper *shakh!* Bring her out and let me show her what a true man can do."

"What's going on?" the girl hisses. "Why is he out there? I thought you said the law was satisfied."

I lurch to my feet. Blood pounds in a pulse of mingled lust and violence, each sensation vying for dominance. I am not my best self in this moment, and for that I am glad. I need some vent for these feelings, and as I cannot indulge lust just now, wrath will have to do.

"Stay there," I growl, too harsh but unable to be gentle just now. "I will deal with this."

She nods. Horror brims in her eyes as Lurodos's voice shifts from Noxaurian to common Eledrian, which she can understand. "Come out, sweet maid!" he cries. "I'm hungry this morning. Let me feast on your succulent fruits until you scream my name—"

I fling back the tent flap and stride out so fast, Lurodos is forced to back away several paces or risk being run down. The Noxaurian smiles cruelly, his teeth sharp in the new dawn light. "Good morning, half-breed," he purrs. "Is she begging you to turn her over to me yet? Are her tears as hot and wet as her—"

"Begone, Lurodos," I snarl, drawing myself up to my full height and meeting him eye-to-eye. "There's nothing for you here."

There's a crowd gathered around the tent—all the same foul onlookers who congregated last night, hoping to hear the salacious screams of my victim no doubt. They watch Lurodos and me with unabashed interest, eager to see us rip each other apart. Ruvaen is among them, I notice with some discomfort. Of course this pavilion belongs to the prince. He has every right to be here and to evict us if he so chooses. But he only stands a little to one side, arms folded, eyes hooded, an expression of mocking amusement on his face. Ordinarily I would consider Ruvaen an ally; he and I have forged a certain degree of respect for one another over the years of our alliance. But Ruvaen is a Noxaurian, a pure-blood fae. He is no more trustworthy than any of these fiends. I cannot count on him to take my side when it comes to Lurodos. While Ruvaen may hate his most brutal warlord, he won't openly side against him.

I am alone. And my people aren't here to stand with me between this monster and the girl. The girl who has no real claim on me at all, but to whom I vowed my protection.

Lurodos sniffs loudly, nostrils flaring. "I don't smell virgin's blood on you, my friend," he says, that leering grin twisting his face once more. "You didn't do it, did you? You didn't *shakh* her."

"What takes place between me and my wife on our wedding night is no one's concern but ours," I answer coldly, even as rage roars in my gut.

Lurodos laughs. "Your *wife?*" he says. "Your warbride, you mean. She is no wife—she is a plaything. And if you don't intend to play, you must pass her on to the next player. Such is the law of Noxaur. Is that not right, my prince?" he adds, turning to Ruvaen.

The prince gives me a narrow look. "Technically our friend Lurodos is right."

My eyes flare. "You said," I answer in a deep growl, "that our wedding ceremony might follow Licornyn traditions, not Noxaurian."

"Indeed." Ruvaen shrugs.

"Does it not follow that Licornyn custom would also hold sway for the wedding night?"

Lurodos throws back his head and howls with laughter. "Are you half-breeds such limp *shakhers,* you can't shaft your own brides on the first go?"

All the Noxaurian spectators join their voices with his, a cruel chorus of cackles and hyena yodels. Even the women in their midst shriek in amusement, teeth flashing, though there's hardness in their eyes as well.

I ignore the rest of them, addressing myself to Ruvaen. "Last night my wife and I consummated our marriage according to Licornyn tradition. We fulfilled the law. She is *mine.*"

Ruvaen quirks a silver brow. "I'm sorry, Taar. But, as Lurodos so baldly puts it, the law of Noxaur requires coupling. Did you spill your seed inside the woman?"

I swallow. Otherwise I don't move a muscle, not even to breathe.

"I'll take that as a no," Ruvaen says with a sigh.

"That settles it then." Lurodos claps his hands together and rubs them, delighted. "You can either fetch her out, Taar, my friend, or I can go after her myself. Either way, she's mine by right of law. And you can be sure," he adds, turning to the rest with a lewd leer, "that within the hour, she'll be moaning and weeping her virgin's tears while I split her in half."

Laughter and jeers batter inside my head. I stare at Ruvaen, disbelief coursing in sickening ripples up my spine. The prince merely lifts his chin, that damned eyebrow of his still slightly cocked. Suddenly I realize he anticipated this all along. He knows me, knows I'm not the kind of man to take a woman by either force or coercion. He is also familiar with Licornyn customs, more familiar, perhaps, than he lets on. He allowed this whole situation to take place because he wanted this very outcome.

And now I know what I must do. I know how I will save my bride.

Lurodos is still laughing, thrusting his pelvis for the amusement of the crowd. Then he turns and takes a lunging step toward the tent flap. I block his way, planting myself firmly as a wall. I stare into his face, our eyes mere inches apart. "If you want her," I say, "you'll have to go through me."

Lurodos laughs again, his lips pulled back in a snarl. "You don't want to play games like that with me, half-breed."

"I do not play games, Lurodos."

The warlord draws back an arm, intending to strike me here and now, initiating what must become a bloodbath. Before his blow can fall, however, Ruvaen's voice rings out: "I would not do that if I were you."

Lurodos turns to his prince. "What's this?" he demands, gnashing his teeth. "Have you two concocted some sort of plot against me? Are you so determined to keep me from my lawful property?"

"Certainly not," Ruvaen replies with an easy grin that turns my stomach. "But, according to Noxaurian law, death's blood is a fine substitute for virgin's blood to seal a marriage. If our good Licornyn king wants to claim his warbride via mortal combat rather than more traditional—or pleasant—means, I have no qualms with it.

So long as you are keen, Lurodos, my friend. Otherwise I'm afraid you must give up your claim on the human entirely."

"A fight to the death?" Lurodos speaks the words slowly, savoring them. He looks me up and down, his expression almost lascivious, as though he gazes upon his intended maiden victim. Finally he turns to Ruvaen. "And are there restrictions on what weapons may be used?"

"You are both riders," Ruvaen says, "Taar a Licornyn, and you a Reptant Master. Let you decide this matter mounted and armed with the traditional weaponry of your people."

A vicious smile slashes across Lurodos's mouth. He turns to me once more and points his long nail straight at my nose. "Mark my words, half-breed: I'll cut off your head and add it to my collection. Then I'll saw off your beast's horn and use it as a toothpick." He licks his lips slowly. "When I'm through, I'll let my reptant feast on its guts even as I feast on my new warbride."

I lean in closer, breathing in his foul air. My eyes burn into his, and I see tongues of fire on the edges of my vision.

"Prepare your soul for hell, Lurodos," I snarl.

13

ILSEVEL

STAND WITH A BLANKET WRAPPED AROUND MY SHOULDERS, listening to the rise and fall of voices outside. I cannot understand the words, but I recognize Taar's voice: strong, clear, and ferocious. He sounds angry. Very angry. This can't be good.

Worse still, the other voice—the one belonging to Lurodos, I'm quite certain—doesn't sound angry at all. There's nothing but triumph and mockery in his tone, like a victory song played over a death-strewn battlefield. My legs shake. I fear I'll disgrace myself and faint, but somehow manage to lock my knees and stay upright. Was everything that happened last night—every beautiful, terrible, unforgettable, breathless moment—not enough? Am I about to be fed to the beast after all?

Suddenly the tent flap flies back, and Taar storms in. He almost runs into me but stops just in time. His bare torso is mere inches from me, heaving chest directly in my line of view. His breath, panting and hot, warms my brow. Slowly I tip back my head, looking up into his shadowed face. My gaze comes into focus on his mouth, his full, parted lips. I remember the shape of them against mine. I remember the burn of them on my skin.

My throat goes dry. For a few throbbing heartbeats, all thought of fear abandons me in an unexpected, desperate surge of hunger. Hunger for *him*. For this stranger. This warlord. *My husband.*

But though we are separated by no more than a sliver of air, it feels as though some great chasm has opened between us. And he does not reach across it, does not take me in his arms and crush me to him. Instead he draws back a half-step, leaving me in a little slice of empty space. I shiver—more from need than anything else. But he sees it.

"You're cold," he says.

I shake my head. He ignores this, however, and takes me by the arm, his fingers firm through the folds of blanket wrapped around me. He draws me unresisting back to the fire, which has burned low since the night. "Sit," he says, and I obey. While he sets to work applying kindling and stoking the flames, I watch him in silence. So many little details stand out to me—the gleam of firelight on his black hair, the fine, sharp plains of his cheek, the chiseled cut of his jaw. His hands. Oh, his hands . . . scarred and strong and nimble, and if I look at them one second longer, the heat in my belly is going to bloom into an inferno. Then what will I do? Sink to my knees and beg him to do to me again what he did last night?

But I remember too well what followed those blissful revelations. The shocks and shivers had scarcely abated before he extricated himself from between my legs and turned his back on me. His voice was rough, almost vicious when he stated: "*I will not touch you again.*"

Gods, I could hate him for that. If I didn't already, that is.

Pulling the fur blanket a little more tightly around my shoulders, I bite the inside of my cheek then force my chin upright. "Are you going to tell me or aren't you?"

"Tell you what?" He glances up from his intense focus on the fire.

"What the uproar outside is about." I clear my throat, determined to make my voice strong and defiant, no trace of a quaver. "Am I to be handed over to Lord Lurodos?"

Taar drops his gaze back to the fire. He doesn't look at me again for a long time but stirs the low embers and sets the flames dancing. He watches that dance for some moments, breathing in and out through his nostrils. Finally he lifts his head, fixing me with a pair of eyes brimming with secret darkness. "It will not come to that."

"Oh?" I lean forward, eagerness suddenly jumping in my veins. "So we are safe to leave?"

The way his gaze darts away from mine speaks volumes. To my unspeakable frustration, he does not answer, but gets up and crosses the room to that upright chest in the back. He pours something into a cup, brings it back to the fire, and sets the cup in the coals he's raked to the edge of the circle. Within a minute, the brew inside begins to bubble. Though I fear he'll burn his hand, he plucks the cup up again, turns it around, and offers it to me by the handle.

"It is safe," he says. "The cup is enchanted. The brew is not."

I sit there, mouth open. Slowly I accept his offering and lift it to my lips. The steam rising to my nostrils is spicy and sweet. I sip, and a bouquet of delightful flavors burst across my tongue, warming my throat, and settling my nervously jumping stomach.

I take another sip and another, all the while watching Taar, who purposefully does not look at me. What am I supposed to make of him? Is this the terrifying warlord who smacked me across the head and hauled me away into captivity? Why should he—this leader of monsters, this barbarian brute—serve me? Maybe it's part of his people's custom, the way bridegrooms serve their brides on their wedding nights. But I'm not really his bride. Am I?

My heart skips a beat. For a moment I allow myself to wonder—to hope, to dread?—if he's about to tell me that he's decided to keep me. Could that be the secret he's unwilling to speak? Well, if so, he'd better think again, because I'm not about to be bought, sold, or owned by any man.

That being said . . . could any other man touch me the way he did last night? I don't think so, can't even imagine it. Fyndra certainly never described any such wonder, and she was horrifyingly forthright when Father sent her to prepare me for my night with the Shadow King. As for Artoris, my only other so-called lover? Nothing about his touch indicated that he knew or wanted to know anything about my body. About what I liked, about what made me sing. He was only concerned for himself.

But last night, even when he was obviously in some discomfort, Taar had remained solely focused on me. A man like that, a man who proved himself to be unselfish and sensitive, observant and exciting, willing to push me but never to pressure me—such a man might indeed make a fine husband. The kind of husband who inspires a lifetime of devotion.

But what's this nonsense? Perhaps that blow he struck to my head knocked my brain loose. I'm not seriously going to sit here daydreaming about becoming the wife of my captor! The man who threw me in a cage, who's responsible for my being in this situation in the first place. And Aurae . . . my sweet sister is still out there. Did she also endure a warbride's wedding night?

Something tells me hers did not play out as mine did.

A serpent of dread coils in my gut. I set the cup of spiced brew aside and stand. I hardly cut an imposing figure, wrapped up in this fur blanket as I am, but I draw myself up straight and demand in the most imperious voice I can summon: "All right, warlord. No more deflection. Tell me what is going on. I have a right to know what my future is to be."

Instead of answering, Taar leaves me by the fire and crosses again to the opposite side of the pavilion. I see a pile of armor and weaponry which had escaped my notice before. His, apparently, for he begins to strap on his pauldrons, his belt, his sword. Only then does he turn to me at last and meet my gaze. His face is hard and stern.

"I am to face Lord Lurodos within the hour," he says. "To claim your life, I must fight and kill him. That, or I will die by his hand."

All heat seems to drain from my body. The fire might as well be radiating frost. I clutch my blanket tighter. "A deathmatch?"

He nods.

"For me?"

In lieu of an answer, he goes back to strapping on his gear, attaching a bracer to his left forearm. I watch him mutely for some moments before finally asking, "Can you kill him?"

"I can."

The words come without hesitation. But something about the quickness of his response convinces me he is not absolutely certain.

"You're risking your life," I say, almost a whisper. "For me." I catch my breath. Then: *"Why?"*

The next moment I'm across the room, reaching out to him. I touch his right arm, the one without a bracer yet. The one around which the wedding cord was wound. For an instant I almost believe I feel it there, a hot, constricting snake. In the same instant I could swear I feel a similar pressure and heat on my own forearm. The sensation is gone before I can quite grasp hold of it, so I simply look up into the warlord's face. There's so much conflict in his expression—confusion, determination, violence, and more. He doesn't know the answer to my question. He truly doesn't. But he's not going to back down from this fight.

I shake my head. Then, lifting my hand from his arm, I step back. "No," I say firmly. "You shouldn't do this. You shouldn't put yourself at risk. You don't owe me this."

"I vowed to protect you."

"Skewer your vows!" I take a short, angry step. My foot treads on the edge of my blanket, pulling it down from my shoulders. Rather than yank it back, I let it fall, and stand once more in nothing but the filmy gauze gown. "This has gone far beyond any reasonable responsibility of yours. Here." I stick out my hand, reaching for the twin knives strapped at his thick belt. "Give me one of those. Send me to this Lurodos, and I'll take care of him myself. I don't need you to do it for me."

His stern brow softens, his eyes gleaming with a flash of . . . that better not be amusement! "And where do you think you'll hide a knife in a gown like that." His gaze rakes over my form, slow and knowing.

Heat jumps in my veins, but I ignore it. I simply slip one of his knives from its sheath. "That's my problem," I say grimly, "not yours. I won't stand by and let you get yourself killed for my sake. You've done enough already."

"I'm the reason you're here, remember?"

243

"Yes, well . . ." I admit begrudgingly, "you were only trying to keep me from having my throat ripped out by those raveners." I lift my chin, tossing a lock of hair back from my forehead. "You gave me a fighting chance. No one can ask for more than that." My hand gripping that knife hilt begins to tremble, but I tighten my fingers and brandish it a little higher.

Taar breathes a long sigh. Then he reaches out and, taking hold of my wrist, adjusts my grip so that the balance is better. "Keep it," he murmurs, his fingers still resting against my skin. "If things go awry, if I do not succeed, you should have a weapon to do what must be done."

He catches my gaze then, his eyes dark despite the dancing firelight. And I realize he's not talking about me using the knife on Lurodos. I wish I could fling the blade across the room, as far from me as possible. What horrors await in my second bridegroom's chambers that death by my own hand would be preferable?

"Thank you, warlord," I say softly, looking down at the weapon and turning it slowly so that it catches the light. It is a larger knife than the one hidden beneath my pillow last night. The hilt is intricately worked and set with a gold stone. I've never seen anything quite like it. It is beautiful in a deadly way. Like the man who gave it to me. "I will . . . keep your advice in mind."

I lift my eyes to him again, surprised to find him still so near, studying me in silence. An impulse to pull his head down and kiss him bubbles up suddenly in my breast. A wild compulsion and a little bit mad, considering we're poised here on the brink of life and death. But I can't help it. I know what his lips feel like now, and the idea of never experiencing that feeling again is almost unbearable.

His gaze drops as well, fastening on my mouth. Is he thinking what I'm thinking? *"Zylnala,"* he murmurs, and reaches for me, his fingers slipping through my hair to the back of my head. I lean toward him, standing up on my toes. My eyes half-close, and my lips part as I draw a last desperate breath—

"Oh, I say, am I interrupting?"

Taar and I spring apart as the tent flap swishes open, and a tall fae man strides into the pavilion as though he owns it. I vaguely remember him from last night: he spoke to Taar in the growling language of the other fae monsters directly after I was auctioned off. His eyes are ice-pale, his hair white but with a sheen of lavender undertone that is quite startling in the firelight. His skin is unexpectedly bronzed, almost honey-toned. It must be glamour, for that combination of coloring could not exist naturally. He radiates beauty and danger, as all the fae do, but of a more refined sort—the sort that will kill you with subtle knives and cruel poisons rather than brutal blows. A dark crown of spikes twists across his brow and looks as though it might bite into his own flesh if he does not take care.

I know at once who this must be—Ruvaen. The Prince of Noxaur, my father's great enemy.

Quick as thought I raise Taar's dagger, assuming a more

balanced stance. The prince looks me over, taking in my revealing gown, my small stature, my utter humanness. And he laughs. He laughs, gods-damn him, as all men do, mocking me and my futility. I take a lunging step, determined to plunge this blade straight into his eye.

Taar's hand falls heavily on my shoulder. He speaks in that growling fae language I do not know, though I hear the reprimand in his voice. Prince Ruvaen shakes his head and holds up both hands as though in defense, still laughing. Then he touches his lips before offering me a sweeping bow. "Forgive me, dear Lady Ragnataarthane," he says, switching deftly to that strange Eledrian tongue that translates itself in my head. "I mean no offense. You really are quite ferocious, and it took me by surprise, you see."

I grit my teeth. How many lives would I save if I threw off Taar's grasp and lodged this blade into the prince's black heart? Would the war finally come to an end? Somehow I doubt it. Some other fae lord would find an excuse to raid our land. There's plenty more where this one came from. Besides I don't think Taar's about to let me slip his hold all that easily.

The prince strides into the room and takes a seat by the fire. "Taar, my friend," he says, "I see why you like her. I never would have believed it last night, but she's cleaned up a treat! And that scowl? It would send the very thralls of Ashtarath scrambling back through the Rift in short order. A prize to be sure. Certainly worth dying for."

"What are you doing here, Ruvaen?" Taar growls, his fingers pinching into my shoulder slightly.

"What?" The prince spreads his arms wide and leans back in his seat, stretching out his legs before the fire and crossing them at the ankle. "Need I a reason to enter my own pavilion? You are the guest here after all, not I. I loaned you this little oasis out of the goodness of my tender heart. All so that you might perform one very specific function, I might add. A function, it would seem, you have failed to perform, although . . ." He slips into his own language again so that I won't understand him. I understand perfectly well the look he sends gliding up and down my body however. I wish I could bend and pick up the dropped blanket without looking like an absolute fool. Instead I lift my chin and stare the man down coldly.

"Feisty too," Ruvaen adds, just for my benefit.

Taar responds in Noxaurian, his voice a dangerous growl.

Ruvaen laughs. "Ah, that would be clever, wouldn't it? And I won't deny, the thought had crossed my mind. Just in case, I had this sent for . . ."

He reaches into the front of his heavily embroidered tunic and produces a vial of some black liquid. It is so black, in fact, it seems to draw the light from the room itself, reducing the world around it to shadows. There's an undeniable pulse to the atmosphere, and it takes me a moment to realize it's my own heartbeat suddenly loud and oppressive. Otherwise all is silent, but more than silence. Like darkness is the absence of light, so this silence is the absence of something far more profound. The absence of *song*.

"Here, my friend," Ruvaen says. The sound of his voice seems to break a spell that held the room momentarily captive. "Take it. Use it. Slaughter that brute for me once and for all."

I glance at Taar. He's looking at the vial with an intensity of focus that unnerves me. It reminds me, in a sickening, twisted way, of how he'd looked at me last night. Hungry. Ravenous. Lustful.

"You know I don't partake of virulium," he says, his voice strangely rough.

"Not as a rule, no. And I certainly wouldn't recommend it for frequent consumption. It plays hell on the innards." Ruvaen tosses the vial casually. Taar chokes on a breath, but the prince catches and twirls it in his fingers before holding it out again. "Indulge just this once. For my sake."

Releasing his hold on me, Taar crosses his arms and braces his stance, as though preparing for resistance.

Ruvaen rolls his eyes. "Lurodos is sure to use it. And if he does, he will rip you apart." The droll smile which had played across his mouth all this time slips into a more serious expression.

Taar draws a long breath. "I don't need demon magic to take down my enemies."

For an instant—an instant so brief, I have to wonder if I imagined it—Ruvaen's face pinches into something else. Something withered and gray, something sickly and frightened. Something so utterly different from the glorious fae prince, they hardly seem capable of sharing the same world, much less the same face. He blinks, however, and the image is gone. Did his glamour waver? Did I just glimpse the truth of Prince Ruvaen behind the magicked illusion?

He slips into Noxaurian, his voice urgent. He even rises from his chair, steps around the fire, and approaches Taar, brandishing the vial. Taar only moves to put himself in front of me, but otherwise is as stone, arms folded, shoulders set. Ruvaen says something that sounds like a curse and waves a hand to indicate me. "And what of your little pet?" he demands, switching to a language I understand, possibly in a bid to woo me to his side. "You know what awaits her if you should fail. Surely you must care something for her wellbeing or you wouldn't be risking your life like this. Do you want her in Lurodos's clutches? There's nothing I can do to spare her, not even for your sake, Taar."

"It is my honor to protect my wife," Taar answers evenly.

My pulse jumps. This is so . . . so ridiculous! So ludicrous, so surreal. Can it truly be happening? Why does he call me his *wife?* We both know that's not what I am.

Ruvaen's teeth clench, his pale eyes flashing fire. "I need you to win today."

"I will. But I will do it cleanly, without tainting my soul."

"And if you fail?"

"I will not fail."

Ruvaen curses again, bitterly, in multiple languages. Then with a sigh, he tucks the vial back into the front of his shirt. Immediately that pulse of *non*-music vanishes, and I breathe easily once more. "I hope you know what you're doing," the prince says. With that he turns to go, striding past the fire, shaking his head.

Before Ruvaen makes it to the tent flap, Taar calls after him, "I require a gown for my wife."

My heart turns over in my breast. Gods, I wish he wouldn't keep saying that word.

The prince looks back, his gaze once more raking over me, no longer admiring so much as speculative. "Very well," he says. "I'll consider it your last request." The next moment he is gone.

Immediately Taar turns away from me and begins strapping on his right bracer, as though nothing had happened. I watch him, questions brimming, uncertain where to begin or if I even should begin at all. Finally I say, "What was that?"

He casts me a look from under his heavy brow.

"That . . . that liquid. That dose Ruvaen tried to give you."

"Demon's blood," Taar answers. He says it so easily, like it's the most obvious thing. Yet, at those words, I feel as though the non-song which had filled the chamber echoes hollowly in the back of my head. "Drawn from the Rift, which tore an opening to Ashtari, the Seventh Hell. Dark magic of the foulest kind."

I stare at him blankly. Is he jesting? Surely he doesn't really believe in the nine hells and the demons that rule them.

"Noxaurians take the brew," he goes on, his voice even, emotionless, "to augment their prowess in battle. But it turns them mad. If they do not succeed in killing within an hour, they themselves will die. Horrifically. The darkness burns too hot and liquifies their innards, which then runs in black streams from every orifice. Take too much, and the same will be your fate—but only after you've slaughtered everyone in sight. Friends, allies, enemies. The bloodlust of virulium does not discriminate."

I lick my lips. "You speak as though you know it well."

He does not look at me. Instead he draws the second of the two blades from his belt, the mate of the one he gave to me. Holding it up, he tests its sharpness on the tip of his finger, not even flinching when blood wells. "Some of my riders have chosen to use it," he says, speaking as though to himself rather than to me. "But it . . . changes you. In ways you cannot predict. Those who have sampled virulium once find they are compelled to take it again. When they do not have it, they think of it all the time, hungry for another taste. I . . ." He lowers the blade, turning it over slowly. The citrine jewel at its hilt glints like a winking dragon's eye. "I do not want to end up like that. So I will not take it, and I've forbidden my people from touching it. Some defy my orders, to their own destruction."

There's something about the way he says that last part, some heaviness and pain. He lost someone to the demon's blood. Someone important to him. He doesn't have to tell me—gods know, he doesn't owe me any explanation. But I find myself wondering who it was. Who *she* was.

Hastily I shake that thought away. After all he could mean

anyone or no one, and none of it is my business. There are more important matters closer to hand. "Lurodos will be taking virulium when you face him?" I ask.

"Yes."

"Would a dose guarantee your victory over him?"

"No."

"The prince . . . Ruvaen . . . he seemed to think it would."

Taar's teeth flash in a grimace. "Ruvaen is Noxaurian. He thinks all his problems can be solved by demon magic."

I bite my tongue, press my lips together. I certainly don't like the idea of demon magic. Until this moment I wouldn't have said I actually *believed* in demons at all, but there was something about that vial, that liquid that defied unbelief. It was truly dark. Full of absence where there should be fullness, full of brokenness where there should be unity. No one should touch such power, alluring though it may be.

But what if Taar dies? What if I am passed into Lurodos's hands? I won't survive whatever follows. And Aurae . . . she's still out there somewhere. Waiting for me to rescue her, waiting for me to come. Are all my hopes to be dashed on the altar of this man's stubborn honor? Could I bear to beg him to compromise that honor?

"You're quite determined then," I say at last.

He flicks me a short glance. "I am."

"Fine. Do it your way." I toss my head and brandish his knife. "I've got this to . . . what? Slit my own throat if it all goes wrong?"

Taar looks at me earnestly. "You should go for the heart. Just like I taught you last night. Up under the ribs, no hesitation. Plunge deep. It will be painful—I won't deceive you on that score. But it will be quick." He pauses, exhaling a ragged breath. "It won't be if you let Lurodos take you."

I grimace. "You're such a comfort, warlord."

With a single step he crosses the small space between us. Though he does not touch me, he bends his head, and his eyes draw near to my own. A voice of absolute darkness rumbles in his chest: "I will not let it come to that."

14

TAAR

⁓⊷❦⊶⁓

I HEARD STRANGE MUSIC IN YOUR SOUL LAST NIGHT, VELLAR.
I stand with Elydark on the edge of the pit, gazing down
at the packed dirt floor far below. He came at my summons,
stepping out from the shadows of Wanfriel Forest like a phantom
and making his way through the Noxaurian ranks. They shivered
and quickly sprang out of his way, careful not to make eye-contact
or rouse his ire. So he passed unmolested through the encampment
and took up position at my side.

A small sigh eases through my lips. I place a hand on his powerful
shoulder. *Last night was . . . strange,* I answer and offer no more.
While Elydark and I are as closely bonded as two souls can be,
he does not need access to some parts of my life. *This morning,
however, is simple, my friend. We must fight. We must kill.*

Elydark tosses his head, his horn shining in the light of the rising sun. He is keen for battle, beast of war that he is. His song in my head is wordless but eager. I let it fill my own heart, bolstering my resolve. And my courage.

The pit is nearly emptied out now. Ordinarily used to hold reptants—who have a tendency to stalk and kill unsuspecting foot soldiers if not contained—it has been deemed a worthy arena for my duel with Lurodos. The reptants have been herded to the other side of the spire and contained with temporary entrapment spells, and the pit is swept clean of their wrinkled skin-husks and other refuse.

Come, Elydark, I say and lead my beast down a narrow walkway on the south end of the pit, which was appointed to us. We have no second, no support. All our people have gone, none of them aware of the insane risk their king has undertaken for the sake of a human woman. Gods, am I really such a fool?

Vellar? Elydark hums in my head, sensing the turmoil in my soul.

I don't bother to answer, to explain. What explanation can I offer when I don't understand myself? I simply adjust the set of my sword's sheath and take a moment to survey the pit from inside. The ground is relatively smooth packed earth, approximately a hundred meters long and fifty wide. Ample room for maneuvers. I sniff, inhaling the stink of reptant and the old blood of their meals. This is certainly not the glorified battlefield on which I envisioned I would one day meet my death. Good thing I don't intend to die this day.

Overhead the Noxaurians and fae mercenaries crowd in, eager to claim the best view of the bloodshed to come. They jostle each other so hard, many topple right over the steep edges. They scramble and slide, causing small avalanches of dirt in their wake, and are then obliged to climb fifty feet to escape.

On the east side of the pit stands the scaffold which was used for the auction last night, moved to serve as a makeshift dais. Servants have carried the two scrollwork gilt chairs from the prince's pavilion and set them out like thrones. Ruvaen lounges in one of these, his leg swung over the arm, a cup of sparkling golden wine in one hand.

She sits in the other chair. My warbride. The prize of today's match. Watching me, her eyes large and dark beneath the fierce line of her brow. Her hands grip the arms of her chair, and she sits so still she might as well be a statue. Only the wind rippling through the folds of her skirts betrays the truth.

When I asked for a gown to be sent for her, I'd expected something simple and sturdy, something practical. But Ruvaen is an enthusiast for spectacle, and he sent something far more enticing. She's clad in black, as might befit a Noxaurian lady, all silk and elaborate embroidery. The corset bodice laces up the front and pushes her pale breasts up in display while simultaneously emphasizing her trim waist and the devastating curve of her hips. Her shoulders are bare, but delicate drooping chains of gleaming black metal drip down her upper arms, symbolic, perhaps, of her captivity. The skirt is full, but with a ruffled slit that reveals all of her bare thigh when she's seated. As she is now. From this angle, I can just glimpse the sheath of the knife she's hidden there.

It's difficult to look at her . . . because, once I look, it's nearly impossible to look away. Every tantalizing glimpse only reminds me of what I saw, touched, tasted last night. A cavern seems to open in my gut, a longing, a hunger I cannot deny. I hate it. Hate this weakness in me. Hate the burning, raging determination that fills my veins, to skewer Lurodos on the end of my sword and spill his guts on this dirt floor. Not for her sake. For mine.

Vellar! What has come over you?

Ripping my gaze away from that scaffold, I turn to my licorneir. Elydark watches me narrowly, his gaze fixed on my forearm. I realize that, even through the armor bracer I wear, I feel the tightness of the invisible cord. It's not real—it's all in my head. But the pain is very real indeed, real enough to make it difficult to wield my sword.

I shake my head, focusing on Elydark. His nostrils flare. Fire burns in the depths of his eyes, anger and uncertainty mingled. *Is this human your hearts-bond then?*

No, I answer at once, and in the same instant, the constricting around my arm relaxes. *I will save her. And I will deliver her to her people as promised. Then I will think of her no more.*

My licorneir turns his head to one side, peering down at me.

You may lie to yourself, brother-soul. But such lies do not work on me.

My teeth grind so hard, my jaw aches. I turn away, refusing to let my traitorous eyes lift to the girl again. Instead I gaze across the arena to where Lurodos even now makes his appearance, accompanied by the wild cheers of the bloodthirsty mob. Foregoing the traditional spiked Noxaurian armor, he wears only pauldrons and bracers like a Licornyn, mocking me and my people while simultaneously indicating to all those observing how easily he expects to take this victory. It has the desired effect on the crowd, who begin howling imitation Licornyn battle cries in between bursts of raucous laughter.

Four slaves lead Lurodos's reptant down the narrow track behind him. The beast lashes its tail and hauls against its bonds, more vicious than I've seen it before, even on the eve of battle. I don't know what its master did to drive it into such a frenzy. Reptants are loathsome creatures, but no living thing deserves to fall into the clutches of that man.

Just as they reach the arena floor, the reptant wrenches against its bonds and manages to break free of one man's grasp. Quick as a flash it turns and rips the head right off the unfortunate man. The onlookers redouble their cheers, pumping their fists and howling with delight as the stench of blood fills the air.

I cannot help glancing at the girl again. She looks terribly pale, her expression rapt with horror as she stares down at the gory scene. One hand moves from the arm of the chair to touch the bulge of her hidden knife.

While the reptant is distracted, feasting on the remains of its victim, the three surviving slaves take the opportunity to chain it firmly to the wall. Then they make a hasty escape up the narrow track, while Lurodos watches with wry amusement. When the beast looks up to snarl at him, he casually boxes its jaw. Catching my eye across the arena, he grins, showing every sharp tooth.

I meet his gaze grimly. My fingers tense around the hilt of my sword.

"Friends, countrymen, brothers and sisters-in-arms!" Ruvaen's voice, augmented by glamour, rolls across the sky. A hush falls on the crowd as every eye turns to watch the Noxaurian prince rise from his seat. He speaks in Eledrian so that everyone listening may understand. Including any humans.

"We have gathered here today," he declares, "that the right of ownership over this warbride may be determined once and for all. Taarthalor Ragnataarthane, *Luinar* of the Licornyn, has pledged to offer death's blood in exchange for virgin's blood to seal the marriage. Whether it be his own blood or that of Lord Lurodos of House Uldreyin, only the gods know."

Even his glamoured voice is nearly drowned out in the hollers, roars, and cackles that explode from the onlookers. The girl's eyes are fastened on him with such loathing. She looks as though she might like to snatch her knife from its hiding place and plunge it into Ruvaen's throat. I grit my teeth, willing her not to be so foolish. As though she heard me, even through the cacophony, she shoots a glance my way. I shake my head once. She presses her lips into a hard line but places her hand back on the arm of the chair, fingers squeezing. I let out a slow breath, relieved. She would not survive any attempt on the prince's life.

"Come forward, my friends." Ruvaen beckons with both hands. Leaving our beasts, Lurodos and I stalk to the center of the arena and stand below the platform. Lurodos offers a deep bow while I merely incline my head. "You must," the prince continues, "vow to honor the bloodtrial law. You will confine your violence to the pit. Let no harm come to those who remain outside this set boundary."

"Aye."

"Then let us bid Tanatar's will be done."

So saying, the prince raises both hands to the sky and commences a longwinded prayer to the God of War, dragging it out for the sake of drama and to heighten the tension in both combatants and onlookers. He always knew how to play a crowd for his own amusement. I take the opportunity to send a prayer of my own to Nornala, Goddess of Unity. May she protect the union forged between me and my bride last night . . . and forgive me for intending to break that union at first opportunity.

The prince finally reaches the end of his prayer. With an ominous, "So let it be," he lowers his hands. "To your mounts now, my friends!" he declares.

Lurodos turns to me, grinning enormously. "Don't worry, half-breed," he growls. "I'll make her scream so loud, you'll hear her from your grave."

I do not answer. I merely look at him, the promise of death in my eyes. His grin falters almost imperceptibly. Then, with a curse, he turns and marches back to where his reptant waits, bloody drool streaming from one corner of its awful maw.

I let my gaze lift one last time to the girl. This stranger with whom my very life and death have become so inexplicably entangled in the span of mere hours. She looks very solemn, her brows tight, her eyes wide. But she catches my look and nods. I plant my fist to my heart in salute. It feels both strange and right to honor her in this way.

Elydark is pawing the turf with massive, knife-sharp hooves when I return to his side. He does not articulate in my mind, but the war song in his soul echoes my own. I stroke his powerful shoulder and whisper in his ear: "Now, my friend. For wrath. For blood. For victory."

Gripping the saddle, I mount in a single, fluid motion. Elydark throws back his head, uttering a deep-throated, ululating bellow. All the watching Noxaurians go still. A hush of dread swallows their excitement. The battle-cry of the licorneir is a terrible thing.

But a cruel laugh breaks the hush as Lurodos yanks free the chains binding his reptant. "What's this, my bastards?" he cries, swinging up into his saddle. "Have you no cheers left for your favorite? Let me hear your gods-damned voices!"

They take up their cries once more, dark words of hunger and gore echoing across the blue sky like a death chant. Lurodos laps it up as his due, turning his reptant round in circles. He holds something high in one hand: a dose of virulium. Glinting sunlight reflects off the glass surface, but darkness radiates from within. Lurodos bites off the top of the vial and pours the contents down his throat. His people redouble their cheers when immediately the madness overcomes him. He begins to writhe and shake, convulsing so hard in his saddle, I half-expect him to fall and be trampled beneath his reptant's clawed feet.

"Let the battle begin!" Ruvaen cries.

This is my chance. A chance I cannot afford to miss.

I bow over Elydark's neck and urge him forward. I must take Lurodos down now, before he's fully succumbed to the virulium's influence. I have seconds at most, but my licorneir moves as swift as thought, leaping across the distance. Perhaps it is unsporting to try to fell my opponent while he is vulnerable, but considering what Lurodos intends to do to the girl, I don't really care.

We cover the arena in a few long strides. Elydark's soulfire— the flaming reality housed within his physical form—erupts around us, burning through crevices in his flesh and licking up my skin to engulf me. We are one in flame and spirit, a terrible force of destruction. I swing my sword arm high, aiming for Lurodos's head.

The reptant roars. Lurodos lurches back in his saddle, roaring as well, a demonic sound that bursts with a spurt of dark ooze from his torn lips. He narrowly avoids my sword stroke and whirls a terrible black-metal flail in repost. It whistles through the air and swipes straight at Elydark's flank, a crippling blow if it lands. But my licorneir, though a large, heavy beast, deftly avoids the deadly spikes.

We gallop past our foe, heading straight for the pit wall. Elydark banks, charging partway up the path, before leaping out and over the reptant's head in a graceful arc of flame. The reptant lunges for his underbelly, narrowly missing. The licorneir lands lightly and puts on speed, but Lurodos and his monster are now at our heels. The crowd roars with laughter at the sight of us fleeing before their champion.

But Elydark is no beast's prey. He dodges nimbly to one side, and I mold my body to his, keeping my seat as naturally as though we are forged into one being. The reptant, too set upon its path, careens forward, while Lurodos shrieks in ravenous madness on its back. Elydark rounds to face them, mighty chest heaving, flame snorting from his nostrils.

Lurodos whips his beast around, smashing his own flail viciously into its haunches. The creature is panting, bleeding, and hungry for some vent for its rage.

Elydark lowers his head. Lurodos sees this through the black tears sluicing out from his eyes. He laughs, spitting more virulium ooze, and drives his reptant into a charge. For a moment my heart tightens. I have no love for reptants; even so I hate to see the creature die because its master is too rabid for blood to care. His mount is more afraid of Lurodos than the licorneir, however. So it charges.

Elydark lunges forward to meet it before I even give the command. His head is lowered, his lancelike horn sharp. The reptant springs, huge claws outstretched, huge jaws open to rip into its prey. Lurodos laughs wildly on its back, black tears streaming from his cheeks, flail whirling in a furious cyclone overhead. Elydark swings his head up, neck muscles rippling. His horn pierces straight through the roof of the beast's mouth, through its brain and skull. With a shake of his head, my licorneir sends the reptant hurtling to one side, Lurodos still on its back. They roll five times before coming to a stop.

The crowd goes berserk, as thrilled at the downfall of their champion as they would be for his success. In their eagerness they jostle and press each other, until several fall over the edge into the pit. They grip the walls, struggling to climb back up again. One unlucky soul tumbles all the way to the ground and lies stunned from the impact.

Are you all right, my friend? I sing into Elydark's head. The reptant's claws caught him a terrible cut across one shoulder. My licorneir shakes his mane and utters another ululating cry. His soulfire rips through me, a triumphant anthem that bursts from my own throat in wordless song.

But Lurodos is not yet defeated. On hands and knees he pulls himself out from under his reptant. With a leap he springs atop the fallen carcass, throws back his head, and howls like an animal. His blackened eyes are lost to demonic hunger. His body seems larger somehow, hunched and warped, and his teeth have elongated.

Movement off to one side. Lurodos whips his head, distracted by the sight of that fallen Noxaurian trying to scramble up out of the pit. Lurodos lunges at the man, who lets out a single, terrified scream. There's a confusion of violence and wet, crunching sounds as Lurodos rips out his victim's throat with one hand.

I don't wait to see more. It's time to put this demon down.

Now, Elydark! I urge, and my beast obeys, leaping like a bolt of lightning from a cloud. I lean to one side in the saddle, my sword carving a deadly arc in the air, ready to cut Lurodos in two as he bows over the fallen spectator. But Lurodos moves with unnatural speed, dodging my blow. Elydark pivots neatly, lowers his head, and begins a second pass. Lurodos is ready for him this time. He brandishes his flail, swings it with all his might. The spikes come into ringing contact with Elydark's horn. It cannot hurt him—such weapons are nothing against a licorneir in flame. But it knocks Elydark off balance. He stumbles, and I struggle to keep my seat.

Shaking his head, Elydark carries me several yards farther. *Are you spent?* I ask and am answered by a roar of heat in my head. I turn him one last time, determined to take off my enemy's head with this pass. Moving as one, my licorneir and I fly across the packed earth.

Lurodos braces for our assault. Even as my sword draws back for a deadly stroke, he hurls his flail. The chain wraps around my weapon, yanking my arm askew. Lurodos springs, grabs hold of me, and yanks me from the saddle. I hit the ground hard, rolling, breath knocked from my lungs. There's dirt in my eyes, grit in my teeth, the throb of my heartbeat drowning out the uproarious howls of the watching mob.

Lurodos is on me before I can drag in a lungful of air. He grips my throat, squeezing, his knee digging into my chest. I grapple with him, manage to elbow him in the face, using the sharp edge of my bracer. His head twists to one side. He turns slowly, looking down at me, black demon's blood pouring from his eyes, his lips, his tongue.

A flash of fire at his back. Lurodos has just enough awareness through the virulium madness to look up and see death descending. He leaps out of the way, dodging Elydark's deadly horn and hooves. I roll over, desperately gasping, and pull to my feet. My sword lies but a few yards away, still wrapped in the chains of Lurodos's flail.

"*Shakh*-damned half-breed!" Lurodos roars, spewing black bile with every word. Hunched and lumbering, he nonetheless moves with strange agility, narrowly avoiding my licorneir's blows. "Can you not fight your own battles?"

He does not understand the truth. He does not realize the deep bond between a licorneir and its rider. They are as one as two souls may be, and to separate one from the other is like hacking off a limb. Nonetheless I send a song straight from my spirit: *Stand down, Elydark.*

My licorneir throws back his head, stamping in protest.

No, I insist, and square my shoulders, teeth bared. *I want him for myself.*

Spattered reptant blood burns in the fire of Elydark's being, filling the air with an acrid stink. The great licorneir shakes his horned head, but retreats, still eying Lurodos closely. I approach, moving in a wide circle around my prey. Lurodos retrieves both his flail and my sword. The spiked ball swings gently back and forth, a hypnotic pendulum. He has every advantage now, but he cannot wait for the prime moment of attack. Virulium drives him to recklessness, and he throws himself at me.

I anticipate him and dodge both the swinging flail and the flash of the blade following soon after. Lurodos strikes again, too wild, and I avoid it, but narrowly. On his third attack, the flail strikes the ground with such force, the spikes stick hard.

Springing on the opportunity, I plant my foot on the chain, dragging Lurodos down, then kick him in the face. Lurodos goes over backwards. I whip out my remaining knife and lunge.

Lurodos is too fast. He blocks my blow with my own stolen sword, then lunges at me, slashing, hewing. It's not pretty, but it's so erratic, I struggle to anticipate him now. All the while,

Lurodos shrieks, a ravening, insane, unending battery of sound. I deflect a blow with my bracer. The power of Lurodos's attack rings with stunning pain up my arm. But though I'm driven to my knees, I adjust my grip on my knife and plunge the blade deep into Lurodos's unguarded side. My angle is wrong; it does not reach his heart.

He screeches. Pain means nothing to him now, caught fast in virulium's grip. He takes hold of the knife, wrenches it out of his side. Black blood gushes from his wound. With a swift backhand, he cuts me across the upper arm, a vicious blow.

I stagger back, pain bursting across my senses. But then I feel it—worse than pain. The burn. The rush. The poison in Lurodos's blood, which now mingles with mine. I've not tasted virulium in such a long time. But I've never forgotten . . .

With a roar I throw myself at my enemy, strike him in the gut, in the face. My blows are hard enough to knock the wind out of Lurodos, at least enough that I can back up, put some distance between us. My breath comes in painful, wrenching gasps. Around the edges of my vision, darkness licks, eager, hungry.

Lurodos bleeds profusely, but he does not seem to feel it. He wouldn't. He's too far gone to feel anything but rage. He's got both my weapons now and stalks toward me, tongue lolling, blood gushing from his side, poison spewing from his mouth. His is the face of death, unrelenting. I take a single step back then brace myself, ready to take him with my bare hands if I must.

Something glints in the air, catching my eye.

The next instant, my own knife plants in the dirt, a few paces from me. The twin of the blade in Lurodos's hand.

I don't have time to consider its miraculous appearance. I simply lunge for it, catch it up. Turning, I'm just in time to deflect Lurodos's blows. Then, quick as thought, I plunge the blade straight into my enemy's black eye.

He screams. The sound echoes from the deepest reaches of his corrupted soul, as though issuing from hell itself. He drops his guard, battle rage momentarily frozen in shock. I wrench my other blade from his grasp. This time when I strike, my blow drives home—up under the ribs, straight into his heart.

A death gasp bursts in his lungs, spattering bile across my chest. He heaves my own sword against me one last time. I avoid the blow and kick him in the face, knocking him over backwards. Lurodos hits the ground, convulsing. Drowning in his own blood. Or rather drowning in the demon's blood which pulses in his veins. He spits a geyser of black. His one remaining eye widens, dark and rolling. Somehow, though I cannot see the pupil, it communicates pure, raw terror. As though here, in his final gasping moments, he gazes into the abyss which is his doom.

Then, with a last hideous rattle of breath, he dies.

Profound silence envelops the arena. The onlookers stare down in shock at what has taken place. I step back from my enemy's corpse, wipe blood from my forehead, and grimace at the pain which suddenly makes itself felt across various parts of my body. Then I turn my face to the scaffold.

Ruvaen stands, having sprung from his seat. He looks down, open-mouthed and smiling. Meeting my eye, he lets out a whoop of triumph, then sweeps his arm and declares to all those watching: "Behold, Tanatar's chosen champion!"

The Noxaurians erupt in cheers. What do they care that it was their own man, their brother-in-arms, their fearless leader, who just died gruesomely before their eyes? Blood has been spilt, and they have relished the spilling. So they cheer for me in their awful voices. A chant of, *"Half-breed! Half-breed! Half-breed!"* echoes in my ears.

I turn from them, disgust curling my lip. My gaze seeks out my warbride. She too has risen from her chair and stands close to the edge of the scaffold, staring down at me. Wind pulls at her hair and whips back her slitted skirt, revealing her naked thigh and the empty sheath strapped there.

She meets my gaze. Just for a moment that stern line of her brow relaxes into a smile.

And the breath is stolen from my lungs.

15
ILSEVEL

❦

YOU MAY MAKE USE OF MY PRIVATE PAVILION FOR the rest of the morning," Prince Ruvaen says as, fingers pinching into my upper arm, he drags me back across the encampment, through the cheering throng of men and monsters. "Tell my good friend Taar how pleased I am with his efforts. Then stitch him up and find a way to thank him for saving your life."

He casts me an insinuating grin with this last statement, even as he pushes aside the pavilion flap. I want to slap him or claw his eyes out. Something in the prince's expression tells me he knows exactly what I'm thinking. His grin only grows as he releases my arm and sweeps a mocking bow. "Lady Ragnataarthane," he purrs.

I glare at him, trying to summon all the hatred in my soul. This fae is the reason for all the death and destruction across my kingdom. This fae is the reason my own life has been so disrupted. If I hadn't already tossed my secret knife to Taar, I'm sure I could find a good use for it right here, right now.

But I did toss that knife. I am helpless as a kitten before this tiger of a man. He knows it. And he enjoys the knowledge.

Determined not to let him cow me, I lift my chin, narrow my eyes. Then, without a word of acknowledgement, I slip into the pavilion and the warm darkness within. To my great relief, Ruvaen doesn't follow. He drops the flap. Instantly the silencing spells take effect, blocking out the ongoing roar of enthusiasm from the fae horde.

I stop short, shoulders stiff, arms straight, my fists gripping handfuls of silken skirts. Then, with a long exhale of breath, I let my body slump, insofar as this tight-laced corset will allow me. Oh gods. He survived. My captor, my enemy, my bridegroom . . . he survived. And my life is spared. For the time being at least.

All the tension I've been holding tight as a bowstring releases for an instant in a single, choking sob. I catch myself before a second sob escapes, however. I cannot come undone. Not now. All those images of gore and violence play out behind my eyelids. I force them back and draw a deep, steadying breath. I must stay strong. For just a little longer. Just until I find my sister and get us out of here.

The pavilion is empty—no sign of Taar. But he's on his way, I'm sure of it. And will he expect me to . . . to celebrate his victory? To offer the congratulations Ruvaen implied? I'm not certain which I fear more: the idea that my champion will demand something of me or the idea that he will simply dismiss me out of hand.

I pace back and forth in front of the low fire. There are no chairs to sit on, as those were carried out to the platform for the prince's use. The only other place to sit is the bed, and . . . I won't even look that way. Not now. Now is not the time to remember the heat of his breath against my skin. Now is not the time to remember how my blood leaped in my veins, how my body erupted with sensation.

My hand strays to the empty sheath strapped to my thigh. The weight of the knife had steadied me, offered me some small comfort amidst the chaos. Now even that is gone. The world has lost all semblance of reason. I'm caught in a wave of confusion, churning and relentless, and I don't know how much longer I can keep my head above water.

The tent flap moves. I whirl, and my traitorous heart leaps in my throat at the sight of the tall, dark figure in the opening. "Warlord!" I gasp.

He stops just inside. Firelight glints in the depths of his black eyes as he lifts his heavy head and looks at me. *"Zylnala,"* he rumbles.

He steps into the pavilion, dropping the tent flap and once more blocking out the sounds from outside. For a heart-stopping instant, I wonder if he's going to take me in his blood-spattered, mud-crusted arms. Heat surges in my veins, either with hope or fear, I do not know. If he reaches for me now, would I resist?

But he doesn't. He passes by me without a word or a look and goes to the cupboard from which he fetched food and drink the night before. A little rifling, and he grabs a bottle and what looks like a stack of fine linen napkins. These he carries back to the bed. He sits on the edge, heedless of the stains he's leaving on the velvet blankets and furs. Pulling off his bracers, he tosses them aside and starts to remove the pauldrons.

"Let me help with that," I blurt and step forward. The long slit of my gown parts, revealing the full length of my leg. I hastily move to cover myself.

Taar pauses. I don't know if he even sees me, his face is so purposefully averted. But somehow I sense awareness in him. Like a chord of dark song, pitched too low for human perception, but humming in his soul. For the space of ten heartbeats, he doesn't move. Then, slowly, he lifts his head, gazing up at me cautiously. "I do not need assistance."

I swallow, my throat tight and dry. "Let me help you all the same," I manage and, moving a little more carefully so as not to expose myself more than necessary, I go to him. My fingers shake as I unstrap the pauldrons and ease them off his shoulders, and I try to convince myself that I don't notice every time I accidentally brush his sweat-glistening skin. Why am I so aware of him? The heat of him, the largeness of him. The smell of him, that reek of mud and blood and victory that makes something in my lower stomach flutter. This is not what I want.

Turning away, I place the heavy pauldrons to one side. When I face him again, I make certain my expression is cool. "Well," I say, folding my arms, "after all your hemming and hawing, you made short work of that business."

Taar gives me a look. I flush, wondering if this was an inappropriate remark considering a man's life was just brutally ended. But then he says, "I should have found an excuse to do that a long time ago." His voice growls in the deepest hollows of his chest. "The worlds are better off without a creature like Lurodos in them."

"On that we can certainly agree," I reply, keeping my voice bright and hoping no telltale quaver betrays the truth of my churning emotions. "So tell me, was it as easy as you made it seem? Or were you obliged to exert yourself somewhat?"

His eyebrow tips. "You think that was easy?"

"Oh, quite," I answer and wave to indicate the bleeding cut on his upper arm. It looks rather deep and strangely dark around the edges. I remember too well when Lurodos ripped Taar's own knife out of his side and slashed back, the blade still dripping with his own blackened blood. The memory makes my stomach knot, but I say only, "No doubt this was all for show. To keep the bloodthirsty masses invested. Most effectively managed, I must say."

He turns, grimacing as he looks down at the wound. A shudder ripples through him, as though the pain is only just hitting him. Without a word he takes the bottle of spirits, uncorks it, and moves to pour it directly onto the cut.

"What are you doing?" I exclaim.

He flashes me a narrow look. "The wound must be cleansed."

"By sloshing an entire bottle all over it? What a waste!"

Another one of those eyebrow tilts. "If the worst sin I commit this day is to waste a bottle of Ruvaen's private store, I won't be spending any breath on penance prayers."

"Nonetheless." I reach out, fingers beckoning. "Let me do a proper job of it. You might as well make use of an extra pair of hands while you have them, right?"

He says nothing, only looks at me, his expression inscrutable. But when I grip the neck of the bottle, he relents. Pulling it from his grasp, I perch on the edge of the bed beside him . . . and am suddenly very aware of everything that took place between us the last time I sat here. When he pushed me into those soft blankets. When he knelt between my legs. When he hiked my hips forward, drawing me to his hungry mouth.

Oh gods. I was just saved from death, from worse than death. How can my mind still be so fixated on all the wrong things?

With a little shake of my head, I splash spirits into one of those linen napkins and set to work cleaning the wound with careful dabs. Concentrating on the task, refusing to let my mind wander. I pull out bits of dirt and debris and gently prod the torn flesh. "It will probably need stitches."

He grunts. An agreement, I think.

"This is your right arm," I point out.

"Yes."

"But you're still going to try to stitch it up lefthanded, aren't you?"

He doesn't look at me. His attention is apparently fixed on the dancing fire. "I'm quite used to tending my own wounds."

I sniff and continue to clean the blood from his skin. "While my mother permitted me to study almost no useful skills growing up, she did insist I learn to make small, precise stitches."

His eyes flick sideways, catching mine. "I am not a tapestry."

"Oh, I was never talented enough to be allowed anywhere near the tapestries. No, no, simple, solid mending work. That's what I'm good for and little else." I tap his massive bicep. "This is nothing more than a ripped seam. I'll have you fixed up in no time."

Taar does not answer at first. His gaze holds mine for a count of ten breaths, then returns to the fire, his brow pulled into a tight knot. Finally he says, "You'll likely find a kit in that chest over there."

I look where he indicates and see a small black chest sitting atop a larger one between two of the tent poles. Investigation soon reveals a compact medical kit. Not something I would expect to find among a fae prince's supplies. I wonder if Ruvaen will mind the way we've helped ourselves to his things. That being said, he's been helping himself to the spoils of my kingdom these last many years; I won't spare him any sympathy.

Returning to Taar's side, I open the kit and inspect the

contents. "I would have thought the fae could simply glamour their wounds away," I muse, selecting a curved needle and some stout black thread.

"They do," he replies. "But glamours won't stop them from bleeding. So, while you will never see a fae with scars or missing limbs, that doesn't mean they aren't right in front of you, hidden to the naked eye. Ruvaen himself does not look the way he presents. In fact I suspect the real Ruvaen is something quite different."

"Really?" I thread the needle, my fingers trembling rather more than I like. "I should have known none of his beauty was real."

"You think Ruvaen is beautiful?"

"Of course. All you fae are."

"But I am not fae."

I grit my teeth, refusing to look at him, refusing to let him goad me into complimenting his outrageous good looks. No doubt he's perfectly aware of the effect he has on women just by walking into the room. Fae or not, he's probably glamoured from head to toe. It's the only explanation.

Knotting the end of the thread, I hold the curved needle up to the light and face him. "Ready?"

He turns, presenting his wounded arm. His skin shivers slightly when I pinch the torn flesh together with my left hand. I can't tell if it's from pain or . . . something else. And I won't think about that. Not while this task needs doing. The cut is straight enough, a neat slash right across the bicep, a good four inches long. I start in the middle and work out, grimacing as I press that sharp tip through layers of skin and muscle tissue. It's such an unpleasant sensation, nothing at all like mending a torn seam, despite my bravado.

Taar doesn't wince. His jaw tightens slightly, but otherwise he offers no indications of pain. He's probably used to it. Up close to him like this, I cannot help noticing all over again the numerous scars riddling his body. I find myself wanting to explore them—to run my fingers along their various textures and shapes. To feel the way they pull across his hard muscles. Even now, covered in mud and blood though he is, I wonder what it might be like to let my tongue slide along those ridges and . . .

"You're trembling, *zylnala*."

Suddenly aware of his gaze upon me, I glance up. He's so close, I could swear I feel the air stirred by his eyelashes. He's not watching my work; he's watching me. Those dark eyes of his take me in slowly, reading my face, searching for secrets. But surely he cannot read my mind. Can he?

"Stop," I say, my voice snappish. "Stop looking at me. You make me nervous."

His gaze drops at last to my stitches. They're neat enough, tight and strong. "Is this your first time?" he asks. "Stitching up a man, I mean."

Heat burns up my neck. Oh gods, I'm not a blusher. So why does he have to bring out this pathetic side of me? "We all start somewhere," I answer shortly, concentrating intently on my work.

He continues watching as I plunge that needle through his flesh and yank the thread taut. "Wouldn't you be more comfortable finding a . . . a fixed point to focus on?" I suggest. "You know, to distract yourself from the pain?"

His mouth quirks slightly. "You are distraction enough."

I freeze, fingers poised in midair.

"That is," he continues, his voice low and contemplative, "your face is incredibly expressive. I can watch your thoughts playing through your eyes, one after the other."

And when I was thinking just now about licking his chest? Did he catch that one?

I bite my lips hard and simply breathe for some seconds. Somewhere in the turmoil of my soul, I must find a ledge of calm. Steeling my spine, I get back to work. Slow, precise. There's a strange darkness on the edges of his skin that I don't understand. If I didn't know any better, I'd say it was rot. But surely a wound like this wouldn't begin to fester so quickly?

"That was really horrible, you know," I say at last, the words slipping softly through my lips.

"Yes," he says, understanding my meaning. "Deathmatches are never a pretty sight."

"I'm glad you killed him."

"As am I."

"But . . ."

"I understand."

We are silent again. I'm relieved that I don't have to try to explain myself, to rationalize the low hum of horror which sits in my gut at the death of that monster. A death which feels so . . . pointless. So random, so without reason. So brutal when performed for the sake of pure spectacle. And I was a part of that spectacle: a trophy, an object. The whole situation makes me sick.

At last Taar breaks the silence. "Were you worried for me, *zylnala?*" he asks softly.

I don't answer. I can't answer. Because an image flashes through my head: that terrible moment when Lurodos dragged Taar off the unicorn and slammed him into the dirt. That moment when I believed he was dead. Such a surge of dread had come over me then, not for myself and what his death would mean for me, but . . . but for *him*. Because I did not want him to die. Not there. Not then. Not in front of that cheering mob.

This is wrong. He is a means to an end, nothing more. Not to mention the cause of my current peril in the first place! I cannot forget that little detail. Perhaps this is some fae trickery, manipulating me into seeing him as my rescuer, as some sort of hero. Perhaps it is a spell that makes me want to grab him, to pull him down on top of me until I'm crushed into the bed while he suffocates me with kisses.

I glance up and find myself trapped in his dark gaze. Am I really so transparent? Can he read my thoughts even now?

Dropping the needle and thread, leaving them to dangle from

his flesh, I quickly push to my feet and back away. "There!" I declare. "That's done."

He looks down at his arm. "You didn't tie it off."

"You can manage that for yourself. Besides, it's time we got going. We must find my sister." The words have no sooner left my mouth when all the warmth in my body seems to vanish, and I'm flooded with ice. Aurae! While I've been sitting here, admiring this massive hunk of godlike manliness, Aurae is out there in the hands of some monster. I clench my fists. "There's no time to waste. Do you have any idea where she was taken? Do you know where to look?"

Unlike my own face apparently, Taar's expression is unreadable. Using his left hand, he deftly ties off the dangling thread and snaps the needle free. Then he rises from the bed, and the light from the fire shifts, casting his features in darkness. He comes toward me, one step, then another. I'm tempted to back away but stand my ground, and soon he is close enough to touch me. But doesn't. He simply looks at me, long and hard.

"I will help you find your sister, even as I vowed," he says. "But you may not like what we discover."

I nod once and hold his gaze. "I need to know. And then I need to get her out."

"Whoever bought her might not be willing to part with her. Not without a price."

"Another deathmatch?" I guess, despair welling up in my throat.

I cannot ask Taar to risk his life in yet another battle.

"Perhaps," he acknowledges. "But more likely an exchange."

All the blood seems to rush from my cheeks. Of course. What do I have to offer for my sister's life other than my own? And, considering it's my fault that she's in the situation to begin with, how can I not make the offer?

"Don't do it, *zylnala*," Taar urges, his voice low and a little rough. "Don't go after her. Think of your sister as dead—a casualty of the battle."

Fire sparks in my breast. I look up at him, and, if I were armed in this moment, I would lash out without hesitation. "The battle *you* led," I spit.

"Yes," he replies.

How I hate him just now. Hate that coldness, hate that calm. Hate the casual way he speaks of my sister's probable fate. I hate myself as well for letting myself be even temporarily seduced by such a man. Such a monster.

"But there's a good chance she isn't dead," I persist. "As long as that chance remains, I'm not going to leave her." Dropping my gaze to the floor, I study my own feet peeking out beneath the hem of this black silk gown. "If I have to exchange my freedom for hers, so be it."

He feels so large and seems to expand still more as he draws a deep breath into his chest. "Whatever happened last night has already happened. Throwing your life away will not undo it."

"Are you going back on your word?" I yank my head up, tossing hair from my eyes and glaring fiercely at him. "Are you saying you won't help me find her after all?"

His face is quiet, solemn. Once more I feel as though I can hear a hum of song pitched too low for human ears. A deep, reverberating note, full of both darkness and truth. I'm not sure if it's my gods-gift at play or merely my own desperation. "Have I honored my word to you thus far?" he asks quietly.

He has. Damn him, he has. Even to the point of death.

I wrap my arms around myself, trying to suppress the shivers suddenly quaking my limbs. Hopelessness threatens to overwhelm me. I want someone to lash out against, someone to fight. But I'm outmatched at every turn. Gods, if only my mother had allowed me to study weaponry alongside my elder brother! I was given basic instruction when I was small, but after my gift manifested, I was strictly forbidden to touch anything sharper than a pair of sewing shears. Maybe if I'd not been forcibly warped into this useless shape, I could actually do something to save my sister and myself.

"Give me the knife," I say suddenly, holding out one hand.

Taar blinks at me.

"Please," I continue, struggling to soften my tone somewhat. "Let me have the knife. I'll go on my own. I'll find her. I'll trade myself for her, and then I'll . . ." My voice trails off.

The warlord drops his hand to the two sheaths at his belt. He draws forth one of the knives then takes hold of my outstretched hand and presses the hilt into my fingers. A spark of fire seems to shoot up my arm where his skin comes into contact with mine.

"Keep the knife, *zylnala*," he says. "It is yours. Consider it a gift. But . . ." He releases his hold on me and takes a step back. The distance between us feels like a chasm. "I will go with you. And I will not allow you to make such a trade."

I stare down at the weapon in my grip. "You can't stop me," I whisper.

"Oh, but I can. Because, until we part ways, you are still mine, warbride. Sealed with Lurodos's deathblood. I am not giving you up to either man or monster."

I cannot speak. My heart lodges in my throat, stifling any protests I might make. I turn the knife over slowly, watching how the firelight glints off its edge. Then, with an effort, I swallow and force myself to look at him once more.

"Very well, warlord," I say. "Have it your way. For now."

16

TAAR

—◦◦◦◦◦◦—

MY FIRST TASK IS TO FIND HER A MORE PRACTICAL gown to wear. Ruvaen's tastes may flatter her figure in ways I scarcely dare acknowledge, but that silk ensemble certainly won't stand up to any strenuous travel.

Ruvaen responds to my request by sending a Licornyn style gown of sturdy *quilen* cloth dyed blue, with a split skirt and trousers underneath, fit for riding. She'll look like a proper Licornyn in no time. A fine joke—Ruvaen knows perfectly well no human bride of mine will ever be accepted by my people. Which wasn't the point of this marriage to begin with.

I stand outside the pavilion while she changes. Part of me wonders if she'll need help getting out of that ornate silk gown, but I'm not about to volunteer my services. Instead I cross my arms and simply wait, wondering all the while how I ended up in this ridiculous situation. I don't regret it. Not exactly. If nothing else, I'm glad Lurodos is dead. That man was trouble, and his ruthlessness brought about the deaths of not only my own people but many innocents as well. He needed to be put down.

Still there's a wrongness to it all—the fact that I spilled blood to earn a warbride whom I intend to abandon at the next opportunity.

Not abandon, I remind myself firmly. *Set free.*

Is that the truth, though? I don't know who she is or who her people are. I don't even know her name. So why can I not shake the feeling that she belongs with me? Tucked safely under the sheltering curve of my arm . . .

"*Shakh*," I growl as pain shoots through my forearm, pinching my flesh like constricting cords, though there's nothing there save my leather bracer. I wish Elydark were here with me. My licorneir moved beyond the range of the spire again once the battle was complete. Not before he gave me a long, warning stare, however. He does not approve of my recent choices, no more than Kildorath or any of my people do. I don't really blame them; I don't approve of myself. But I'm in this far now, I might as well forge on until I find the other side. Save the sister if possible. Get them both out of here, away from the Grimspire and Ruvaen's folk. Make certain they are safe.

Then away with all speed, back to where I belong. To my own kind, my own realm. My own dark path.

Something sharp strikes my cheek, a glancing blow. Startled, I put up a hand and turn to the whirring blur darting past my face. I narrow my eyes. Snatching out with one hand, I wrap my fingers around the small angry glow of a pixie, caging it in my grasp. It screeches and curses, trying to break free. I hold it up to peer into its tiny, furious little face. It's long upper lip rolls back to show its gnashing teeth.

"What's this, Pompkin?" I demand with a growl. "I pay you well for information, and you reciprocate by pelting me with pebbles?"

"No more than you deserve!" a piping little voice shrieks back. "I am a warrior of the mighty Hopdiddle Clan, yet you treat me like a common page! *Fetch this, carry that, find me a juicy tidbit of gossip.* Disgraceful!"

"You took the payment," I point out dryly. I'd handed over a scrap of human writing on a piece of parchment torn from an old ledger book years ago. Worthless to anyone save a pixie. They cannot resist the written word however they can get their grubby little hands on it. They believe if they ingest it, the power captured in those words will be transferred to them. Foolish creatures, but useful when motivated. "You owe me. Come now, out with it, Pompkin. What did you hear about the other human warbride? Is she still here at the Grimspire?"

The pixie curses me soundly, but that's common courtesy among its kind. It finishes by spitting at my eye, missing by a foot. Then it sighs and stops fluttering its wings, settling into my grasp.

"Fine," it admits at last. "There was another human female sold at last night's auction. To Ravagol."

My blood runs cold. I recognize that name: it belongs to a warrior who serves under Lord Dormaris of Lunulyr. Neither titled nor wealthy, Ravagol makes his living by sheer brutality, serving as his master's prized attack dog.

I've known all along that whoever spent his hard-earned coin on a warbride wasn't going to be the kind of man who should ever lay hands on a woman. But Ravagol? He is a beast. Unlike Lurodos, he never bothers to disguise his monstrous aspect with glamours, but proudly displays all the outward signs of his twisted soul. Though he has profited well off every war he's been in, no fae woman would willingly accept him as her husband. If he was ever to take a wife, this is the only way—by force and by cruelty. I suspect he's done it before. And will likely do it again.

I shake my head slowly, breathing out a curse. If only I could convince my own impetuous warbride not to pursue this matter further. She's not going to like what she finds.

I release the pixie, who spits at me one more time before flitting off. Just then the tent flap moves, and *she* steps out. My bride. This stranger now clad in the traditional garments of my people.

I catch my breath. The gown is simple enough. The sturdy blue cloth fits her figure well without constraint. Tooled leather sleeves crisscross over her upper arms and her exposed collarbone, and a series of intricate belts wrap her trim waist. The skirt is long, full, and slitted to the hips on both sides to reveal the tightly wrapped trousers and soft boots underneath. She's braided her hair back from her face but left the long waves loose across her shoulders.

She is . . . beautiful. There is no other word more worthy, more suited to her. Somehow, seeing her like this—covered and modest, not a single tantalizing glimpse of gratuitous skin revealed—only calls to mind more vividly the softness and sweetness of her naked form.

"What?" she demands. And I realize I've been staring at her for some moments unspeaking.

I force myself to look into her brown eyes. "*Zylnala,*" I say, my voice thick in my throat, "allow me to escort you to the town of Cramaer. It is a half-day's ride from the Ashryn Shrine. You should find help there among your own kind."

She blinks. Then her stern brow crumples. Bravely she manages to steel herself, to fight back a sudden onrush of tears. "Have you had news then? Is my sister dead?"

I don't like to tell her. I don't want her to know the truth. Because whatever we discover, it will surely break her. "I don't know," I answer at last, truthfully. "She might be, but . . ."

The girl pulls herself up straight. Her hand goes to rest on the hilt of the knife I gave her, strapped in its sheath to her belt. "Take me to her," she demands. "Now."

The Lunulyr encampment stands on the north side of the Grimspire, set apart from the Noxaurians, but still near enough to benefit from the spire's influence. The tents are all constructed of deep blue silk which, when combined with a thick atmosphere of oily smoke, gives the impression of falling dusk, though it is still only midday.

Dormaris's pavilion stands in the center, not so large as Ruvaen's, but impressive in its own right, structured like a five-pointed star. I have spent little time with the Lunulyrian lord, but rumors aplenty have reached my ears. It is said he joined Ruvaen's struggle against the humans simply to indulge his own curiosity. As a connoisseur of warfare, he sought to educate himself on how humans conduct their wars. He is not a brute like Lurodos, but a scholar and a sportsman. In many ways he is the more dangerous of the two. I should not like to cross him.

"When we stand before Dormaris," I whisper to my warbride as she trots to keep up with my long stride through the orderly rows of blue-silk tents, "let me do the talking. He is a subtle man and will twist your words and your will in a heartbeat if you do not stay on your guard. It would be best if you did not attract his attention at all."

She shoots me a nervous glance. "Is he the man who bought Aurae then?"

Aurae. Her sister. Strange that I should know her name and not the name of this woman at my side.

"No," I answer. "That man is one of Dormaris's warriors."

"Why do we not go straight to him then?"

"That would be a mistake. The man in question, Ravagol, is an unpredictable savage. But Dormaris is reasonable. He might be persuaded to help us."

Her pursed lips communicate her displeasure, but she trusts me enough to swallow her protests as we come to a stop outside the large pavilion. Dormaris's family crest—a crossed sword and battleax on a bloodred field—flutters overhead. I sent word in advance of my coming, and his guards, recognizing me, do not hesitate to step inside and alert their master to my arrival. I subtly move to position myself in front of the girl, assuming a wide stance that could easily turn into a defensive crouch if needed. My few interactions with Dormaris over the years have been courteous enough. But I'm not a fool. I know better than to relax my guard around a man like him.

The pavilion curtain swings back; Dormaris himself steps forth. He is obliged to duck, for he stands over seven feet tall, and the coiled black horns sprouting from his forehead only add to his great height. He wears a wine-red robe, open in the front to reveal the chiseled body of a warrior. Hair the same color as his garment flows down his shoulders, braided and ornamented with small bones and skulls. The effect should be barbaric, but instead, he looks strangely refined. Almost kingly, one might say.

His sharp, golden-eyed gaze passes over me to fix on the girl half-hidden behind me. Something flares in the depths of his pupils. Something I don't like. I shift my stance, moving to shield her. She grabs my arm, however, and peers around me, determined not to be blocked. Her fingers are tense and tight against my skin.

"Lord Dormaris," I say, my tone pitched to a low, careful tone of respect. "I come seeking one of your men: Ravagol, the warrior. I've been told he returned to your encampment with a warbride last night."

The warlord's gaze snaps back to mine. "*Luinar* Taarthalor," he says, and places a hand to his chest, inclining his head. "Indeed, yes. Ravagol boasted to many of his new prize. A most unexpected turn of events."

I don't quite know how to interpret the look on his face. He speaks in common Eledrian, however, which the girl understands. She leaps out from behind me, heedless of risk. "Where did he take her?" she demands. "What did he do to her?"

Dormaris tilts his head, his black horns catching the midday sunlight in their coils. His eyes move from me to her and back again, his expression curious and cautious and something else I can't quite define. "It would perhaps be easier," he says at last, "to show you rather than to try to explain what took place."

"What?" The girl's fists clench, and she takes an aggressive step forward. She's so small compared to his majesty, the sight would be almost comical were it not for the desperate look on her face. "What are you talking about? Where is my sister?" I place a restraining hand on her shoulder, but she twists free, reaching for her knife. Before she can draw it from its sheath, I grab her arm firmly and wrench her back. She staggers and falls against me, and I hastily slip my arm around her shoulders, pinning her in place. "Let me go!" she yelps.

I bow my head and growl in her ear. "You will not help your sister by offending Lord Dormaris."

She strains in my grasp one last time before going still. Letting out a small huff of air, she nods once. I don't release her but instead lift my gaze to the fae lord. He has taken a step back, and both his guards have half-drawn their own weapons. I don't understand it. Any one of these men could break her in half between his thumb and index finger . . . and yet they all stare at my warbride with an intensity that borders on fear.

"Do you have her under control?" Dormaris asks, eyeing the girl.

I nod and, though it should go without saying, add: "She is no threat to you, lord."

Dormaris narrows his eyes. Then, with a sharp word to his guards, he turns and strides through the encampment. We follow after, even as more armed men and women fall in around us. We are soon surrounded by ferocious Lunulyrian warriors. None of this makes any sense to me. Dormaris knows I am an ally, bound by my vows to Prince Ruvaen the same as he. And the girl? Anyone can look at her and see that she is harmless. Brave, reckless, determined, yes. But harmless.

We pass through the ordered rows of Lunulyrian tents. The stink of burned flesh intensifies, and the smoke in the air thickens. Something is wrong. Very wrong. I'm not sure what, but I do know that, if I had my way, I would spare my bride whatever revelations are coming. She walks at my side, her face set in grim lines.

Neither of us is prepared for what Lord Dormaris reveals.

We come to a swath of the encampment that has been flattened. Tents ripped from the ground, thrown down, poles broken, silk torn. Spatters of blood and gore everywhere. Signs of dragging, deep gouges in the earth. And in the center of it all, what appears to be a great blast of some kind.

I come to a stop, my warbride close beside me, and stare out at that scene of destruction, uncomprehending. Dormaris strides forward until he stands almost in the center, turning slowly to look at the carnage. "Ravagol brought her here," he says, his tone almost musing. "Having won her in auction, he returned at once, first to show her off to his fellows, then to consummate the marriage according to Noxaurian law. It is the way things are done," Dormaris adds, with a dismissive shrug. "Noxaurians always were a barbarous lot. Her screams could be heard across the camp, but then . . ." He sweeps an arm to indicate the scene around us. "Then something changed. And it was my people I heard screaming in the night."

What he's implying is unbelievable. "You're saying the warbride did this?" I demand. There are hewn limbs, scattered entrails. I spy a severed head, half-hidden beneath a collapsed tent. "You're saying she killed Ravagol?"

"*Killed* Ravagol?" Dormaris chuckles darkly. "My friend, she did more than that. She ripped him to little pieces. We've not yet found all of him. Then she turned and did the same to all those nearby. I lost twenty warriors last night before she was finally subdued."

I look down at the girl beside me, studying her face for some sign of confirmation. Surely if her sister was such a deadly warrior, she would know something of it. But the girl looks confused. Horrified.

She looks up at me, her eyes limned with tears. "He . . . he's saying Aurae did this?"

I nod.

"But . . . how?"

"Do you not know?"

She shakes her head. "It's not possible. Aurae is . . . she's sweet. And gentle. She couldn't hurt a mouse. And she certainly couldn't . . ." Gulping down a sob, she whirls on Dormaris. Though every bone in her body trembles, she demands fiercely, "Where is she? Where is my sister?"

"Your sister?" Dormaris answers musingly. "You are of the same blood then?"

The girl nods. "Bring me to her. At once."

She speaks with all the imperious authority of a princess. Oddly enough Dormaris inclines his head. "This way," he says and guides us on through the carnage to where the smoke is thicker in the air.

"*Zylnala*," I say, laying a warning hand on her shoulder. "Don't go. Don't make yourself see this. It can do no good."

She does not answer me, does not look at me. She simply strides forward, her face set, even as smoke stings her eyes.

Dormaris leads us to an open place on the far side of his encampment. There we find what the smell had already told me we would: a pyre. Bodies piled up and burning. The remnants of last night's carnage, cleansed in fire. It is nearly burned out, and little remains but ashes and the twisted husks of corpses.

"No," the girl whispers. "No, no, no . . ." With each word, her voice rises until it becomes a wail of such horror, such sorrow, it echoes across the whole encampment. It strikes me like a song of mourning, plunging straight to the depths of my gut where my own losses reside, suppressed but unforgotten. For a moment it nearly knocks me to my knees.

Somehow I find a ledge of reason inside my head and manage to steady myself, to remain present in this place of burning flesh and horror. I peer through the smoke, searching for the girl, only to see her hurtling toward the pyre.

"*Zylnala!* Stop!" I cry and charge after her. I fear she will cast herself into the remaining flames, determined to join her sister in death. I catch her just as she reaches the hideous pile and, wrapping my arms around her waist, haul her kicking and screaming back. I press her to my chest, murmuring in her ear like she's some crazed animal. "She's gone, *zylnala*. She's gone.

Her pain is over. Let her go. Let her go."

The girl pounds at my chest, tears at my face with fingers curled like claws. But I do not release her. I hold her as she screams, and her pain batters my heart like a war hammer. I don't know how long we sit like that, before that hideous mound of death, surrounded by the watching eyes of Lunulyrian warriors. After some time I realize she is clutching something in her hand, something she'd dragged out of the fire. A bit of cloth, burned and stained almost beyond recognition.

"It's hers," the girl sobs, clutching that cloth to her breast as I hold her. "It's her prayer veil. She was wearing it when . . . when . . ." She cannot finish. She buries her face in that scrap, and I press her to my chest, my arms enfolding her.

Lord Dormaris approaches, his gaze wary. "She was gods-gifted," he says, addressing himself to me. "The War Gift. I've heard stories of the phenomenon but never seen anything like this."

I nod, comprehension slowly dawning. My bride did tell me last night that she was possessed of magic. A gods-gift would explain it. And though such gifts are rare, when they do occur, they often run in families. I had glimpsed the younger sister during the temple attack, lying unconscious. She had seemed small, delicate, and very young. Not at all a deadly instrument of war. But the gods are like that sometimes—bestowing gifts where least expected, all for their own ultimate and inexplicable purpose.

That purpose has come to an abrupt conclusion here, in a

pile of smoking corpses.

"Is this your warbride?" Dormaris asks, nodding to the girl in my arms. "Are you interested in selling? I will pay you handsomely. After all, if she is another gods-gifted—"

"She isn't for sale," I growl.

The Lunulyrian lord holds up both hands and takes a step back. "Ah, well . . . they say the War Gift only manifests once in a generation anyway. A pity."

I don't wait to hear more. Scooping the girl up in my arms, I cradle her close and carry her away from that scene of horror and all those wide-eyed and fearful warriors. I carry her out of the encampment entirely, into the encircling wood, beyond the range of the spire's influence, to where the shadows are deep and cool and sheltering.

17

ILSEVEL

T HE PATTERN OF BEADED EMBROIDERY IS STILL visible. Through the blood. Through the ash. Delicate starbursts and flowers, each shining bead placed with such care. Aurae wore it often, devout in her prayers as I never was. Of the two of us, one might think she better deserved the protection of the gods she so loved.

Aurae. *Aurae . . .*

It simply cannot be true. That site of destruction, of bloodshed, of horror. How could any of it be my sister's doing? I still remember the day her gift manifested. We all waited in terrible suspense. After what happened to Faraine, well . . . one never knows what gift the gods will choose to bestow on those they've touched with their power.

But Aurae's manifestation was something special. At first nothing happened. She simply sat quietly in a pool of sunlight in the center of the sacred Hall of Gods, her head bent beneath the very prayer veil I even now hold in my hand. Then, as though hearing some song none of the rest of us could, she rose and began to move. She was always a graceful creature, even as a little child, but these movements were something else: absolute control harmonized with absolute release of inhibition. Every part of her body synchronized, from the top of her head, to the tips of her fingers, to the soles of her feet. She was light dancing on running water, she was leaves caught in an autumn breeze, swift and shining.

Though no music played, I began to vocalize, catching the spirit of her movement and giving it voice. My own gift had already manifested years before, and my song blended with her dance so perfectly, it was like we were made to exist together. Though she was five years my junior and my opposite in temperament, we felt a wholeness in each other's company. Music and dance. Rhythm and song. Sisters in heart and soul.

Father was disappointed, of course, but he'd long ago given up expecting the gods to bless his children with gifts he could sink his teeth into. So he cursed the priests and kicked over an incense brazier, but when he was through, declared that at least Aurae was a pretty enough little thing, and he'd find some use for her eventually.

Aurae herself lived to spread sweetness and light wherever she went. She was much like Faraine in her earnestness but, unburdened by Faraine's particular gift, she was able to live a more carefree existence. She assumed the role of caretaker of her own volition, offering me comfort during the Shadow King's courtship, and volunteering to ride with me on my Maiden's Journey. She was always more concerned with the needs of others than herself. Even last night, even when faced with the prospect of imminent death, did she not urge me to sing for our fellow prisoners?

It's simply not possible Aurae bore the War Gift. I cannot believe it. I won't believe it. That fae . . . perhaps he could not lie outright, but he's playing some game, of that I'm certain. Could it be he tricked me into believing Aurae is dead? I did not rifle through that pile of burned bodies to find her. I saw that charred hand clutching the scrap of veil, but what if . . . what if . . . ?

I jerk my head upright, pulling my awareness back to the present. Where am I? There are trees all around me, dark and deeply shadowed, with only occasional splashes of sunlight making their way through thickly-laced branches and leaves. Heavy, rhythmic hoofbeats rock the earth underneath me, and I realize I'm on the broad, red back of a unicorn. Taar's unicorn. And these are Taar's arms wrapped securely around me.

Guilt floods my veins like fire. It's such a terrible rush, I fear I will simply combust then and there. Why? Why, why, why did I end up here in his arms? Why did he choose to bid on me, to save me from degradation and death? To give me pleasures beyond anything I've ever known . . . all while my sister was brutally murdered in a bloodbath, her body broken and desecrated in flame. I cannot comprehend it.

"Take me back." The sound whispers from my lips, cracked and broken.

Taar does not respond. I'm not sure he heard me.

"Take me back," I say again, this time with force, though the words sound more like dull grunts without articulation. "Take me back, take me back, take me . . ."

Suddenly along with the guilt comes a raw spark of hatred for this man. This man who holds me, who made vows of protection over me, who fought for me, bled for me. And all for what? No reason. None at all. Pure, random chance landed me with him. I didn't deserve this. If it was to be either of us, it should have been Aurae, sweet, gentle Aurae. He should have seen her, been moved to compassion for her, and let me go to the monsters. The fact that he didn't makes him a monster too, worse than any of the rest . . . or so my crazed soul insists in that moment. Some small part of me knows I'm not thinking rationally anymore. I don't care.

Whipping the knife he gave me from its sheath, I slash it across his arm, right in that soft place above his bracer. It doesn't bite deep, but the shock brings a roar of surprise bursting from his lips. He yanks his arm back, and his unicorn utters a terrible, rumbling bellow, rearing up on its hind legs.

I don't wait for a second chance. Freed momentarily from his grip, I slip from the saddle, hit the ground hard, and lie stunned for a moment. I hear him shouting: *"Zylnala!"* and the word seems to galvanize my limbs.

Pulling myself upright, I stagger, stumble. Then I run. Blindly. I don't know where I am or where I'm going. I know only that somehow I've got to get back to that encampment, got to find Aurae. Because she's not dead. She cannot be dead. *I will not allow her to be dead.*

Branches slash at my face. Still gripping the knife in one hand, I hack them away, pressing and pushing through the dense undergrowth. My soft boots pound on uneven ground, and tree roots seem almost to rise up, attempting to trip me as I go. If I didn't know any better, I'd say this forest was sentient. I could almost swear I hear laughter whispering through the leaves and crackling in the branches.

"Zylnala! Stop!" Taar's voice bellows behind me. His unicorn's massive hooves vibrate the ground under my feet as his body crashes through the trees. "You don't know where you're going! The Wood is dangerous, it will devour you!"

I hear him. But I don't believe him, or rather, I don't want to believe him. All I care about now is getting away from him, of getting back to my sister. Of setting right everything that has gone so horribly, horribly wrong.

A grove of alders appears before me, all pale gray bark and

dense greenery. They seem to open up, a road appearing through their midst. I turn my feet that way, desperate for an easier path to pursue. Taar's warnings ring in my head, but I plunge forward, heedless, and stagger into the shadows of those trees.

Immediately they close in behind me. And suddenly I know this is no forest of the mortal realm. It is like something from the fairy tales I heard as a child. The trees seem to shift before me, assuming vaguely humanoid shape. They reach for me, lewd fingers prodding at my body, ripping at my skirts. I yank free only to stagger into the waiting arm-branches behind me. They grasp me, fondling my breasts, clinging to my neck. Other trees close in, and I hear the rip of cloth, feel more dry fingers creeping up my thigh. Empty-hollow eyes and cavernous mouths leer before me, so many of them. A scream bursts from my lips.

Light erupts in my eyes, an explosion of heat and brilliance. The trees screech, their hollow throats uttering unholy sounds unlike anything in my experience. Rippling roots burst forth from the soil as the alders fall back. My confused vision takes in random flashes—images of the red unicorn, slashing with its great horn, hewing branches and skewering trunks. Fire snorts from his flared nostrils and sparks in his wild eyes. Terrified of that fire, the trees crowd into each other, desperate to flee both flame and horn.

My knees buckle. I sink to the forest floor in what is no longer an alder grove but a little clearing in a patch of sunlight. Lungs heaving, I struggle to draw a complete breath.

A shadow falls across me. I look up at the dark silhouette of my warlord husband, standing with sword drawn before me. Blood trickles down his arm from the cut I gave him. Only then do I realize that I dropped my knife sometime during my struggle with the alders. It lies at his feet. He picks it up, turns it over.

Then he kneels and offers the knife to me.

I stare at that beautiful blade, the citrine jewel winking in the handle. For a long moment it seems to take up the whole of my vision.

Then, with a sharp intake of breath, I take hold of the hilt and slash, aiming the point of that blade straight for his eye. He blocks the blow. As though he expected it. Perhaps he did. And he does not take the weapon from me, but merely draws me to him, pressing my head against his shoulder as great, tearing sobs wrench from my throat, from my soul.

"There, there, little songbird," he croons, his voice rough and yet somehow gentle. "Rage if you must. Weep if you must. Break if you must. But do so in my arms. Let me hold you as you fall to pieces. You are safe to break with me."

I don't know when his words cease to be words and become song: wordless sound full of meaning, rich and deep as a secret well, springing from the depths of his soul. At some point, his unicorn joins him. Its voice is a multitudinous resonance, like the very voice of the soil from which this forest grows. Their song, joined in harmony, washes over me, painful and yet cleansing.

Slowly, slowly, guilt releases its hold on my heart. Guilt that fate should contrive to keep me alive while not protecting my sister. Guilt born, not of sin, but of circumstance. As it recedes, however, sorrow sweeps in to replace it. But this is worse still . . . for while guilt offered me a handhold of rage with which to steady myself, this sorrow is deep, a turmoil of dark water that will drown me if I fall into its depths. I close my eyes, pressing into Taar's chest, shivering as that wave of sorrow overwhelms me.

Only I find I'm not alone here. It's dark, it's horrible . . . but the song remains. The song of Taar and his unicorn, wrapping me up tight, preventing me from being entirely swept away. So the sorrow washes me, cleanses me, but does not drown me as I feared. Because I'm not alone.

He's here with me. This stranger. My gods-damned husband.

I lean into his strength and sob until no tears remain.

"LET ME HOLD YOU AS YOU FALL
TO PIECES. YOU ARE SAFE TO
BREAK WITH ME."

18

TAAR

———◦⊱✦⊰◦———

I T IS ALWAYS STRANGE, STEPPING IN AND OUT OF THE between-worlds space in which the Forest of Wanfriel grows.

The fae use Wanfriel to navigate safely across realms, traveling via secret gates to appear in the human world and disappear back into Eledria at need. Most of the gates are ancient things, established long ages past by fae kings and queens of tremendous power. But Ruvaen has used the magic channeled by the Grimspire to open numerous temporary gates into the mortal realm, allowing him to conduct his raids and escape again undetected back into the mysterious depths of the Between.

One such gate lies before me now—the gate Lurodos and I used just two days ago in our ill-fated attack on Ashryn Shrine. I can feel the magic weakening. A gate between worlds is a dangerous spell, and these temporary portals are chaotic at best. I would not use it again if I had another choice.

But I vowed to carry my warbride back to her people. And this is the shortest route.

I signal silently to Elydark, and he comes to a stop a few paces from the gate. This appears like nothing more than two whisper-thin pine trees, straight as arrows, growing so close together, their branches are hopelessly entwined. In the narrow space between their trunks, the air moves strangely, that unsettling twisting, churning of the atmosphere that betrays a thinness in the veils of reality. Beyond that churning, a hazy landscape swims before my straining vision. The human world.

"We're here, *zylnala*," I say softly. She stirs at the sound of my voice, as though waking from deep sleep. She gives her head a little shake and lifts it from where it's been resting against my shoulder for these last several hours. I point to the gate before us. "Through there lies your world. The town of Cramaer sits between those two hills, no more than a few short miles. I will take you there if that is your wish. It is the nearest human settlement, not far from the temple. Unless there is somewhere else you would rather go?"

She does not answer. In the short time that I've known her, she's been nothing but defiance and fire contained in this small, human frame. Now she is limp in my arms, as though all the strength has simply gone out from her body.

Uncertain that she heard me, I repeat my question. When she

continues to offer no response, I urge Elydark forward. Passing through the gate is an unpleasant experience, even with a licorneir companion. Beings like Elydark are created to exist in many layers of reality, often simultaneously, but my body is merely flesh and blood. To send it through the veils is like feeling a layer of skin peeled away, and what's left underneath is soft and vulnerable to exposure. Both seconds and years pass over me in a whorling storm as time shifts and moves in the wake of our passage.

Then we stagger through, out into that magic-depleted air. Elydark tosses his head, displeased by our return to this realm, which is so unsuited to his very being. The girl shudders violently. I'm only just in time to help her lean out and vomit up everything in her stomach, missing my leg by inches. Humans are even less suited to world-traveling than my kind.

But it's done now. She lifts her head, wipes her lips with the back of her hand, and looks dully around at the landscape. It is winter in this part of her world—the trees are bare and gray, the fields fallow, the road before us empty save for sharp-whistling winds that send ripples across muddy puddles collected in the furrows.

"Is this where you leave me then?" she asks, her voice low and hoarse. It's the first she's spoken in many hours, since I saved her from the hungry arms of the alder trees.

"I shall carry you to within sight of the town," I say. "Do you have people there who can help you?"

She is still for a long moment. Then she nods.

"Is there anywhere else you would prefer to go?"

Another long pause, followed by a short shake of her head.

"Very well then."

I urge Elydark forward, and we make our way down that empty, mud-choked road. Nothing about this sits well with me. The girl is so determined to keep her secrets. I truly know nothing about her, this living enigma who has somehow fallen into my hands. I wish I did not have to leave her, wish I had time to explore more deeply into her mysteries. Something tells me there is a great deal to be discovered, and those discoveries will be well worth the effort.

But that is a pleasure for some other man. The man who eventually succeeds in gaining her trust . . . and her heart. Not for the husband she never chose, the one who bought her against her will, who carried her into captivity. I certainly do not deserve her trust. I do not deserve her love.

And I don't seek it. My responsibility is through. I saved her from Lurodos. I helped her discover the fate of her sister. Now I will deliver her to her own kind and be off. My people need me. Ashika, Kildorath, and the others await my coming at the Luin Stone, but they cannot wait much longer. The Hidden City needs the protection of its Licornyn Riders. We have already been away too long.

My gaze strays from the road before me, down to the dark head of the girl slumped against my chest. Though I try not to, I cannot help being aware of the round softness of her body, of the way she nestles between my legs. The sensation brings other memories to life—the smell of her in my nostrils, the taste of her on my tongue. Gods above, why does she affect me so? It's been some time since I was with a woman, yes, but she is a stranger. Our time together was always meant to be brief. One night of passion and then goodbye. That was the agreement. I certainly cannot offer her more.

And yet my arm, wrapped loosely around her waist, tightens slightly. I feel again the constricting burn of the *velra* cord eating into my skin. My heart rate increases, and my breath grows tight in my chest.

Vellar, Elydark's song murmurs in my head, **do you sense danger ahead?**

No, my friend, I hasten to assure him. *No, all is well.*

Why does your heart beat so fast then?

I don't want to tell him. I don't want to admit the sickness, the anger, the fear churning in my gut. Perhaps if I do not tell him, I can make it not be so.

We come to a turn in the road at last. The town lies before us, huddled between two hills, all squat gray buildings in this sad gray landscape. Clouds roll in, carrying mizzling rain with them. Everything about the prospect is bleak and sad and colorless.

"We're here," I say, my voice deep in my chest. "This is as far as I dare go. Humans cannot see Elydark or me either while I ride him. But they will see you floating in mid-air, and you'll be hard-pressed indeed to explain it. Best if you dismount and walk on from here."

She nods. With my assistance, she slips from Elydark's back

and lands lightly on the ground below. She looks so strange, this human girl, standing in the human world, but clad in the garments of my people. She huddles in the folds of a Licornyn cloak, her gaze downcast. The damp air plasters strands of dark hair against her cheeks.

I draw a breath through clenched teeth. Then, untying one of my saddlebags, which I prepared in advance, I hand it down to her. "There," I say. "Supplies. Food, spare clothing. A little human coin even. It's not much, but . . . I hope it will serve."

She nods, clutching the bag to her chest.

"And you are quite sure there are people here who can help you? Who can return you to your family?"

"Yes, I am sure." Her voice is soft and low. She draws a deep breath which shudders slightly. Then: "You have done enough, warlord."

She speaks the words without malice or bite, but I hear the accusation nonetheless. Even now she blames me for her pain. And how can I deny it? Perhaps I could have done more. Perhaps I could have protected both her and her sister.

It is done, however. My choices, whether good or ill, cannot be unmade. I have nothing more to offer her save regret and a hope that her life, once free of me, will prosper.

So I nod. Then, on impulse, I lean in my saddle, reach out, and touch her cheek with one knuckle. She shivers but does not withdraw, and I let my finger trail down to her chin, tipping her face back so that I might look at it. At last she lifts those brown eyes of hers to meet my gaze. Gone is that fire, that spark, which had so heated my blood in the dark, secret hours we spent together. All that remains are ashes.

"Be well, *zylnala*," I murmur. And what more is there to say to this woman, this wife, this stranger? I wish I could offer something, some acknowledgement of what these last few hours have meant to me. But I myself do not understand. An impulse comes over me to lean down and kiss her, and I almost give in to it. But what would be the good of that? She is not mine. I may not casually take such pleasures from her.

Retracting my hand, I turn Elydark's head about and set my back to her, determined not to look over my shoulder. Not to seek a last glimpse of that forlorn figure, standing there in the big, gray, winter-caught world. *Go, Elydark!* I sing into my licorneir's head. He breaks into a canter then a gallop. I lean over his neck, eager to cover the distance between us and the gate, eager to leave this world behind.

Within a few paces, I gasp. A sudden searing pain shoots up my arm. It's so sharp, so unexpected, light seems to explode in my head. I struggle to draw breath and nearly fall from the saddle.

Vellar? Elydark's voice hums inside me. ***Vellar, you are suffering.***

I'm fine, I answer grimly, shaking my head, shaking that shock out of my senses. *Get us out of here.*

You should not let her go. Your hearts-bond belongs with you.

She is not mine. A growl rumbles in my throat, even as my song

323

rings silently in my licorneir's head. *We are not bound.*

Elydark responds by pulling up abruptly, half-rearing and tossing his horn. **You are wrong,** he says. **You are wrong, brother-soul. You are bound to her by the vows you made.**

Vows spoken under duress are not binding. I speak the truth with absolute conviction and drive my heels into Elydark's flanks, determined to leave this place. I must go, and quickly. I must get away from her before . . . before . . .

Another searing pain races up my arm, bursts in my head, and ripples through my body. With that pain, something else awakens—something dark and deep. Head swimming, I look down at the stitched-up cut on my bicep. Am I seeing things? Is the skin beneath those stitches blackening before my gaze? Dark tendrils shoot out from it, eating into my flesh, crawling up my shoulder.

Virulium. The truth hits me like a blow. Lurodos slashed me with a blade stained with his own poisoned blood. And now that poison is spreading.

Vellar? Elydark's voice bugles in my mind, frantic and furious. But I cannot answer. My eyes roll back in my head. I slip from the saddle, fall, and collapse in the dirt on the side of the road, even as darkness swarms in to claim me.

19

ILSEVEL

———

A T SOME POINT, I SUPPOSE, I'M GOING TO HAVE TO come up with some sort of plan.

My feet move of their own accord, one step after the other. They don't seem concerned with avoiding the puddles in the road, but splash through them, soaking the hem of my gown. I feel strangely disconnected from those feet, from this body. From this whole world. But soon I'm going to have to face other people again, going to have to give them my name, tell them my story.

Or what if I don't? By now everyone in this part of the country must know about the temple's destruction. Soon word will spread, and my father will hear of my disappearance and presumed death. He will rage at the loss but not mourn, and swiftly turn to scheming up ways to salvage the alliance with the Shadow King.

My mother might shed a tear, and Faraine will certainly weep for the loss of her two sisters. But does that necessarily mean I must return to them, to offer them comfort? To step back into the role King Larongar determined for me?

Will I marry the Shadow King after all?

Bitterness burns in my belly. All my desperate scheming, and what did I accomplish in the end? My letter brought Artoris to the temple and, with him, the fae. Had I never written to him, had I simply submitted to my father's will, married the man he chose, stepped into the life ordained for me . . . so many lives would have been spared.

Perhaps it is best for me to return. To learn the meaning of submission, to bow my head, lower my voice, and be the version of myself that is needed. Like Faraine. Gods, why could I not have modeled myself after my elder sister to begin with? If I had, maybe Aurae would still be alive.

Besides now I've seen the ravages of the fae invaders for myself. I've looked into the eye of Prince Ruvaen and known him for the monster he is. My teeth set in a grim, fierce smile. If marriage to the Shadow King is the only revenge within my grasp, so be it. I will marry him. And he and his monstrous warriors will sweep through the ranks of the fae, slaughtering them like pigs. So will my sister's death be avenged.

Plod, plod, plod. My heavy feet carry me down the center of the street into the town. All is strangely silent. Perhaps the rain drove everyone inside, though I'm not sure this accounts for the ghostly stillness in the air. Someone will spot me soon though, surely. Will it be difficult to convince them of my identity? I lift my head and look to the ridge across the valley where Lamruil's temple stood. Smoke still rises from the ruins. That conflagration must have been visible for miles around. Perhaps the townsfolk fled into the surrounding forests when they saw it, fearing the fae would set upon their town next.

I proceed to the center of town where the largest of the houses stand in a square, facing one another. All their windows are empty, their doors shut fast. No one steps out to greet me. "Hullo?" I call, my voice echoing strangely. No response save for a cold wind, which snaps through my cloak.

With a sigh I turn to the largest house, a three-story structure built of local stone, shingled instead of thatched, with proper glass panes in the front windows, likely the home of the town elder. It seems as good a place as any to wait for the townsfolk to return. I take a step toward that fastened door, intending to knock, hoping someone inside will hear me.

Before I can take a second step, however, a bugling cry echoes up the street behind me. My heavy heart lurches. I whirl on heel. To my utmost surprise, the big red unicorn gallops down the street, heading straight toward me. Huge and powerful, the glow of his spirit so bright, bursting out of the confines of his physical flesh in tongues of flame, he is a magnificent creature in any setting. But here, in contrast to these gray buildings and this potholed street, he is positively terrifying.

Taar is not with him. My brow tightens. Something must be wrong. The last I saw him, the warlord had turned this beast's head about, and they were galloping swiftly across the damp landscape, eager to see the last of me and my world. Why would the unicorn return alone?

I brace myself, clutching the bag of supplies Taar gave me against my chest, and wait for the unicorn to draw near. Some small part of me half-expects the mighty creature to run me through the heart with his horn, though for what reason, I can't say. I've gotten the distinct impression the unicorn does not care for me. Call it a hunch.

To my relief, however, he stops a few paces from me, tosses his fiery head, and trumpets another bugling cry that echoes up and down the fear-frozen street. I scowl up at him. "What?" I demand.

The beast lowers his head again, looking at me. In his burning eyes, I feel rather than hear a strange but undeniable . . . song. Like the music of his soul, full of meaning far deeper than words, meaning just beyond my ability to fully grasp or comprehend. I can only pick up bits and pieces: fear, tension. Distress.

"Has something happened to your master?" I ask.

The unicorn snorts fire and paws at the ground with one hoof. I bite the inside of my cheek, uncertain what to do. I only just parted from the warlord less than half an hour ago. What could possibly have befallen him between now and then? Did he run into a party of Miphates? Surely I would have heard or seen something.

But I can't deny the reality of this massive unicorn, standing here, huge and burning and . . . and *singing* at me. Singing a song I cannot hear but which I feel in my bones. It's eerie and a bit painful and absolutely impossible to ignore.

I glance around at the empty town once more. Still no sign of anyone. What am I supposed to do? Will I simply enter one of their houses, pop my feet up on a stool, and wait for the townsfolk to return? Or I could go with this unicorn and . . .

Shaking my head, I turn to the beast again. "Whatever it is, whatever has happened, it is none of my concern. Your master and I have parted ways. We're done."

The unicorn's eyes flash. He snorts and stomps. Tongues of fire spring up from the paving stones around his hoof. I leap back a pace or two, then glare at him. "I don't owe him anything!" I snarl. "So he saved my life . . . what of it? He also endangered it in the first place. We're done. We're *done*, do you understand me?"

The great beast begins pacing back and forth, the song rippling from its spirit so urgent, so desperate. I feel that song pushing, pushing, pushing inside my head, as though trying to force meaning into my incomprehension. Finally it bursts through, and I hear what almost sounds like a word, only it's clearer than a word. More like a force.

Please.

A shuddering breath escapes my lips. There's something so awful about such a glorious being begging for help. Begging for *my* help, no less. But there's something beautiful here too. In that one word, I hear the love the unicorn bears for his rider, and . . . well, the truth is, that love is not unmerited. I may hate the man for what he has brought into my life, but I cannot deny his honor. His courage. His strength and resolve. He risked his life for mine when he had no reason to do so. No one would have blamed him had he simply washed his hands of me and gone about his day without a second thought. Most men would have.

"Fine!" I growl, anger and resignation warring for dominance in my breast. "Fine, I'll go with you. But not for long, do you hear me? I'm coming back."

The unicorn, understanding me perfectly, kneels on the paving stones, apparently expecting me to climb onto its back. The fire licking across his skin douses, leaving behind solid flesh. I hesitate. I've seen these creatures flaming in battle, seen how that flame overwhelms their riders. Taar looked like a living torch when he fought Lurodos in the pit. If this unicorn suddenly erupts once more in flame, I'll probably be incinerated on the spot.

"Skewer it," I mutter and scramble into the saddle, clutching a handful of mane with one hand as the unicorn rises. My head whirls with vertigo. My gods, but this beast is tall! A worthy mount for his rider. I've always been drawn to horses, riding being one of the few outdoor activities my mother considered suitable for my upbringing. But I was usually mounted on dainty hunters bred specifically to carry highborn and delicate ladies.

This is nothing like that. It reminds me instead of the time I snuck out and rode Gloridel, my father's destrier. Age and retirement had made him docile, but he still rippled with muscular strength. I'd not been able to urge him into more than a canter, but the ground had absolutely quaked under his feet. The thrill of feeling all that power under me had rather spoiled me for other steeds. Though I was punished severely once caught and never allowed near Gloridel or any of the other war horses again, I never forgot that feeling.

This is something like that, only on so much greater of a scale as to be almost laughable. This beast is not only massive in size, but also in the overawing force of his spirit, which no mere horse could hope to equal. There's an undeniable sense that so much more of him exists than can be contained within the physical confines of this body, no matter how tremendous that body may be. It's like his spirit is meant to be a star, burning bright in the vaults of heaven, but has been compressed to fit this form, all without losing any of the power of his true nature. It's terrifying, overwhelming, and completely exhilarating.

I wind my fingers through his mane, holding on tight as he springs into motion. It feels like no more than a single leap before we leave the town behind. By the time I blink and draw a breath into my tight lungs, we're already out in open country, speeding down that lonely dirt road. The wind is cold, sharp against my face, but I peer ahead through slitted eyelids, searching.

Finally I see him—Taar, standing in the middle of the road. His back is to me, his arms slack at his sides. He seems to be staring out across the landscape, but when I look beyond him, I cannot see what has captivated his attention. There's nothing but the forest ahead, no sign of any life, of any enemy or threat.

I let out a breath through my clenched teeth, more relieved than I like to admit to see him upright and whole. But why did the unicorn come out of his way to fetch me? I don't understand it.

The unicorn slows his pace, coming to a stop several yards back from his rider. Shaking his mane, he utters a strange sound, like a growl and whimper combined. His cloven hooves prance in place, churning up the mud of the road. Taar does not react, does not turn at the sound of his unicorn's voice. He stands like a statue, and only the wind stirring in his hair betrays any sign of life. I bite my lip, frowning. Should I call out to him? There's something unnatural about his stance.

"What is he looking at?" I say, leaning over the unicorn's neck to speak the words to his back-tilted ears.

The unicorn shivers. Fine cracks seem to open up across the skin of his neck. Red light flares through, radiating heat, like fissures in the earth revealing magma at its core. He's suddenly much too hot for comfort. Fearing a sudden burst of engulfing flame, I hastily slip from the saddle. It's some distance from his back to the ground, and the landing jars the bones of my ankles. I back away from the unicorn hastily, heart pounding. He tosses his head again, rumbling another strange growl that sounds so wrong coming from his throat. It's not an aggressive sound, however, but pleading.

"What do you expect me to do?" I mutter, oddly hesitant to raise my voice and call Taar's attention to me. He looks so odd standing there. I can't explain it. It's as though some perception I've hitherto been unaware of is trying to warn me of something. Like a song, singing from a great distance.

I glance at the unicorn again. Those hairline cracks are spreading swiftly across his hide, the fire underneath intensifying. Gods, this can't be good. I pull my cloak around myself, a flimsy shield of sorts. Then, because I don't know what else to do, I turn to Taar. "Warlord?" I call out softly.

He doesn't hear me. Perhaps I wasn't loud enough. I clear my throat and take three steps toward him. "Warlord?" I call again, a little more forcefully this time. "This gods-blasted beast of yours chased me down and brought me back to you. He seems to think something's amiss." I take a few more hesitant steps, my brow tightening. "*Is* something amiss, warlord? Did you . . . did you send for me?"

Now that I'm nearer, I can hear him breathing—deep, heavy, labored breaths. His chest expands and contracts hugely, the muscles of his shoulders moving with the effort. Though his arms continue to hang loose, his fingers keep curling with claw-like tension, then relaxing, then curling again.

My lips are dry and cracked, despite the moisture in the air. I lick them uneasily. Then, though I can't explain how I do it, I reach out to him—not with my hand, but with my spirit. With that part of me that feels music, that understands the language and shape of song in ways that defy mere language.

I'm hit by a wave of something dark. It stops me in my tracks so abruptly, I gasp for breath. I stagger back a step, shaking my head. The impression is gone already, leaving nothing but aftershock in its wake. What was that? That sourness of sound, that discord? I've heard my fair share of amateur musicians attempt to play or sing—I've heard weak voices fail to hit notes, untrained fingers stumble over strings. But those were always mistakes; they never effected the rightness of the song being attempted.

This, however, was no mistake. This was purposeful. It was like the song itself was being . . . bled somehow. Broken, drained, purged of what made it music. A dissonance, a breaking of all melody into madness, done with absolute intent.

I blink and shake my head. A dull ache throbs at my temples, but . . . but did I just imagine it? That *un*-song? Surely I must have. Whatever that was, it was too brief to have been real. My ears ring, but the only sound I hear now is Taar's deep breathing and my own thudding heart. They work in strange synchronization, making a little counterpoint song all their own. Why do I get the strange feeling that these sounds are all part of a paper-thin reality? That the true world, the true song, exists underneath in that space I cannot quite hear . . .

Suddenly I want very much to turn on heel and run from this place. I look back over my shoulder, half-prepared to flee, but the unicorn stands in the middle of the road, blocking my escape. He too is breathing hard, and those cracks across his skin are spreading fast. His eyes burn, little flickers of red light dancing like trailing lashes from his lids.

"Oh gods," I breathe, more a curse than a prayer. Steeling my spine, I turn to the warlord again. Uncertain what else to do, I take another two steps toward him. "Taar?" I call tentatively.

At the sound of his name, he turns.

I choke on a scream as the nightmare that is his face appears before me. Black tears pour down his cheeks, running in rivulets from his engorged eyes and spilling through his beard to splatter on his heaving chest. His lips roll back from his teeth, and oozing bile spills over his jaw, spurting with every breath he heaves.

He cannot see. Not through those tears. And yet I feel the moment when his focus fixes on me. His mouth twists in a hideous smile.

"*Run,*" he growls.

Deep down—down underneath the panic-thrilling jolt of terror racing like lightning through my veins—some reasonable part of me knows that I shouldn't. If I run, he will give chase. He simply won't have a choice in the matter. If I'm to survive, my only hope is to stand my ground.

But reason has no place in my mind now.

I whirl in a flurry of skirts and cloak and hurtle back down the rutted road as fast as my feet will carry me.

20
TAAR

MY PREY IS RUNNING. I MUST GIVE CHASE.

The joy of the hunt thrills through me. I feel it calling to me—that lust for the crack of bone in my jaws, the gush of blood down my throat. That sensation of a beating heart stuttering out its last, desperate pulse in my grasp. The need for carnage burns in me, filling me up from my core.

I see nothing but movement, heat, and the brilliant vibrance of fear emanating from that shadowy bit of nothing that is my quarry. I must have it. I must make its fear mine, must possess it in that intimate moment of sheer terror just on the brink of death. Blackness boils in my veins, and gods! I've missed this! I've craved it in secret, fighting, resisting, but all the while yearning. There's nothing like this feeling, nothing like this absolute power coursing through my soul. Nothing like this hunger which must and will be satisfied.

"You'll never feel more alive."

The voice whispers in my memory, seductive and soft, like gentle fingertips trailing down my neck and spine.

"Believe me, my love. This is the very soul of existence—the dance of life and death entwined. You must experience it for yourself. And when you do, you'll know the truth. You'll know what you were always meant to be."

She was right. She was so *shakhing* right, as she always was. I knew it the first time I tasted the dose she offered. That night, when the two of us together burst from the darkness and set upon that company of human soldiers, who had dared camp too near the edge of our territory. I still remember what it felt like, tearing into their flesh as they screamed. Those screams were music to my ears, and their blood was hot and delicious. My very soul feasted on their deaths.

Why did I give it up? Why did I forsake the very essence of existence? I was a coward, afraid of what I'd experienced, afraid of what it might make me become. Not anymore. I'm ready now as I wasn't back then. Ready to embrace the truth of being. Ready to transform.

"We are death," her voice purrs in my head. *"We are the oblivion from beyond the veil, that which makes mighty men cower in their beds in the dead of night. We are the last great*

dread of mortality, and we are unstoppable."

I know it. Oh, Shanaera, my love, I know the truth at last! How could I have ever doubted you?

So I lunge after that fleeing form. I am the wolf pursuing the deer, driven by an instinct so primal as to be irresistible. I am the truest form of myself that I have ever been, the most real, the most whole. The world around me is blotted out, a veil of darkness come over my vision. I don't have to see—the senses driving me are more powerful than vision, more powerful than any sense by which a mere man perceives his world. I stretch out my hand to take hold of my prey, to snap the life-cord. I can already taste the sweet flow of spinal fluid, the savory stickiness of marrow. My heart hungers for her death, her pain.

Suddenly—light. It flares in red brilliance, piercing through the black film like lances straight into my eyes.

Vellar!

That burning voice bursts in my head, reaching through the darkness into this realm of death and hunger where I exist, then reaching deeper still. All the way down to where the quivering worm of *manhood* still writhes in the center of my being.

Vellar! Hear my voice! Do not fall into the demon's song!

My worm-self struggles, rearing its sickly head, trying to assert dominance. I stagger back from the light, throwing up both hands, bellowing to drown out the thunderous roar of song in my head. Where is my prey? She has gone beyond my perception, hidden behind that being of light. But I need her, I need her death.

"*Give me to drink,*" urges the ravenous voice in my head. Shanaera's voice? I'm not sure anymore. It's deeper somehow, and many. A legion of voices made one and ravenous. "*Give me to drink, Taarthalor. Pour out blood unto me.*"

Turning from the light, I stagger then run back into the embrace of darkness. There is more prey out there, waiting for me and my hunger. I can smell it. I will find it. I will spill its blood.

I will offer my sacrifice of worship to the darkness which indwells me.

21

ILSEVEL

❦

I FLING MYSELF TO THE GROUND AS THE UNICORN LEAPS. My chest hits the mud, air knocked from my lungs, and I'm aware of nothing for some moments beyond terrible heat soaring overhead in a burning arc of light.

Then, pulling myself upright and twisting around, I see the unicorn rear up on its hind legs, standing between me and his master. Red light flares from his horn in a burst like lightning. But these sights mean almost nothing, for my vision is but a frail thing compared to the sound, the song. The absolute fury of the unicorn's soul, rising up against the darkness of that *un*-song, which seeks to overwhelm it. For a moment I don't know which will vanquish the other. I know only that these two forces cannot exist in the same plain, not without bringing this whole world down with them.

It lasts no more than an instant—the light and the dark, the song and the *un*-song.

I'm shaking my head, gasping for breath, and my physical eyes blink into focus on the world around me again. The unicorn stands before me, shuddering, his red hide covered in flames. Beyond him, hunched over like a monster but moving fast, is Taar, fleeing across the field, making for the not-too-distant forest.

I breathe out a quivering sigh and let my head come down to rest in the muddy road. Then, with a curse, I push up onto my trembling arms. I'm absolutely spattered in muck from head to toe. When the wind blows, it cuts right through the wet cloth and into my bones, but though I shake in every limb, I don't feel the cold.

Fearing my knees will simply give out and leave me toppled over once more, I slowly get to my feet and face the unicorn. He turns his great head about, looking at me from those flaming orb eyes, like two suns trapped in his skull. His massive chest expands and contracts so hard, as though it struggles to contain this great soul within the physical confines of flesh and bone. Any moment now he might explode.

"You . . . you saved me," I pant.

The unicorn throws back his head, uttering a ferocious bugle.

I shudder, gripping the folds of my soaked cloak. Gods above, I could have sworn I *felt* Taar's hand close around my neck, snapping my spine, breaking me to pieces! My mind still isn't fully convinced it didn't happen. Taar's retreating form has nearly reached the line of trees now. Soon he'll disappear into those deep shadows.

I press a hand to my chest, as though I might still my own frantically beating heart. How did this happen? The signs of demon's blood are unmistakable, but he'd so adamantly refused to take it this morning. What could have changed his mind? There's no enemy in sight, not a single living soul but me. And what will happen to him now?

"If they do not succeed in killing within the hour, they themselves will die."

I hear his voice in my memory, the warning he spoke just a few short hours ago. Is this then to be Taar's fate? Since the unicorn prevented him from killing me, will he succumb to the poison's influence?

"The darkness burns too hot and liquifies their innards, which then runs in black streams from every orifice."

"Oh gods," I whisper. "Oh, gods above, no." The unicorn is watching me. I feel his burning gaze and turn to him desperately. "What am I supposed to do?"

He does not answer, not even a trill of song in my head.

I rub a hand down my face, wiping mud and muck away. Utter helplessness churns in my gut. I can't fight Taar! I can't subdue him, and, even if I could, I couldn't stop the demon's blood from killing him as he described. Am I supposed to just let him murder me? But if that's what the unicorn wanted, if that's why he brought me out here, why would he interfere?

A scream erupts across the sky, swiftly followed by another and another. I spin in place, turning in the direction of those voices. People emerge from among the trees—the townsfolk, who'd fled into the forest to hide from the fae. I can see them, spilling out into the field: men, women, and children. Taar has found fresh prey.

Teeth grinding, I turn to the unicorn. "Are you going to burn me alive if I ride you again?" I demand.

He shakes his great head. A shiver seems to ripple across his flesh, and those hairline cracks close up, one after the other. The light sinks back down inside his body. I can feel the tension in him, the concentrated effort it takes, but within a few moments, he becomes once more a big red beast of flesh and blood. He kneels and tilts his great head expectantly to one side.

"Skewer me," I growl. "Skewer me six ways to hell!"

Then I fling myself at the unicorn, scrambling up into the saddle. He scarcely waits for me to swing my leg over and grab a fistful of mane before he sets off galloping across the fields. His stride is long and fluid, and his feet never seem to touch the ground. I might as well be flying, clinging to his back, bowed low over his neck, and praying to any god who can keep up that I won't fall and break every bone in my body.

People flee across the field, screaming and frantic in their need to escape. Women clutch their children, while men brandish makeshift weapons, their faces stricken with terror. They do not see the unicorn, do not seem to see me either, which is just as well.

He dodges them nimbly, moving with such lightness, they might as well not be there at all.

We come to the edge of the forest where a little road emerges from the trees. There are abandoned carts here, sacks and supplies, all the signs of hastily-made escape. And there, in the center is Taar, bent over a fallen donkey. The donkey lets out a last panicked bray, hooves flailing, just as Taar rips out its throat with his teeth. He leans back, head up, mouth gaping. Blood and black bile roll in streams down his jaw and throat.

A flicker of movement draws my eye. I look beyond the donkey carcass to the cart it was pulling. A child crouches behind one of the wheels. Wide-eyed and terrified, left behind by its family in their flight.

The same instant I become aware of the child's presence, Taar does as well. His head whips to one side, his awful, black-pooled eyes fastening on that tiny figure, who scrambles away, trying to escape out the back end of the cart. Taar's mouth opens wider. Elongated black teeth jut from his jaw.

I don't have time to think. I drive my heels into the unicorn's flanks, and he responds without hesitation. Muscles bunching, he springs forward, soaring over the heads of the last few fleeing townsfolk, aiming straight for Taar. He lands between Taar and the child, pivots with unnatural grace, and rears. Flames lick up his flanks and shoulders, and I realize I have mere moments before I'm about to be engulfed in fire.

Releasing my hold on both mane and saddle, I slip from the unicorn's back, right over his rump and tail. I land hard, the wind knocked out of me, heat and flame erupting in my vision. I roll away, arms upthrown to shield my face. When I come to a stop, I'm lying on my stomach, staring into the face of the child, who has scrambled out from under the cart and stands in the open, mouth gaping in a silent scream. His round eyes are fixed on the unicorn, whom he can absolutely see in this flaming state.

"Run!" I scream. The child doesn't hear me, enraptured by the horror and beauty of that sight. Gritting my teeth, I scramble upright, ignoring the aches and pains bursting across my body. I stagger, catch my balance, and rush to the child, gripping him by the shoulders. "Go! Get out of here, now!" I cry, shaking him hard.

He blinks at me, taking in this wild, mud-spattered woman who has appeared as though out of nowhere. Something about the sight of me jars him back into reality. With a squeak he whirls and races down the forest road after the other townsfolk, his little bare feet slapping against the cold, wintery ground. I breathe out a sigh, glad to see the last of him, then start to turn toward Taar and the unicorn.

Something strikes me across the temple.

I stagger, fall, but never hit the ground. A strong hand catches me by the shoulder, wrenches me back upright. Sparks burst in my vision; pain explodes across every sense. For a moment I cannot comprehend what's happening to me.

Then I find myself staring up at Taar.

He's so massive. Great and looming, a mountain of a man. No, not a man . . . a monster. Though there is still some trace of the Taar I knew, the darkness bursting from his eyes and mouth has warped him into something terrible. His long black teeth no longer fit in his sagging jaw, and the ends of his fingers have lengthened as well, the nails transformed into cruel talons. His spine is hunched, bones protruding, threatening to burst through the skin in jagged burs. Blood mingles with the bile dripping from his tongue, pouring from his eyes.

Donkey blood—not human.

This thought pulls at the back of my fear-wrung mind. He did not kill any people but went for the beast instead. Does that mean there's some part of this creature that is still Taar? That is still fighting to resist the pull of the demon poison?

His huge hands grip my head, one on either side. I feel the terrible strength of them, how easily he could crush my skull like a bit of delicate porcelain. I stare up into his face, into those abyss eyes. Through the throbbing of my pulse, I feel it—that *un*-song, that unmaking, that dissonance. It pulses out from the core of him, swallowing up all that was once harmony and wholeness in his spirit.

But he's still in there, deep down. He's got to be.

"*Taar!*" I scream his name, the sound tearing from my throat. Just at the end of that scream, I deepen my voice, let it become something more. Let it become *song.* My gods-gift ripples across my tongue and bursts in his ears, echoing and reechoing, filling the forest with one clear, desperate note.

Taar roars and shakes his head. He takes a step back, blinking globs of black tears. For an instant—so brief, I wonder if I imagined it—I glimpse his eyes, staring out at me through that viscous film. He takes another step back, and his talon-tipped hands release their grip on my head. I drop to my knees, gasping in relief. Still he retreats, one staggering step at a time, his body and being quaking in the aftermath of that single burst of song.

"Taar," I gasp again, my voice too ragged to be musical. I tip my head back and try again, a bare whisper of sound. *"Taar."* This time it works: the gods-gift emerges from my lips again, clear and true.

He screams. His awful hands go to his own head, clasping over his ears as though to block out the noise. Dissonance ripples out from his mouth, from his soul, a pulse of power that knocks me flat. I stare up at the spinning branches of winter-bare trees overhead, at a distant, cloud-strewn sky.

Then all goes dark.

I don't know how long I lay there, flat on my back in the middle of that forest trail. When I open my eyes once more, the clouds have rolled on by. The clear sky beyond them is purpling with twilight, and a few faint stars are just visible in the highest reaches.

Slowly, painfully, I push up onto my elbows. Gods, everything hurts! All the mud on my clothing and skin has dried into cakey flakes, and I'm fairly certain I've cracked a rib or two. I look around at the abandoned carts and knapsacks littering the road around me. The escaped townsfolk hadn't the courage to come back searching for their goods. The donkey carcass looks particularly grim in the half-light, surrounded in a pool of blood. An opportunistic raven sits on its belly and gives me an evil look.

There's no sign of Taar anywhere. Or the unicorn either.

Shuddering in every limb, I get to my feet. I'd much prefer not to; in fact I'd be perfectly happy to put my head down and simply drift back into unconsciousness. But with the cold of night settling in, that would be a fatal mistake. If I want to survive this night, I need to get moving, keep my blood warm. Can I make it back to the town on foot? Surely it can't be too far. I take a step down the road.

Then I stop. And look back into the forest.

What has become of Taar? Has it been an hour already? I don't know how long I was unconscious. Has he succumbed to the poison, his innards liquified and drained from his corpse?

I wrap my arms around my stomach, trying to stifle the sickening sob welling up inside me. I couldn't help him. I couldn't save him. In the end my gods-gift was just as useless as it has ever been. That single burst of fear-inspired song may have saved my life, but it couldn't save his.

Why did the unicorn come for me? The question picks at my brain, refusing to let go. He believed there was something I could do . . . but what?

It's too late now. They're both gone. And the hour is probably spent. Taar is dead. He's dead; he must be. And I couldn't help him, any more than I could help my sister. I'm right back where I was before, only now I'm cold, wet, haggard, and bruised across every part of my body. My feet are heavy as I turn them down the forest track. But with no other options available to me, where else am I to go? What else am I to do?

I stop again. Turn and gaze over my shoulder into the forest. There's something there, some faint glimmer of light. I can't really see it, but I feel it, thin and delicate and trailing through those trees, and . . . and it seems to be wrapped around my wrist somehow.

Frowning, I stare down at my forearm. For a moment I seem to see again that cord with which the skinny young priest bound my hand to Taar's. Was it just last night? It hardly seems possible. So much has happened in the intervening hours, I scarcely feel like the same person I was then. It must have been some other Ilsevel who stood with her hand clasped in the grip of a powerful warlord stranger.

"*It is* velra," he'd explained when he saw the confusion on my face, "*woven from the roots of the* ilsevel *blossom, which is sacred* to my people. *The influence does not last more than a few hours, but it temporarily binds us to one another.*"

Am I still bound to Taar? Is the cord still alive? It seems to be, for when I move my arm, I could swear I see it glinting through the trees up ahead. And if it's still alive, does that mean that he . . . ?

I don't wait to question further. Renewed energy burns in my veins, an unexpected surge of hope and determination. Gathering up handfuls of my skirts, I spring from the path and forge into the forest in pursuit of that delicate gleaming.

22

TAAR

IVE ME TO DRINK! GIVE ME TO FEAST!"

"*I thirst! I hunger!*"

I feel her thirst and her hunger as though it is mine. I feel her need for blood, for death, for unmaking. The voice in my head still sounds like Shanaera sometimes, begging me, entreating with all the desperation of her soul, wringing my heart of life's blood.

But it isn't truly Shanaera I hear. It never was.

"*I will have my feast, Taarthalor. One way or another.*"

Beneath the ravening, beneath the horror, that small, worm-like part of me that is my mortal soul coils up in dread, knowing what is to come. I have not given that hunger what it demands, so it will take from me instead. I've seen it happen before; I've seen the corpses of those who went too far into virulium's madness to be reclaimed, the husk-like shells of their remains lying in pools of their own liquified innards. Worse still, however, is what waits on the far side of that agony. For how can a soul so corrupted hope to be claimed by the Goddess? No, it is not to Nornala's light that I will go after death.

Hell will claim me. It will feast on my heart for eternity.

I stagger blindly, my eyes dark to the world around me, my soul deadened to all but the screaming clamor in my ears. Some distant part of me is aware of the rush and roil of water, and I stop, recoiling from that flow, as all those maddened by virulium do. Unable to progress, unwilling to retreat, I drop to my knees. This, then, is where I will meet my doom. My body burns inside, my blood boiling, sweat mingling with the foulness pouring from my mouth and eyes, from my nose and ears. Not much longer now.

Vellar.

A bolt shoots through my heart, a silver lance of song.

Brother-soul.

I shake my head. This is not what I wanted. Elydark . . . he should not be here with me. If he is, it can only mean that my licorneir is likewise succumbing to the poison.

Go! I cry, my voice desperate in my head, all but drowned out by the clamoring roar of the burning dark. *Go, Elydark, get out of here! Don't follow me in this death!* He cannot survive our soul's sundering. But he can still hope to ascend to the goddess.

He need not join me on this path.

I feel him, feel the pain of his song striving even now to break through the dissonance. ***Where you go, I go, brother-soul.***

Then he begins to scream.

23

ILSEVEL

STUMBLING AND EXHAUSTED, I FOLLOW THAT GLIMMER of nothing through the lengthening shadows of the forest. With every step I take, I feel time slipping away from me. How many seconds remain to Taar's hour? Is he even now gasping out his last, agonized breaths as the demon's blood tears him apart? Will there be anything left of the man to recognize when I find him? Perhaps I never will find him . . . perhaps this cord of connection will simply vanish when his life ends, and I'll be left alone out here, in the middle of the woods, in the dead of winter. A widow.

That word, so strange and ridiculous, brings a huff of semi-laughter to my lips. I forge on, redoubling my speed. At least this cloak Taar gave me seems to slip through underbrush easily, the clinging branches finding no purchase on its glossy folds. Otherwise I'd be making poor time indeed. My breath pants in little icy clouds before my face, and my ribs ache with the effort to draw air into my lungs.

What exactly will I do if I manage to find my warlord husband? I still don't have a plan. That singular burst of song seemed to have some effect on him, enough to convince him not to shatter my skull with his bare hands. But I can't very well just go . . . sing at him. Can I? Gods-gift notwithstanding, I can't imagine how it will help.

Oh, why didn't the gods grant me the War Gift instead of my sister? I would not have misunderstood the sudden outpouring of magic like she did. I would have recognized the true power inside me and used it. I would have saved Aurae. I would have saved myself. I would have prevented all of this from happening in the first place.

Instead the gods made a mistake. That, or they maliciously chose to do exactly as they did. I'm not sure which idea gives me less comfort.

When I was a child, before my gift manifested, I used to dream that I was meant for some great and glorious purpose. People used to speak of my impending gift with reverence. I was meant to be an instrument of the gods in this world, a savior of kingdoms and shaper of destinies. What a joke. It was all nothing but vanity and foolishness in the end . . . and now the gods laugh at us all from their high heavens, while we muddle along in the mess they themselves orchestrated below.

Furious blasphemy roils in my chest, heating my blood and driving me faster and faster in my hopeless race against time. I'm just working up to a series of good teeth-grinding curses, when I burst suddenly through a thicket and into an open space before a rushing river. I stop short.

Taar is there. Kneeling with his back to me. His attitude reminds me so starkly of when I saw him on the road, it makes my stomach drop. Only this time I know what to expect when I look at his face. I know the blackness of corruption that will pour from his mouth and eyes. I brace myself, uncertain what to do. Approaching him seems foolish, but now that I've come all this way, am I simply going to stand here and . . . watch whatever horrible end comes over him?

That's when I see the unicorn. I nearly missed him entirely, for his spirit has gone completely dark, and his song is utterly suppressed. He stands beside his kneeling rider, a shadow among shadows, only just visible to my naked eye. His muscular neck is bent, his long horn resting across Taar's bowed shoulders. The two of them are so still, one could almost believe they'd been turned to stone.

I rub unconsciously at my right forearm, feeling again the tightness of the invisible cord. What am I to do now? I have no better idea than I had when I first set out. But I can't very well turn around and go back. I'm here. I must do something.

"Taar?" I call softly.

He doesn't move or offer any indication of hearing me. The unicorn, however, shifts ever so slightly. A single eyelid lifts. A faint gleam of light peers out at me, the last glimmer of a soul nearly snuffed from existence.

I hesitate a moment. Then, with a fatalistic shrug, I glide closer to the two of them, man and beast. Reaching out a trembling hand, I touch the unicorn's broad cheek. His eye closes once more, but I feel something down in him—a thrum, a pulse. A song? It sounds strangely familiar. Just a few simple lines of melody, not heard so much as felt.

I withdraw my hand again, turning from the unicorn to Taar. My stomach knots. He is so horrible, so gross with that black ooze pouring from his eyes. I cannot see the man who made love to me only last night. He's gone.

Tears spring to my eyes, trickle down my cheeks. I dash them away, frustrated, furious. Why should I weep for this stranger? This enemy, my captor. He doesn't deserve my tears, and yet . . . and yet here I am, mourning his death before it's fully claimed him. Unable to lift a finger to prevent it.

The unicorn shifts again. The movement startles me, and I draw back a pace, but he only adjusts the angle of his horn. It no longer rests on Taar's shoulder but instead seems to point to his bicep. I find myself looking at that cut which I'd sewn up only a few short hours ago. My eyes widen. It's *pulsing*. All the stitches are blown, and black ooze dribbles from the cut. Though I can't explain it, darkness seems somehow to pulse from that point, radiating through the rest of Taar's body.

Realization dawns: *this* is the source of his poisoning. That dagger he stuck into Lurodos was tainted with demon's blood. When Lurodos pulled it from his side and slashed back at Taar, he infected him. It took time to react, being but a taint of poison rather than a full dose, but the effects were, in the end, the same.

The unicorn's eye fixes on me again, a last, flickering gleam. I know that light will go out any moment, but . . . "What am I to do?" I ask softly. "I can't stop the poison. I'm sorry, but I'm useless here!"

Another faint trill of music in my head, familiar and gentle. I've heard it before. Somehow I feel that if I can just remember where and when, it will make all the difference.

"Please," I say, reaching out and touching the unicorn's dark cheek once more. "Please, what is this song? Can you tell me?"

The song intensifies, sinking deeper and deeper into my head. Not music I can hear, but fuller, clearer, stranger. The sensation transcends mere physical perception to become a truer form of music than any I've yet experienced. My gods-gift responds, leaping in eagerness to embrace this new sound that is no sound. There's so much greatness in it, so much potential, and it beckons to me.

Suddenly I draw a sharp breath. I recognize that song: it's the wordless melody Taar sang over me last night when he healed the cut in my hand. I look down at my palm, at that delicate white scar. *"The Goddess of Unity is alive in the song of the licorneir,"* he'd said. *"That song, when channeled correctly, may remind split flesh what it means to be whole."*

I swallow the lump in my throat, then look up at the unicorn once more. "I can't sing."

The music in my head becomes irate, if such a glorious sound can be anything of the kind.

I grimace. "All right, fine. I *can* sing. But I *don't.*"

This isn't good enough for the unicorn, who stamps his hoof, shaking the ground. I flinch. "Why should I sing?" I growl. "Aurae is dead. The gods gifted me with a useless power, one that I could not use to save her, while they gave her a power she could never hope to control. There is no rightness in this world, no fairness, no goodness. So why should I sing, damn it? Why should I?"

The unicorn's song presses against my resistance, a tidal force crashing over a wall of stone. Every time it breaks, it reforms and crashes again, wearing me down. Just as a manmade structure cannot hope to withstand the encroachment of the sea, so my bastions crumble under the eternal burning of this being's soul. Perhaps if it came at me with anger or vengeance or sorrow, I could be stronger. But this is a song of love—deep and abiding. Love for this man who kneels before me. The bond between them is profound and mysterious. I cannot pretend to understand it, but neither can I deny its existence.

I drop my gaze from the burning eyes of the unicorn, looking at Taar once more. I hate him, or at least, I think I do. I'm not sure. While I want to blame him for Aurae's death, I cannot blame him more than I blame myself. And now he's dying from a poisoned wound he received while fighting to save my life. Somehow I can't bear the idea that he should die after all this. Not after everything we've been through. Not while I walk away free and clear.

"All right." I meet the unicorn's gaze once more. "I'll sing. But . . . I'm not sure I know how."

The unicorn shakes its head as though to say, ***It doesn't matter, just follow my lead.***

Uncertain what to do, I place a hand on the unicorn's cheek once more and rest the other atop Taar's wound. It's hot—the black ooze scalds my palm, and I'm forced to pull away. Biting my lip, I stretch out my hand again and let it simply hover over the torn flesh.

Then the unicorn begins to sing: a deep, rolling, beautiful song. It seems to flow from that coiled horn into my skin, into my skeleton, down into the very center of my being. I'm not sure I could resist responding even if I wanted to—an answering song simply bubbles up inside me, pouring from my lips. It's a song of light and dark, a song of heights and depths. A song of unmade things being made new and whole. A song of unity, far more prayerful than any prayersong I ever uttered while kneeling before an altar.

Something burns in my veins. It takes me a moment to realize what it is: magic. Raw magic, channeled from the unicorn via its voice, mingled with mine. My head whirls, and my vision is full of light, despite the deep gloom of the twilit forest around me. I feel as though the three of us—me, Taar, and the unicorn—are held in a little sphere of gentle, silvery song.

But as I open to the song, other things encroach on my awareness. I feel the discord in this wound. It's like I can hear it, the wrongness of his marred flesh, the dissonance, the brokenness. All things working against unity and healing. It frightens me, but I lean in to the unicorn's voice. Slowly, surely, I begin to hear new lines of melody. A harmony to that brokenness that might somehow bring healing.

I glance up at the unicorn. He watches me, his song never ceasing, his power coursing in pulsing waves through his horn. Though part of me fears I'm about to make a muck of the whole thing, I start to sing that new harmony. My voice plays around the unicorn's song and somehow, slowly, draws a connection between it and the dissonance of Taar's wound. It's like my voice was a missing link, the necessary counterpoint to make sense of the whole. It's strange and eerie, but for the first time in my life, I feel the true *power* of the gods-gift which I've carried for so many years.

I'm so caught up in the song, in the harmonies I'm making, in the beauty the unicorn and I are creating from the brokenness, I almost don't notice when Taar begins to stir. He groans, the sound loud enough to break my intense concentration. I blink. Visions of light and dark and dancing soundwaves retreat from my eyes, and I see the world around me once more. Still singing, I peer into the warlord's face. His color is much improved. The black bile seems to have evaporated from his face, leaving behind nothing but faint stains. His brow puckers; his mouth moves.

Then, as though fighting against great weights, he slowly turns to me. Though my head is full of music, my ears nonetheless pick up the growl of his husky voice: *"Zylnala?"*

His eyes drop shut again. With a little moan, he topples to one side, there on the river bank. My song breaks in a little, "Oh!" and I bend over him, frightened, my hands gripping his arm. I lean close, struggling to see in the dimness.

His wound . . . it's open and raw, but the poison is gone. It'll need to be restitched, but there's no more of that festering blackness, no trace of demon's blood.

I look up at the unicorn, breathing hard suddenly, as though I've run a mile at full tilt. "Will he be all right now?"

The great beast looks solemnly back at me. Though I cannot understand his words, the meaning of his song fills my head: **He will never be the same again.**

24

TAAR

❦

I COME TO BESIDE A RIVER, PROPPED UP ON SADDLEBAGS, my body covered in the rough cloth of a travel blanket. My face is damp with either sweat or rain. The heavy clouds are gone from overhead, and open, starlit sky arcs in endless splendor before my eyes.

Where am I? The question rings dully in my head. Beneath that clear expanse, I could almost make myself believe I am home once more. But no, these stars are too distant, not the near and clear burning orbs I know, and their constellations, though similar, are not those I remember from childhood.

Then I drag a lungful of air into my chest and taste the bitterness of mortality in the atmosphere. And I know: I'm still in the human world. Gods-damn it.

Memories churn in my mind, confused, dark, and . . . violent. I taste blood on my tongue and some other, bitter coating that makes me gag. If I didn't know any better, I'd think I was coming back down from . . . from . . .

My eyes flare open. Twisting, I look at my arm, struggling to see the wound, the dark spread of virulium poison. My swimming vision is met only with a row of neat stitches. Fresh stitches, unless I miss my guess.

Brow knitted in a frown, I slowly turn to take in more of my surroundings. Elydark is close, his form faint and shimmery in the gloom. An image fills my head suddenly: a vision of my licorneir, burning and huge as a star, appearing out of pitch darkness and chaos. Is it a vision exactly? Or is it rather a song, filling my mind with a reality too big for my small perceptions to comprehend? I'm uncertain. All I know is that I was burning, I was lost, and Elydark came to me.

Only . . . he didn't come alone. There was another with him, a small figure riding on his back, alight with glory.

Angel. The word comes to mind, but it isn't quite right. I shake my head and try again. *Zylnala.*

Surely I must have hallucinated all of it—the violence, the bloodlust. Gods, did I rip out the throat of a donkey with my bare teeth? No. No, it must have been a dream brought on by fever. Surely the poison tainting my cut was so little, it could not have driven me to such madness.

But when I look down at my chest, the ugly stains of virulium blot my skin. I know those stains. And I know as well this aftershock of burning in my veins which accompanies the come-down following a demon-rage. If that was real, then what about . . .

I shift my gaze, desperation suddenly twisting my heart. And there! I see her—that little figure, huddled in a Licornyn cloak a few feet away from me, her arms wrapped around her drawn-up legs, her chin resting on her knees. She's staring off down the river, watching the water rush away into the night.

My warbride.

At first I don't even try to fathom what she is doing here. I simply sit, still and quiet, drinking in the nearness of her. Drinking in the truth that my last remembered vision of her, standing in the middle of that road, pale and forlorn before the backdrop of that human village, was not my last vision after all. Somehow fate has drawn us back together; for the moment I won't worry how or why. Relief floods my soul, and I let it come, let it wash over me. My eyes, hungry for her, take in every little detail they can soak up—that dark spot on her cheek, the deep furrow of her brow, the way her lower lip protrudes in a natural pout that is indescribably tempting. Other details clarify more slowly, such as the tears staining her cheeks. And the way she keeps surreptitiously rubbing her forearm.

That final detail sets off something in my head. Slowly I look down at my own forearm, resting on the ground beside me. It still aches, but with remembered rather than present pain. The reality of the vanished *velra* cord remains. I can almost see it glinting there, a delicate thread of gold, the coils slack for the moment, but binding. Though there is nothing overtly visible, my eyes seem to follow those coils, tracing the pattern they make on the ground as they lead inevitably to . . . her.

She meets my gaze when it lands upon her again. That stern brow of hers tightens. "Warlord," she says, her voice cold.

I grunt. Not, perhaps, the most courteous response, but the best I can manage in my current state. I push upright and glance down at my freshy-stitched wound again. It's a miracle to see healthy flesh and no trace of black stain.

Memories stir—images of screaming strangers fleeing before me. And that voice in my head that I remember too well, urging me to carnage. Then her. This girl, her face appearing through the darkness like a burst of sunlight. Did she . . . did she sing over me? Was that her voice I heard, blending with Elydark's in a song of power, coursing through my veins? Surely that cannot be. Licorneir only bond to one rider at a time, and only that rider is gifted with the ability to hear his mount's unique song. It is a sacred thing, the soul-bond, not something a third party may enter into.

And yet Elydark could not channel the healing power of his magic directly. The force of his song would have killed me, incinerating me from the inside out. That degree of power, of pure, raw magic, must be filtered, or it is too intense, too wild, for creatures of flesh and blood to endure.

It's more than I can fathom. Not with my head still pounding and my body aching and the near brush with death still hovering on the edges of my awareness. Breathing out a sigh, I lean back against the saddlebags, tilting my head to gaze up at the sky. The stars gleam and dance, mocking me faintly with their airy freedom. A thin sliver of moon sails just above the treetops, offering enough light for my half-breed eyes to discern the world around me almost as clear as day. I breathe in another lungful of magic-depleted air, nauseated at the prospect of spending the night in this realm. But I'm not strong enough just now to reenter Wanfriel. For the time being it's safer to remain where we are.

The girl coughs. Not an actual cough, but a pointed clearing of her throat. It draws my gaze back to hers. She peers at me rather uncertainly. Her human eyes do not see well in the dark. "Your unicorn," she says without preamble. "He fetched me back."

A frown pulls the corners of my mouth. I turn again to the wavery impression of Elydark, standing among the trees some little distance off, keeping watch. He does not look my way, but his feelings are as open to me as ever when I reach for them: anxiety mingled with relief, all underscored by a certain resentment. He blames me for this entire situation. And he isn't wrong to do so.

Heaving a sigh, I push upright once more, facing the girl. "Did you . . . ?" I hardly know how to phrase my question so simply nod at my wounded arm.

"Yes," she answers shortly. "I didn't know I could. Apparently my gods-gift is good for something." She snorts and rubs her upper arms with her pale hands. "Who would have thought?"

Ah! That's right: she is gods-gifted. This must explain her ability to connect to Elydark. Surely she could not have even perceived the licorneir song otherwise, much less sung that complicated harmony. Gods spare me, I don't know of any practiced *velhariar*—soul-healer—who could bring a victim back from virulium poisoning! Miracles compounded on miracles.

"I . . . am in your debt, *zylnala*," I say at last, filling the long silence between us.

She snorts again. "You've both endangered and saved my life so many times in our short acquaintance, I'm not sure any debt remains. I'd prefer to consider us even and leave it at that."

I nod. "Nonetheless, thank you for returning. For saving my life."

Her full lips compress into a thin line. "Did I have any choice?" She lifts her forearm, fist clenched. "Or did *this* have something to do with it?"

For an instant my eyes deceive me, almost tricking me into believing I truly see that glimmering gold coil of *velra*. Whether seen or not, it is certainly present. When she moves, I feel the tug on my own flesh, the pressure constricting my forearm.

My mouth goes dry, my throat tight. It is a struggle to form words. "I am . . . not sure. But yes, I think so."

Her eyes flash. "Do you want to explain it to me then?"

I don't. I'm not sure I can.

When I offer no answer, she gets to her feet, pulling her cloak tightly around her slender frame. She looks unexpectedly imperious, with her jaw set and her head high, even as her hard eyes stare down at me. What a queen she would make.

Shahk. Did I just think that?

"I couldn't see it before," she growls. "But just now, sitting here in the moonlight . . . I can almost catch a glimmer of it out of the corner of my eye. And I feel it. Every time I get up and try to walk away, every time I try to leave you here and . . . and . . . and get on with my life, it tightens." Her teeth flash, a ferocious grimace. "Three times I've tried to walk away. You're safe now; I've done everything I can. Even your gods-blighted unicorn doesn't seem to care if I stay. I've given back whatever I owed you, and we are through." Slowly she shakes her head. Her shoulders slump as a little sigh escapes her lips. "Yet somehow I find myself back here. And I can't even say if I chose it."

I turn away, unable to bear that accusatory gaze of hers.

"Well?" she demands, taking a step toward me. Her stance and tone might be intimidating were she not such a waif of a mortal female.

Breathing a sigh that contains a faintly whispered, *"Shakh,"* I rub a hand down my face. There's no avoiding it, however. I must tell her, to the best of my ability.

"In Licornyn tradition," I say at last, "there are two wedding ceremonies. During the first ceremony, the *velra* cord is fastened, and the wedding night takes place. This you already know."

Even by moonlight I can see the faint blush that pinks her cheeks. She looks away from me, pinching her lips again, and nods shortly.

"The second ceremony," I continue, careful to keep my tone even and low, "is held a month later, on *silmael*, the night of the new moon. Then the bride confirms that her husband has honored his vows and makes her own vows in return. According to tradition, the time in between is spent entirely in one another's company. Husband and wife are not to be parted, and this"—I lift my arm, and, though I'm sure it's just a trick of the eyes, could almost swear I see the coils of our binding glint in the air between us—"is a symbol of that bond. Only I've never heard of it manifesting quite so literally."

She studies me intently, struggling to discern the sincerity of my expression by moonlight. I lift my face to give her as clear a view as possible. "So," she says slowly, "you're telling me it's not normal for a couple to be actually *bound* like this?"

"I have certainly never heard of anything like it."

"Then . . ." She draws a long steadying breath. "*What in the nine hells happened to us?*"

The words emerge in a voice so tight and tense, and yet somehow convey more force than if she'd shouted at the top of her lungs. I sit before her, my legs outstretched, my wounded arm somewhat numb and limp. The question echoes in my own head, utterly inexplicable. And yet I must offer her some explanation. "Perhaps," I suggest, "it has something to do with your gods-gift."

"What?"

"You are in possession of a rare magic, bestowed upon you by the gods themselves. These gifts are great mysteries, little understood even by the most learned scholars of magic the worlds over." I shrug. "It could be that, when you sang to me, your gods-gift reacted to the dormant magic of the handfasting ceremony and . . . awakened it somehow."

She blinks down at me, her eyes pools of darkness ringed in silver. "It's a theory, I suppose." Bowing her head, she buries her face in her hands for a moment, breathing deeply. Is she weeping? Trying to hide her tears from me?

"*Zylnala*," I begin, once more starting to push myself upright.

"Tell me this," she interrupts, dropping her hands and catching my gaze once more. "Did you do this on purpose? Did you know this would happen, know I would be bound to you?"

I shake my head. "I did not."

"And if you had known . . . what would you have done then?"

An impossible question. How could I know what I would have done had I fully understood the situation? If I'd realized the vows I made would attach me to this girl with bonds far stronger than anything I'd imagined? Even leaving her presence made me susceptible to magical influence that my natural half-fae resilience should have fought off with ease. Would I have put myself at such risk for a stranger? Hardly. It's too much commitment, too much responsibility. It's one thing to make love to a woman for a single night; it's another to be saddled with her for an entire month.

But I do know what would have happened to her if I'd simply turned a blind eye and walked away.

"I cannot say for certain," I answer at last. "What I can say is this: I'm glad that I saved you. I'm glad you did not fall into Lurodos's hands. I'm glad you are here with me now." I stop myself there, unwilling to go on. Unwilling to confess that putting her down and sending her on her way to that human town had almost been more than I could bear. What right have I to say such things? It's likely not even real, just this gods-damned binding spell at play.

She nods, accepting my words despite the slight curl to her lip. "What will you do then? Is there a way out of it?"

"Yes. At new moon, should you refuse to speak your vows, our binding will be broken."

"But you said that was a month away!" Her whole body quivers as though she's ready to boil over. "Is there anything we can do now? Tonight? This instant?"

I shake my head, adding quickly before she can lay into me with another furious tirade, "If anyone should know the answer, it will be Onor Gantarith of Elanlein."

"Oh? And where is that exactly?"

"The Hidden City."

"Well, that clears it up immensely, doesn't it?"

I let her dry sarcasm wash over me, concentrating on the plan forming in my mind. Though it's hardly a plan; more like a hazy image, an impression. I see myself astride Elydark, galloping across the wide-open plains of my homeland, the girl sheltered in the circle of my arms. Her chestnut hair tickles my face, and her lithe body nestles comfortably between my legs, as though she was made for me. In my vision, she feels so right in that context of vaulting blue sky and sweeping grasslands—a bold heart come home to a bold country.

It's all foolishness, of course. Foolishness born, no doubt, from this damnable *velra* bond, which manipulates my senses. Because she is human, she will never be welcomed by my people. It is forbidden to bring her kind to the Hidden City. Even I dare not thwart the law of the Elders.

And yet what other choice do I have? I cannot be far from my people for long, much less an entire month. And I cannot leave her here without risking more susceptibility to dark magic influence . . . a risk that would soon prove deadly where I'm going.

"You'll have to come home with me," I say, my voice firm. "We will speak to Onor Gantarith, explain what happened, and have the bond severed. Then I will fulfill the original promise I made to you and drop you off at the nearest human settlement."

I can feel the protests, the arguments and accusations building up on her tongue. Something makes her swallow them down, though from the expression on her face, they settle like bile in her gut. She says only, "And where is home for you, exactly?"

There's no delivering this news gently. "My people dwell in the land of Cruor."

I could not have shocked her more if I'd tried. She takes a step back, then another, gripping the folds of her cloak tightly. "You're going to . . . take me into *Cruor?*"

I nod.

"*You* are from *Cruor?*"

"I am from Licorna. But Licorna was destroyed, and there is nothing but Cruor left. The Licornyn folk still dwell on the fringes of the land, and I am *Luinar* of the Licornyn."

"What does that mean?"

"I am the Licornyn sovereign."

"A king? You're a king?"

"If you like."

"If *I* like?" she echoes, her mouth gaping as she stares back at me. A shudder races down her spine. "I've heard tales of Cruor. It's supposed to be a nightmarish land riddled with monsters."

My mouth quirks slightly. "Yes, but we have some lovely views."

She throws up her hands then and stomps several paces away from me before stopping abruptly. I don't know if she reached the end of the invisible tether holding her to me, or if she simply couldn't keep going. Shoulders sagging, she looks back, her face edged in moonlight. "So the king of the unicorn-riders is stealing me away into a monster-ridden nightmare realm." A sharp breath issues from her lips, a silent huff of laughter. "It sounds like something my nursemaid told me would happen if I didn't finish my boiled vegetables."

"It's really not so bad as all that." I lace my fingers behind my head, leaning back on the saddlebags. "My people have learned to navigate Cruor with some degree of safety. So long as you are with me, you will be safe enough."

She doesn't answer, not for a long time. She simply stands there, looking at me, while the night breeze stirs her hair and pulls at the edges of her cloak. I become increasingly aware of the urge to get to my feet, to close the space between us, to reach for her. I grimace. It will not be easy to keep my hands off her for the entire month, not with this damnable heart-bond dragging at me every waking minute. But I know she is not right for me. This stranger, this human, whose name I don't even know.

She's shivering. It comes to me suddenly that she must be very cold out here, exposed to the wintry elements after sundown. Humans are not made to withstand such extremes of temperature. Her breath makes little cloud-puffs before her lips, and I can hear her teeth chattering.

Though I'm still rather numb and more lightheaded than I care to admit, I get up and set about building a fire. The only fuel close at hand is soaked through from the day's rain, but I call Elydark over and perform a simple *rhuenar* spell, which he infuses with a spark of his own magic. The kindling immediately catches, and a blaze springs to life. The girl watches all of this from a distance, shoulders hunched, eyes wary. But she slowly approaches the warmth, drawn to it almost against her will.

"Here," I say, digging into the saddlebags and tossing her an *ume* cake, hard but nourishing. "It's safe for human consumption, I swear."

She looks down at the round little cake in her hand. "I believe you. No fae would try to tempt a mortal palate with something like this."

I chuckle. "It tastes better than it looks. And the ingredients are simple: powdered root vegetable, lard, and a bit of *kiteri* honey for flavoring. It might break your teeth, but it will fill your belly."

Settling down before the fire, she sits as close as she comfortably can, still hunched in her cloak. She studies the cake in her hand for some moments before finally saying, "I'm not really hungry."

"It has been a long time since you ate," I point out, remembering the bread I served her last night. Only I dare not think about last night. I stare into the fire, determined not to let the dancing flames paint sensual pictures in my head. "We have a long journey ahead of us. You must keep up your strength."

She is silent for a long while. Then a dainty sniff reaches my ear. I glance up and see that she is crying. The tears simply pour down her face, and she does nothing to stop them, doesn't even seem to be aware of them. She holds that cake in her small hands and watches the fire burn as though watching her very hopes and dreams go up in smoke.

I chew the inside of my cheek. I remember what it feels like to lose family. My parents perished on the same day, gruesome deaths which I dare not let myself dwell upon. And Shanaera . . . her loss haunts me every hour. She died three years ago, and yet I am still so affected by it as to hallucinate her half-rotted face in the middle of a battle.

This girl—she is so young, her experiences narrow, her losses few. While I wouldn't presume to know her, I would guess she's led a sheltered existence until recent history, passing through the ravages of this world relatively unscathed. This loss of her sister is a new and heart-crushing experience. The fact that she's still upright, still full of fire, still willing to use her gift to help her miserable captor . . . it speaks to the greatness of her heart, the strength of her courage.

"Please, *zylnala*," I say at last. "Try to eat. Your sister would want you to try."

She looks down at the cake in her hands but still makes no move to taste it.

I draw a slow breath, considering. Then, hoping I'm doing the right thing, I ask very gently, "What was your sister's name?" I already know it of course. But something tells me it will do her good to speak it out loud.

"Aurae," she answers, her voice quavering slightly. She sniffs and hastily wipes her tears with the back of one hand. "Her name was

Aurae. It means *radiance*. It . . . it suited her."

For a moment we sit together in that space of remembrance. Though I never knew the sister and only glimpsed her once in life, I hold the memory with honor and reverence along with this grieving woman. So the stars turn slowly overhead, as they have for ages, observing both the losses and joys of the mortal creatures dwelling in this world below.

"Under the circumstances," I continue after some time has passed, "would you be willing to share your name with me?"

She looks at me over the flames. I can see the calculation in her gaze as she tries and discards several false names in a row. But she knows already that I will see through them. At last she sighs and, with resignation, says: "Ilsevel."

My eyebrows lift. "Did . . . did you say *Ilsevel?*"

She nods.

"And . . . in your language, what does it mean?"

Her head tips to one side. "I don't know. My father told me it was a kind of wildflower he saw once when traveling in a strange land. He liked it and carried the name back with him."

I blink, uncertain what to say, uncertain what to think. Because I know that name. And I know its meaning. It is a Licornyn word that translates quite simply to: *soulflower.*

Suddenly my body is warm, flushed. *Ilsevel* blossoms are as vital to our daily existence in Cruor as air and water and flame. I tear my gaze away from her, afraid she will see something in my eyes which

I'm not certain should be seen at all. Because a strange and utterly unexpected sensation has bloomed in my chest: hope. Hope that none of this—my encounter with this girl, her captivity, the auction, our wedding night, Lurodos's spilled blood—happened by chance. Perhaps there are more powerful forces at work here.

Perhaps the gods themselves ordained our meeting.

25
ILSEVEL

I T'S HARD TO FATHOM THAT ONLY TWO EVENINGS AGO, almost exactly, I was kneeling at the altar of Lamruil, desperately praying with my whole heart to escape the life which lay before me.

What is it they say? Be careful what you pray for; the gods might actually be listening.

I huddle into my cloak against the chill wintry wind, watching our small campfire dance across the spell-dried wood. The events of the last few hours seem to play before my eyes, confused and twisted. One moment I see myself with Aurae, rattling along in that cage wagon, clinging to each other with our trembling hands. The next I'm riding on a unicorn, cradled in Taar's arms as we progress through a strange forest of shifting shadows that I suspect is not part of the world I know. A blink, and I'm back on that enormous bed in the dimly lit pavilion, my wrists bound, awaiting the arrival of my stranger bridegroom.

The bridegroom who sits across from me now. Still a stranger and yet, inexplicably . . . not.

I flick a covert gaze over the flames, studying the face of the man with whose life I've become curiously entangled. The revelation of my name shocked him into silence; he's not spoken a word since then but seemed utterly intent upon his own study of the fire. I cannot blame him. I was shocked myself when the word *ilsevel* issued from his lips during the handfasting ceremony. He'd said the very cord which was used to bind our hands together was woven from the stems of ilsevel blossoms. The same blossoms, no doubt, which my father took a fancy to when he traveled long ago into the land of Cruor—or Licorna, as it must have been back then. Back before the war began. Back before Taar and I were enemies by necessity.

I study him now from beneath my lashes. This stranger, this husband. This monster, who very nearly ripped me apart. Possibly the only man in my life who has ever sought to prove himself worthy of my trust.

My stomach knots at that thought. Am I really such a fool as to give my trust so easily to a man I don't know? I've been deceived before. I've loved where I shouldn't, devoted all the energy of my heart to an idea I had invented about a man who was, I know now, entirely unworthy. I won't be so quick to give my heart away again, and yet . . .

And yet Taar would die for me. He's proven as much already. Surely that must count for something.

With a little shake of my head, I turn my gaze away from him, looking instead into the looming trees nearby where his unicorn stands, shimmering, almost translucent. A ghostly image, but so heartbreakingly beautiful. Even from a distance, I could swear I hear him singing. My heart stirs, remembering what it felt like to have that song burning through me, body and soul. It was like . . . I don't know how to describe it. It was like being deaf and having my ears miraculously opened to hear music for the very first time. A revelation. An awakening. I cannot help but be glad to have experienced it.

I suck in my lower lip, biting down hard. How can I indulge in such thoughts? Aurae died; am I glad of that? Is her life worth the trade for these new experiences of mine? Certainly not. And this excitement burning in my veins at the prospect of traveling with Taar into his strange realm, of spending more time in company with the proud warlord . . . these feelings must be suppressed. Whatever his intensions were or are, this man is responsible for the death of my sister.

And if he knew who I really am . . .

I shudder, pulling my cloak a little tighter across my shoulders. Whatever happens next, I must guard that secret. I must never let him know whose daughter I am or what part I'm meant to play in this war between our peoples. And, as soon as the bond between us is broken, I will return to my father's house, wed the Shadow King, and do my part to bring an end to this war once and for all. Surely this is the only way to honor Aurae's memory.

Two hot tears race down my cheeks, one on each side. I dash them away swiftly, ashamed. Because I lived, and my sister did not. Because my foolish bid for freedom led to such destruction and death. Because . . . because . . .

Because I'm glad this marriage cord prevents me from parting with Taar. Because here I am, bought and sold, bound in magical chains, and yet . . . the hope of freedom burns brighter in my breast than it ever has before.

"Gods-damn it," I whisper so low that the crackle of the fire devours any sound. My gaze flicks once more to the face of my husband, all those sharp, chiseled plains edged in red glow. "I'm not going to fall in love with him. I swear it."

EPILOGUE

SHE STANDS ON THE BRINK OF THE CLIFF, RIGHT AT that last pivotal edge before the drop. Some small part of her—a part that still feels anything at all—searches for that old sensation. What was it called? Fear. The dread of the plunge and the prospect of pain, all underscored by that horror of the unknowable existence in the dark beyond the end. A simple set of emotions, but so infinitely varied in their subtleties and hues.

She feels none of that now. No dread, no horror, not even the faintest unease. Even if she should cast herself over this brink, even if she should shatter every bone on the stones far below, there would be no end for her. Not yet, in any case.

Behind her, huddled close to the fire, the mage continues his endless lament. "I cannot return to Evisar!" he declares, spitting the words through clenched teeth. "Not without the princess. I am Morthiel's last hope, and to return empty-handed? It's not to be borne."

She doesn't answer. She stands up on her toes, leaning out a little farther into that void. Daring her old body to react. Perhaps there's still some instinctual urge for survival lying latent down inside. But nothing. No thrill, no terror, not even a little vertigo. She sinks back onto her heels. She would sigh if she had breath with which to do so, but her ragged lungs hang limp in her breast.

"Besides," the mage continues, running his fingers through his pale hair, "that gods-damned half-breed took the talisman. It would be suicide to try to reach Evisar without it, and it will take months to write another. Meanwhile what if the fae work out how to use the spell? They will lay siege to the citadel with everything they've got. It will require all the magic my people have amassed for decades to ward them off. And what will that mean for Morthiel?"

She rolls her eyes heavenward, idly studying the stars in their distant dance above. She doesn't care about any of the mage's petty little plans. Yes, the loss of the gods-gifted princess is a blow . . . but she doesn't think it's a mortal blow. While Mage Artoris assumes the girl died in the battle, she suspects otherwise. After all she knows Taar. She knows how her beloved thinks. He would not leave a damsel in distress to perish at the hands of monsters. No, no. He probably rescued the girl, took her captive. Her lips quirk in a vicious smile. He always did have a dangerously self-destructive need to protect the small and the weak. It is his one great vice.

"I'll have to return to Beldroth," Artoris declares at last, stirring his fire with the end of a long stick just to watch the sparks fly. "Gods skewer me, I never wanted to see that cursed place again! But I must inform the king of Ilsevel's death and urge him to somehow fulfill the marriage bargain with the Shadow King after all. He has other daughters; one of them can surely take Ilsevel's place. It's going to take a troll army to defend Evisar if the fae come marching on our gates."

He turns then to where she stands, right there on the edge of that drop. If he's concerned for her safety, it does not show in either his voice or expression. "I won't keep you and your people here, Shanaera," he says. "I know you must return to Cruor, to replenish your strength. I need you there in any case. Evisar is going to need a steady supply of unicorn blood if we are to survive what is coming. Can you do that?"

Can she? Can she lead the warped corpses of men who used to be her battle brothers into the stricken land that was their home, hunting down the very creatures whom they once held in sacred reverence? Can she be the monster, devouring and hungry, that she needs to be in order to survive? In order to bring about the righteous end she has secretly purposed in her heart?

She smiles at the mage, her half-rotted mouth twisting. "Absolutely I can."

And while she's hunting down licorneir, she will keep her eye open for Taar and the little princess. Because something tells her—call it an intuition, perhaps—that when she finds one, she will find the other. Then all will be made right. Her kingdom will be delivered, these gods-damned Miphates will be obliterated, and she and Taar will reign as king and queen over the newly liberated Kingdom of Licorna.

Forever.

TO BE CONTINUED

DON'T MISS ILSEVEL AND TAAR'S
CONTINUED ADVENTURES IN

HEART
TORN

WARBRIDE: BOOK 2
COMING SOON

ABOUT THE AUTHOR

SYLVIA MERCEDES makes her home in the idyllic North Carolina countryside with her handsome husband, numerous small children, and a menagerie of rescue dogs and cats. When she's not writing she's . . . okay, let's be honest. When she's not writing, she's running around after her kids, cleaning up glitter, trying to plan healthy-ish meals, and wondering where she left her phone. In between, she reads a steady diet of fantasy novels.

But mostly she's writing.

A hybrid author, Sylvia publishes both traditionally and independantly, and enjoys the exciting pace. She's the author of more than twenty bestselling romantic fantasies, including the acclaimed Bride of the Shadow King trilogy.

Visit her website to discover more titles:
www.SylviaMercedesBooks.com

Made in the USA
Middletown, DE
11 June 2024